The BURNSTONES Game

In Search of the Last Door

T D Delaney

First published by Busybird Publishing 2020

ISBN
Hardback 978-1-925949-78-0
Paperback 978-1-925949-76-6
Ebook 978-1-925949-77-3

This is a work of fiction. Any similarities between places and characters are a coincidence.

Cover image: Kev Howlett
Cover design: Busybird Publishing
Layout and typesetting: Busybird Publishing
Editor: Beau Hillier

Busybird Publishing
2/118 Para Road
Montmorency, Victoria
Australia 3094
www.busybird.com.au

*I acknowledge the Traditional Owners of country
throughout Australia and recognise their continuing
connection to land, waters and culture.
I pay my respects to their Elders past, present
and emerging.*

Dedication

*This book is dedicated to Bangerang Elder Wally
Cooper, who gave me friendship and wisdom
To my mother, for teaching me the wonder of nature
and seeing all people as equals
To my children Joshua and Emily, for inspiring me
to make the world a better place and for sharing endless
nature adventures with me
To my daughter Emily, my environmentalist, forever
marching by my side
To my niece Jade Rhianna for countless hours of
encouragement and story support
To my brother David, son Joshua and daughter
Emily, for showing faith and investment in my venture
To Emily, Chris, Anthony, Charlene, Eva and Iris
for the video
To Merrin, Lorna, Krystal, Bron and Kate ever at
the ready to help and support
To Blaise, for patiently guiding me down this self-
publishing path
And to my priceless friends and all of those above
who listened and encouraged my dreams*

Contents

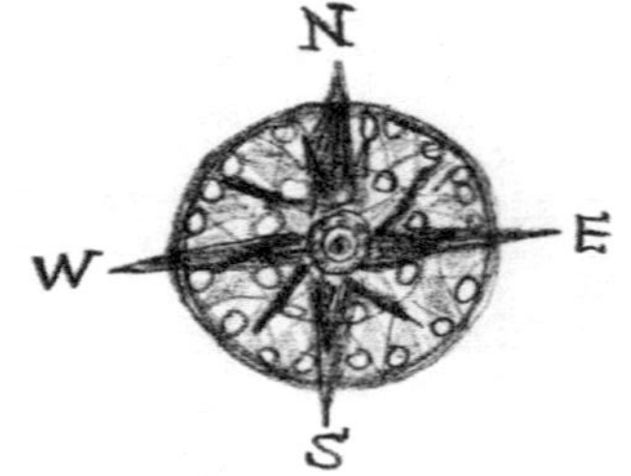

THE BURNSTONES GAME
MAP
HIGH LANDS
FOREST LANDS
SAMBIA COAST
LOW LANDS
THETHYS SEA
LAND OF FENNA SAMARTIA
SEA LANDS
ARAWAK SEAS
TURTLE COVE
GLESSARIA ISLAND
PACIFIC OCEAN
DESERT LANDS
MUNGO
MELBOURNE
N
E
S
W

TWO WORLDS COLLIDED

1

An Enchanted Separation

SATURDAY

Jackson began waking up. As he stirred, he felt the ground was cold beneath him. He pushed himself up into a sitting position and blinked dust from his eyes. Slowly, his sight adjusted to his surroundings. The ground was covered with a fine, sandy dirt. He could see grey rock walls, the inside of a cave. About five metres away, a shaft of sunlight streamed into the cave from an opening to the outside, providing some light in the semi-darkness.

Jackson turned and looked behind him. The cave seemed to go back a long way. He tried to remember where he was.

Out of the corner of his eye, he saw a slight movement. He squinted at what first appeared to be a pile of loose rocks in the shadows. He saw movement again. Jackson stood and stepped a little closer. Everything was still. Again, he stepped cautiously forward. As his eyes became accustomed to the dim light, he realised it wasn't a pile of rocks – it was a person. A female, lying facing away from him. Long fair hair flowed over a dark green cape. A finely crafted bow was strapped to her back. A quiver lay on the ground nearby, the arrows spilling out unevenly in the dust. The body moved again, stretching out, coughing. Jackson stepped back.

The girl had responded to hearing his footsteps, sitting up and turning around suddenly. 'Jackson, Jackson … where are you?' a frightened voice called. The girl was not able to see clearly and held a hand above her eyes.

Jackson was even more confused but he knew his sister Tess's voice. 'Tess,' he responded, 'I'm here.' Jackson couldn't believe his eyes. 'It's okay, Tess. Yes, it's me. I don't know what's going on,' he began as he walked towards her and reached out his hand.

Tess pulled herself up and brushed off the dust from her clothes. 'Jackson, what happened?' she asked in a worried voice. 'Where are we? Why are you wearing those clothes?'

Jackson glanced down. He noticed his arms, between his elbow and hand, were covered in some type of leather guard. He held out both of his arms, turned them over and examined his attire. He looked down at his legs and saw long leather boots. Jackson quickly recognised the outfit. He was dressed as the character of Eadric in the *Burnstones* game he had been playing. He had the character's dagger hanging from his belt and the dual swords crossed over on his back.

'I don't know what's going on,' Jackson repeated. 'Look at what you're wearing.' He pointed toward Tess's clothes. Glancing down, she saw that like her brother, her forearms were protected by leather bracers. Her waist belt was adorned with a dagger and pouch. A bandolier belt stretched from her hip, across her chest, over her shoulder and across her back, holding a quiver and bow in place.

Tess also recognised her outfit. It belonged to the character Emerald from the *Burnstones* game. How could this be? The siblings remained quiet for a moment, looking at each other, around the cave, and at their clothes, trying to fathom the enormity of what had happened. 'Maybe it's a dream,' Jackson said quietly.

'Then how can we both be talking about it?' Tess questioned him, ever ready with a logical challenge for her big brother. Jackson shook his head. He had no answer. 'Wait, what was that noise?' Tess asked, turning her ear toward the cave opening. Jackson hadn't heard anything. 'There it is again,' Tess reported. The noise grew stronger;

now Jackson also heard a dog barking outside somewhere. 'It sounds like Buddy,' Tess said, moving toward the cave entrance.

'Wait Tess, don't go out there, it could be dangerous … and anyway, why would Buddy be here?' he added. With that, a small dog appeared at the cave opening, gave a happy bark and scampered down the two metres or so of dirt and rocks that sloped toward the cave floor.

'It *is* Buddy!' Tess announced, scooping him up into her arms and snuggling her face into his. 'We found you,' she said happily. Jackson was even more confused. What did she mean? 'Remember, Jackson, we lost him. We were looking for him in the park. It was raining … we … oh, Jackson, what's happened?'

Jackson thought for a moment. 'I don't know,' he said, 'but I have a strange feeling about this.'

Tess had the same feeling. For a moment Jackson and Tess just stared at each other, trying to grapple with the situation. Tess snuggled Buddy close to her, his tail wagging happily.

'Tess,' Jackson began hesitantly, 'the clothes …' Tess glanced down at her brown leather skirt and forest green leggings fitted into strong brown boots. Nothing made sense. 'Tess, I don't think we're dreaming. I think that somehow we've gotten stuck in my *Burnstones* game.'

Tess frowned, stopped patting Buddy and looked at her brother. That was a really scary thought. She wanted to find out for herself. She scrambled up the rocks, pulling herself up the last little bit until she could see out of the cave opening.

'Wait, Tess. Wait,' Jackson called, scrambling up after her. He pulled himself up next to her. Brother and sister became motionless, unspeaking, their heads silhouetted shadows against the glaring daylight from outside. Their eyes took in the enormous landscape before them. Time stood still as they stared at a vast desert world. Strange rock formations rose up from sand dunes for as far as their eyes could see.

Jackson sucked in a breath. 'The Desert Lands,' he told Tess. 'It's the first level in the game.'

Tess turned her gaze from the outside world and looked at her brother's face. For once Tess, a very chatty girl, could think of nothing to say. She reached for her brother's hand, which reassuringly took hold of hers. He looked at his younger sister. She was clearly terrified. He would have to take responsibility for keeping her safe. Loose sand and pebbles rolled down into the cave behind them as their boots disturbed the pile of rocks and dirt they were perched on. Jackson felt overwhelmed. He had no idea what to do.

Jackson turned and slid down to the cave floor. 'We need to think this through,' he began. 'We need to make a plan to get out of here.'

Tess slid down after him and sat on a large flat rock. She looked up at her brother, wondering how they would ever work out what to do.

Jackson was biting his lower lip unconsciously, deep in thought. He too sat on a rock, hesitating for a moment. 'Well, we need to think. We need to remember things about this game.' He nodded to himself. 'Yes, that's what we need to do. We need to remember. We need to work it out. We have to think. Somehow we'll have to find our way to the Last Door.'

Tess let out an anxious laugh and shook her head with disbelief. 'You can't be serious, Jackson. That's impossible. We can't do that. Look at us. We're human, not game characters. We can't fight with skills and magic. We'll be killed!' To prove her point, she pinched and wobbled the skin on her cheeks. 'See? Normal human.'

Jackson couldn't disagree. They definitely still looked completely human. The only thing that had changed in their appearance were their outfits. 'Yep, we are human, but there's no other way. We have to find our way out of this somehow. Do you have a better idea?'

Tess stood and started pacing the cave. 'Jackson, remember when we were reading the description for this game? There's so much danger. The characters can die. And if we can't find the Burnstones we'll be stuck in here forever … or worse, we'll be killed by giant creatures. I don't even know, what's the point of trying?' Tess was feeling very stressed. 'What's going to happen when we get to the Last Door, anyway? Can we go through it? Will it even have anything to do with getting home?'

Tess's anxiously high voice faded from Jackson's awareness as he sat deep in thought, mulling over all that had transpired when he'd been playing his new game with his friend Mackenzie. *Was that yesterday?* he wondered.

After a minute or two, Tess broke the silence, 'What are we going to do?' she asked.

Jackson looked up at Tess with a blank expression. 'I don't know,' he admitted. Jackson stood up. His movement stirred up dust particles that sparkled in the shaft of light streaming into the cave. Buddy, full of curiosity, trotted around, sniffing behind rocks. Jackson pulled the dagger from his belt, looking it over. 'Hope we don't need to use this too often,' he said, waving it around for Tess to see.

Tess shook her head and walked over to where some of the bows had fallen from her quiver and lay in the dust. She picked them up. Something shiny caught her eye. 'Jackson, look – it's your phone. That's weird. Why would it be here?' She picked it up and wiped the dust off onto her tunic.

Jackson walked over to take the phone. 'I must have dropped it. Last thing I remember, it was in my hand when we went over to the park.' He hesitated. 'I guess we're not going to have answers for a lot of strange things that are happening. We shouldn't be in this game for a start. None of this makes sense.'

'Is it working?' Tess asked, reaching out to take the phone back, hoping to examine it. Jackson pulled the phone toward himself, preventing her from taking it. He pushed the ON button and waited. The two held their breath, staring at the phone. The phone screen lit up. Tess clapped her hands. 'Quick, see if you can call someone.'

'As if that's going to work. Anyway, even if I could, remember I can't make phone calls, I can only text,' Jackson reminded her.

She remembered now; their mother had decided Jackson could only have a texting phone. She'd been worried that he would make too many phone calls and run up a big bill. *Drat!* thought Tess. How she wished they could make just one phone call home now.

Jackson had already started spelling out a message to his best friend Mackenzie: 'I AM STUCK IN GAME. PLEASE HELP.' Jackson pushed the send button and watched intently to reassure himself the message had left his phone. After a few anxious minutes, Jackson breathed a sigh of relief. 'Mackenzie has answered my message.'

Tess moved closer and peered at the message. 'WILL COME TOMORROW.'

Jackson looked puzzled for a moment. 'He doesn't get it. Mackenzie thinks I'm still at home and I want him to help me with the game.'

Back in their family home, Jackson's console flickered on and off.

Tess shook her head. 'Tell him again. Tell him we are inside the game.' Jackson nodded and began typing a new message to Mackenzie. Then, he stopped and looked up at Tess. A worried look came over his face. 'What is it? What's the matter?' she asked.

'The phone's gone dead,' he said quietly. 'The battery is flat.'

'Great, just great,' Tess complained. 'What else is going to go wrong?' While Jackson and Tess grappled with the situation they found themselves in, things had really become distressing back in their parents' home.

2

The Recollection

SUNDAY

It had been a long night. Neither Mrs Taylor nor her husband had slept. Their children had disappeared and could not be found. Police cars lined the street. Curious neighbours stood outside their homes, chatting about the unexpected events unfolding before their eyes. This was a quiet suburb in Melbourne; the neighbours were not used to such drama. Slowly, the police met with each of them to ask questions. No one had any answers. No one had seen anything. Torches had searched every centimetre of darkness in the park over the road to no avail.

In the Taylors' kitchen, policemen sat at the table, asked many questions, wrote reports and drank endless cups of coffee. Police Constable Mathews came in from the cold. The sun was just beginning to illuminate the sky as dawn broke. He shook his balding head as he looked toward his commanding officer, Sergeant Bourke, who sat at the table checking his paperwork and making phone calls. 'No good Sarge,' Constable Mathews reported, 'The dogs keep losing the scent in the park. It's the strangest thing. Never seen anything like it.'

'Did you walk the whole perimeter and the side streets?' Sergeant Bourke enquired.

'Yep, the whole lot Sarge, and a few times over. The dogs follow the track into the park and then the scent disappears around the rear corner of the park, near a clump of trees. The dogs won't go any further. They're not interested in sniffing out the boundaries at all,' he explained. 'Never seen anything like it.'

Mrs Taylor sat in the lounge room on the sofa, next to her husband. She looked pale and distressed. Mr Taylor held her hand in his; he knew it was little comfort at such a time. He had watched his wife all through the night and felt so helpless. Anxious waiting and no sleep were beginning to take their toll. 'Margaret,' he started, 'why don't you go and lie down? I'll stay with the men.' He motioned toward the kitchen.

Margaret looked toward the window. 'No, I can't, I just can't,' she protested.

'Margaret,' Mr Taylor tried again, 'you're exhausted. You've done all you can, you've told them everything you know.' Mrs Taylor put her head in her hands. 'It won't help the kids if you run yourself into the ground,' he gently reminded her. Mrs Taylor was shaking her head. 'Look, just lie down for a while,' he suggested. 'I'll put the electric blanket on and get you a mug of warm milk.'

'But the men need food,' Mrs Taylor protested.

Mr Taylor waved his hand. 'I can make them sandwiches and I promise I'll let you know anything that happens.'

Mrs Taylor looked at her husband, his chin now shadowed by the growth of overnight whiskers; dark lines were crinkling under his eyes. 'Well, I suppose if I must,' she conceded. 'And then you'll lie down for a while?' she bargained with him.

'Agreed,' Mr Taylor responded as he stood to help his wife up off the sofa.

'I won't sleep,' she insisted.

As the day wore on, police came and went. The local area had been searched over and over. They had no clues, no leads, nowhere to go. The disappearance of the Taylor children was a mystery. A computer technician sat at the family computer, scanning through documents and emails, looking for anything that might provide a clue – or worse, indicate a connection between the children and a possible abductor. Mrs Taylor had found this suggestion extremely distressing this morning, but had agreed to allow the technician to do his work.

Mr Taylor now sat at the kitchen table, staring through the large sliding glass doors that provided a view of the backyard. He wasn't looking at anything in particular though. After multiple cups of strong coffee, he was in a daze.

Three plates of leftover sandwiches dried out on the table in front of him. The police had appreciated the food but Mr Taylor had no appetite. Every ounce of his being was stressed. The children he adored were missing and he, their father, could do nothing. He felt alone and useless, a failure as a protector. Mr Taylor had never imagined he could feel so terribly bad. Slowly his eyes misted over and a tear trickled down his worn-out face.

SATURDAY (Recollected)

Back in the cave, Jackson and Tess thought through their situation, trying to remember what had happened and how they had ended up in this dangerous situation. Together, they tried to recall the events leading up to finding themselves in this strange and confusing place. Jackson recalled how he had started his day playing his new console game on Saturday afternoon with his best friend Mackenzie. He had finally been given the *Burnstones* game as a birthday present. Jackson recalled the fun they'd been having as they created new characters and began to play. As the two players progressed, they began to get used to playing with a split screen.

Hadwyn, the Mercenary, had to swing the longsword frantically as the Giant Trap-Jaw Ant moved menacingly closer. At its frightening mouth were huge snapping mandibles. Hadwyn was much shorter and no match for the beast that towered at least double his height. Behind

Hadwyn, his battle companion, Eadric (who was smaller still), clung desperately to rocky crevices on the cave wall.

Hadwyn and Eadric were on a quest searching for a Burnstone, a transparent red rock made of amber that contained the remains of an ancient lizard. The cocooned and motionless reptile had been trapped long ago and hidden by the giant ants in the upper hollows of the caves, somewhere in a giant ant's nest. The ant tunnels were almost dark, but for a dull red glow providing some guidance on their path. Could Hadwyn and Eadric get passed these oversized monstrosities alive?

'This game is sick,' Mackenzie exclaimed as he continued to use his character, Hadwyn, to fight off the huge ants that kept coming at him in the dark tunnel. Mackenzie couldn't wait to get further into his friend Jackson's new game. 'Oh no, I'm getting low on life,' Mackenzie called out.

Jackson laughed. 'You know Mac, as great a fighter as you are, I think maybe we should've read a bit about the game before we started. It's a pain having to restart all the time.'

Jackson and Mackenzie were exploring the first level in Jackson's new console game *Burnstones: The Awakening*. Jackson had waited all year for this game and finally, on his thirteenth birthday, it had arrived. They had wasted no time reading the blurb on the game case.

Burnstones: The Awakening — **Adventure/RPG**
Millions of years ago, rising seas destroyed the
great pine forests of Europe. Trees wept a sticky
resin as they died. Many creatures became entombed
in the resin. Over time, the sea water turned the
resin into hardened amber stone. The creatures
became frozen in time.

The imprisonment of these creatures upset the natural order. Natural predators teeter on the edge of extinction; prey has become predator, growing unnaturally gigantic as they roam the lands and seas, creating havoc. These powerful creatures guard the Burnstones that maintain their power and position, and will not relinquish them easily.

Choose your character carefully. Will you work alone or with companions? Can you achieve the mastery required? It will take great skill and knowledge to traverse five lands as you seek the Burnstones. Without them, you cannot complete your quest to restore the natural balance of the lands. Without them, you cannot pass through the Last Door.

'Maybe we should look at the instructions for the first level again?' Jackson suggested. Mackenzie had been quite happy to start the game without knowing too much and just find out things as he went along. He rather liked flying by the seat of his pants and dealing with the unexpected, but he also knew his friend wasn't quite as experienced at gaming as himself and needed a bit more information to help him along the way.

Eadric climbed higher in the cave, far above the cave floor, up toward the dirt nests dug out by the ants. He carefully placed a hand, then a foot on any protruding rock or tree root he could find. Hadwyn held his defensive position below, swinging his sword as hard and as fast as he could, but he was losing life fast. Eadric's hand reached out into a hollow, toward a glow of red: the Burnstone. It was within his grasp.

At that moment, Hadwyn's sword was ripped from his grasp and clanged to the rock floor. Hadwyn had been knocked off balance and now lay on the cave floor. The Trap-Jaw Ant towered over him, the mandibles wide open, and within seconds the kill was executed.

The split screen went black on Mackenzie's side.

'Oh damn,' Jackson complained. 'I've got the Burnstone. How am I going to get out of here alive?' Jackson asked. Mackenzie chuckled at his friend's dilemma and watched his character descend into the waiting ants below. There was nothing he could do but wait for his screen to reload. 'Oh damn,' Jackson yelled again, as his character also fell victim to the Trap-Jaw Ants. 'We might as well start again.'

They decided to stop the game altogether and grab some snacks. Munching on potato chips, Jackson read from the on-screen manual. '"You are entering the Desert Lands, a forgotten Australian landscape. Nearing the end of the last ice age, cold arctic winds dried up the ancient lakes of Garnpung, Leaghur and Mungo. Humans compete with towering megafauna to find scarce water supplies. The spirit of the Leliyn Lizards is imprisoned within the Red Burnstone. Your quest is to find it. There are some who will help you. There are others who will fight to the death to stop you. In an arid and dangerous land, now you must compete to survive."'

Mackenzie and Jackson looked at each other. 'Piece of cake!' Mackenzie announced. 'Maybe now we can move on? Sometime this week maybe?' he heckled Jackson. 'Stop reading and get Eadric moving, will you? The day will be over if you don't hurry up.'

'Maybe you should choose a different character next time, or a different weapon?' Jackson suggested.

'Yeah, and maybe a destructive spell, like a fireball,' Mackenzie suggested. The two boys looked over their character choices to discover further clues and hints to aid their play. 'No, I like the Hadwyn character. I reckon he'll do a lot of damage with that longsword. He's kinda cool and smart like me.' He laughed.

Jackson shook his head. 'Mm … yeah I think I'll stick with Eadric as well,' Jackson agreed. 'He's handsome and charming like me.'

Mackenzie picked up a cushion and threw it at Jackson, laughing. 'Hey you. I'm a nobleman. You should learn your place,' Jackson said, throwing the cushion back. 'Your weapons don't look as classy as mine. Check out the jewels in the handles, mate,' he challenged. The Eadric character had the dual swords held in a leather brace on his back.

'Really?' Mackenzie replied. 'Well, I'm betting you'll need someone as clever and experienced as me to get through this thing. Says your character has more charm than ability. My character is smart and strong. You'll be standing behind me in battle, no doubt.'

'Is that so?' Jackson shot back. 'Considering you just let yourself get killed by the Trap-Jaw Ant, I'm thinking you'll still need my help. You can't do it without me.' With that the two friends restarted the game, squirming around in their bean bags as they battled, working rapidly with their game controllers and staring fixedly at the television screen. The game continued …

Jackson and Mackenzie had become inseparable friends since Mackenzie and his mum, Teri Jones, had moved into the old rented house at the end of the street. Jackson's mum, Mrs Taylor, wasn't fond of Mackenzie. He was a year older than her boy and she considered him 'street-wise'. She also worried that he came from a single parent home and perhaps was being raised with different family values. She had only met Mackenzie's mother once, outside the secondary school, and had noticed how shabbily the woman dressed; Mrs Jones didn't appear to have the same standards of dress or pride in her appearance. Mrs Taylor had also learnt over time that Mrs Jones was often at work and left the boy home alone without supervision or guidance. It wasn't something she approved of. She knew that teenagers left on their own were a recipe for trouble.

Mrs Taylor had had many discussions with her son Jackson about his growing friendship with Mackenzie, but to no avail. They remained friends thick and fast. Jackson was in his second year at secondary school and had been having trouble with some bullies. His best friend Sean had moved to another school at the end of last year and it had left a gap. Mackenzie, who was new to the school, met Jackson in guitar lessons after school and they just clicked. Before

Mackenzie came along, Jackson had been spending a lot of recesses in the library just to feel safe. The fact that Mackenzie was fourteen, almost fifteen and in an older year level at school didn't seem to stand in their way.

As their friendship developed, Jackson had no more trouble with bullies. In the end, Mrs Taylor agreed they could be friends and allowed them to spend time together on weekends, provided it was under her roof. She thought it might do Mackenzie good to see how a normal family lived.

The boys' adventure in the lounge room was loudly interrupted. 'I can help,' a cheeky voice piped up from the doorway.

'Oh yeah right, we need help from a twelve-year-old girl for sure!' Jackson scoffed, flicking his hand dismissively toward his younger sister.

'Well, you were still twelve last month!' Tess retaliated, referring to the fact that Jackson was only eleven months older than her.

'But you're the one who's so annoying, not to mention spilling your orange juice on my new game this morning before I'd even had a chance to try it out. You've probably wrecked it!' he continued.

Jackson felt very frustrated having a younger sister so close to his age. She wanted to be with him all the time, but he wanted to branch out on his own now he was older. He'd had years of having to do everything with her, sharing extracurricular activities and always having her around after school. He really felt he had done his bit as a protective brother, keeping her company when she was younger.

His parents expected him to be tolerant of her intrusions on his privacy, his time alone. He had complained about having to look after her, and about her taking or breaking his belongings. She was so clumsy. He felt his patience was wearing thin. This was his birthday, his time with his mate.

'Be a nice big brother, Jackson,' his parents would insist, 'you need to be her role model.' *Well,* he thought, *I've really had enough of this babysitting stuff.*

'But it was an accident,' Tess interrupted. 'I didn't mean to spill the juice. I tripped. Anyway, I know all about the game,' she declared.

'I read all about it online before you got it.' Tess liked to keep up with her brother and try to impress him.

'I don't think so,' said Jackson. 'I'll be lucky if this game keeps working. I bet something doesn't work properly. I had to wash all the juice off and dry it on the heater. I've had enough of you, and if you don't get out of here and leave us alone, I'm going to tell Mum,' he threatened.

'You're so mean, Jackson,' Tess retorted. 'Mum will hear you being mean to me,' she warned, standing with her hands on her hips.

'Hey guys, settle down,' Mackenzie interjected. Mackenzie didn't have brothers or sisters, so he often wondered why they fought so much. He really liked Jackson. They got on well, especially with their music and gaming interests, but he had noticed that Jackson became quite immature with his sister. *Too close in age, perhaps?* he wondered. 'Maybe we can let Tess have a turn?' Mackenzie suggested.

'No way, it's my game and it's the first time I've played it. She butts into everything,' Jackson protested. Tess stuck her tongue out at Jackson and sat down on the seat behind them. Jackson glared at her. Mackenzie looked intently at Jackson and pointed to the game.

'C'mon mate. Let's get back into it?' Jackson and Mackenzie continued to play the game. Distracted for a time, the three of them watched with great interest as the new game unfolded on the screen. 'Fantastic graphics,' Mackenzie declared. 'One of the best games I've seen. The characters are so lifelike and the scenery is unreal. See that water?' They all agreed, the picture quality was almost as good as watching a movie.

The sound of distant thunder interrupted the late afternoon. The warm November day was cooling down fast as a cold front approached the city from the south. Within seconds, a small scruffy dog was scratching at the back door, looking for refuge in the house.

Tess got up from her seat and headed toward the door. She smiled at the little dog as she opened the back door and he jumped into her arms, trembling. 'What a funny little thing you are,' she told him as she wiped the first droplets of rain from his long, sandy coloured hair. 'Nothing is going to hurt you,' she continued reassuringly. 'It's just a little thunder.' Rain droplets were evaporating on the hot cement steps. 'See silly, even the rain is going away.' Tess chuckled at Buddy as she ruffled his quivering head. 'Let's go and watch the boys.'

Tess was right. The few raindrops that had appeared no longer fell. The wind had completely stopped and the birds had gone quiet. If Tess had looked towards the back fence, she may have noticed the large dark mass of clouds gathering in the eastern sky. Lightning was flickering occasionally from deep within the clouds, providing a fascinating light show. The imposing black clouds silently drifted toward them.

3

Lights Out

Inside the house, Jackson and Tess's father, Mr Taylor, struggled to see the holes where the screws were meant to go. He was trying to replace their front door with one his wife had discovered at a garage sale a few months before. It was an old door – *possibly European beech*, he thought to himself as he ran his hand across the light-coloured wood. Mr Taylor was a builder and he recognised the fine, short grain.

The door was decorated by a wrought ironwork tree, with the finely crafted branches and leaves spreading the full length and width of the door. He had pointed out to his wife that at the end of the five largest branches, there appeared to be empty indents where perhaps there were once decorative stones. Nevertheless, her heart was set on it so they came home with it.

Mr Taylor had found it difficult to fit the new door into the old door frame. It was going to take all his experience and skills to achieve the final goal. There was an intricate green and bronze doorknob, matching the colours of the wood and metal work. Mrs Taylor wanted him to install an electronic doorbell 'somehow' into the door knob. 'Margaret, can you turn the light on?' he called to his wife in the kitchen, holding the door in place with his shoulder as he secured the last screws into the hinges. It seemed very dark for 5 pm. *Unusually dark*, he thought.

Mrs Taylor switched on the lights for her husband to see his work as she continued to the lounge room. 'Tess, come here. You can help me bring the washing in. I think a heavy rain is on the way.'

'Oh no, Mum!' protested Tess. 'I've just started watching this game!'

'I won't have any arguments, young lady,' Mrs Taylor continued. 'Come along. Here's a basket for you.' Jackson turned and laughed mockingly at his sister Tess. 'That's enough out of you, young man,' his mother scolded. 'You'll being doing your share when Mackenzie goes home. It'll do you both good to get off those stupid electronic games for a while and get a taste of the real world,' she warned them. 'You need to stop living in a fantasy world, no good will come of it.'

Tess disappeared outside with her mother while Mr Taylor continued, fitting wires under one of the door panels. *Finally*, he thought, *progress*. When he'd accidently dropped the door knob, he discovered that the top of the knob could come off. Once removed, it revealed a hollow area inside, perfect for the wires and buzzer to be situated. With a bit of delicate drilling, he would be able to position the buzzer in the very centre; once the knob was reassembled, it would look like it hadn't been touched.

In the next room, Mackenzie and Jackson roared with laughter and excitement as they squirmed around in their bean bags, manoeuvring their characters in battle.

> *Oversized Whistling Spiders were impeding the way to the ant nests deep within the earth. The dark-brown furry creatures hissed as the stiff bristles around their mouths moved backwards and forwards against each other. The normally docile creatures had been provoked into aggression by the entry of Hadwyn and Eadric into their silk-lined burrow. Bones littered the burrow floor, evidence of the spiders' recent meals.*

Hadwyn and Eadric pushed forward side by side, but the spider numbers were growing, coming at them from both sides. Swords and knives glinted in the half-light as they desperately sought to push back the spiders that continuously plunged towards them from the front and both sides, their mouths snapping with dangerous pickaxe fangs.

'What'll we do?' Jackson asked Mackenzie excitedly, beginning to question their decision to access the ant tunnels by going through the spider burrows.

'Wait! Wait! I have a Statue spell!' Mackenzie answered, fumbling with the game console, seeking the spell button. Mackenzie selected the Statue spell and pressed down.

The spiders froze in their tracks, giving Hadwyn and Eadric a few seconds to escape. Hadwyn and Eadric ran further into the burrow until they located an 'up-tunnel', built off the main tunnel and going straight upwards to an ant chamber. The ants created up-tunnels to ensure they had air pockets when heavy rain flooded their tunnels. Eadric jumped onto Hadwyn's back and then jumped further, using several protruding ledges to get higher. Hadwyn followed. Within seconds, both were high above the cave floor and within centimetres of the ant chamber.

'You have to bang on the back wall to get through to the ant chamber,' Tess interrupted as she ran back into the room.

'SHOOSH Tess! We know!' grumbled Jackson.

The sound of the approaching spiders spurred them on. Hadwyn and Eadric began furiously hitting the dirt wall with their weapons. The spiders hissed louder and louder.

'Any good spells?' Mackenzie asked Jackson.

'Yes, yes,' Jackson nodded, as he selected a spell from his controller and yelled, 'Fireball!'

Hot flames flew from Eadric's outstretched hand and enveloped the spiders below. Within seconds, all that remained were charred spider parts scattered along the burrow floor and a few smouldering strings of spider web silk hanging off the walls. The wall of the ant chamber began to crumble as the two characters smashed their weapons against the dirt wall. The red glow grew brighter. Hadwyn put his sword back into the scabbard hanging from his belt and motioned to Eadric to stop. Hadwyn knelt down in front of the gap in the wall, reached in with both hands and retrieved the treasured red Burnstone. Hadwyn opened a pouch on his belt and carefully slipped the glowing red stone inside for safekeeping.

A magnified view of the Burnstone appeared on the TV screen, showing the beautifully preserved lizard suspended lifelessly inside the red stone. They had succeeded in locating the first stone but were uncertain of the next part of their journey. It was time to consult the map.

'Well boys, time to call it a day,' Mrs Taylor interrupted as she came in the back door. 'You best get home quick smart, Mackenzie, before this storm hits.'

Jackson looked at Mackenzie apologetically. 'Oh well, I guess we can finish the level tomorrow?'

Mackenzie smiled at Jackson. 'Sure Mrs Taylor, and thanks for having me. Oh yeah, and thanks for lunch,' he added. 'Great game Jackson,' Mackenzie told his friend as he got himself up out of the bean bag. 'Wow, there's at least five levels for us to get through yet. Might take us days,' he exclaimed. 'See ya tomorrow.'

Jackson nodded. 'I'll try to get through the first level later tonight,' he told Mackenzie quietly.

'Give me a call if you get stuck.' Mackenzie laughed.

'See your friend to the door, Jackson,' Mrs Taylor instructed.

Mackenzie stood waiting at the door while Mr Taylor tested his workmanship on the door. 'Seems to be working okay now,' he announced, opening and closing the newly fitted door a couple of times and then pressing the buzzer.

'Hey, that buzzer is interfering with my game,' Jackson called from the lounge room.

Mr Taylor looked through the lounge door to where Jackson was continuing to play his game. The game screen was flickering. 'What? Oh, never mind. I still have to make a few adjustments,' he reassured Jackson. 'If it keeps playing up, we'll get Harry to look at it.' Harry was a fellow electrician. Mr Taylor didn't want to create an electrical circuit overload; if the wires melted, it could cause a fire.

'I thought I told you to see your friend to the door?' Mrs Taylor called from the kitchen.

Mr Taylor then opened the door for Mackenzie. 'Good day, young fella,' he said good-naturedly.

'See you Mackenzie,' Tess called out as Mackenzie disappeared from view. Mrs Taylor returned to the kitchen, where she began preparing the evening meal. Mr Taylor was busy packing up his tools.

'Jackson, help your father take the tools out to the shed,' said Mrs Taylor. Jackson had been standing in the doorway for a while, looking at her sheepishly.

'Yes Mum …' he replied. 'I was wondering, Mum, if I could show Tess my new game?' he ventured.

'Now listen here, young man,' his mother interrupted, 'I think you've had enough electronics for one day.'

'But Mum, it's my birthday,' Jackson protested, 'and I had to go to school because it was Friday.'

'Today isn't your birthday, Jackson,' she confirmed.

Tess appeared at Jackson's side. 'And I haven't even had a turn.'

Mr Taylor walked up behind his two children in the hallway. 'Come on, Margaret. Let's cut them a little slack,' he suggested.

Mrs Taylor shook her head. 'It wouldn't hurt you to spend a little time with them instead of just doing your thing and letting them stay on stupid electronic games all day. Suits you, I guess,' she reprimanded him. 'I'm absolutely sick of these wasted days. I'm the only one doing any work around here,' she complained.

Mr Taylor glanced at the door he had just spent several hours installing but didn't comment.

'It's not fair, I haven't had a turn at all,' Tess continued to protest, hoping to swing the argument in her favour.

Mrs Taylor ignored her daughter and continued admonishing her husband. 'Why don't you do something with them for a change? You're always at work or the cricket club or down in that damn shed … meanwhile, they get no exercise and don't have to use their brains at all. They just sit and stare at the idiot box!'

'Now come on Margaret,' Mr Taylor interjected. 'Here's an idea: how about Jackson shows Tess the game now, just until tea time? And I'll take them fishing tomorrow and get them out of your hair. How about that?'

Mrs Taylor looked at the three faces frowning in her direction and then at the saucepan, which had begun to boil over on the stove. She walked over and pulled the lid off, then turned back toward her husband. 'Oh well, I guess Saturday is a lost cause. Fine, you get them up at 6 am. They can help you get the fishing gear and make a picnic lunch.'

Tess squealed with delight and ran back into the lounge room.

'Wait, wait!' Jackson called, following close on her heels. 'Just wait and I'll show you how to pick your character,' he told her.

Tess was already seated in a bean bag and had begun exploring the buttons on the game controller. Tess wasn't listening to Jackson. She surveyed the female characters set out on the screen before her. 'I do like the green character, the one with the skirt and leggings. She's even got a hooded cape,' she began. 'But I like that purple one too, she looks like a fairy, look at her ears. Wow. She looks like she's from Robin Hood's forest …'

Jackson interjected, 'Listen, you can spend till tea time mucking around with the character setup, but we won't get to play any of the game. You still have to pick three spells before we can even start. I'm just going to use the Eadric character. I've already set him up before and we don't want to waste time.'

Tess followed her brother's advice obediently for once, pushing the buttons at his suggestions. It wasn't often she got to play a game with her big brother. She was going to show him how clever she was.

'Just pick the green character, Tess – yep, that's right. Now pick three spells from the top of the screen. See – Invisibility, Charm Stare and Replenish Quiver. That'll do. Come on Tess. We've only got about half an hour.'

'How do I use the spells?' Tess asked.

'It doesn't matter, Tess. We'll work it out as we go along. It's really easy, don't worry,' he said convincingly.

Tess looked admiringly at her chosen character. 'Look, she's just like me,' she announced happily.

'Okay, now wait till I start the first level,' Jackson instructed Tess. Tess waited in her bean bag, playing with her long blond plait.

'Oh, this is so exciting Jackson, I'm going to be a great warrior woman.' Jackson didn't respond, his eyes intent on the television screen, his hands busily working the controls. 'What spells do you have?' Tess enquired.

'What? Oh, Fireball, Skin Shield and Furious Strike,' Jackson rattled off.

'Can't I have a Fireball?' Tess asked.

'Okay Tess, we're in!' he announced, ignoring Tess's question. 'Now use those buttons to choose your direction, and those ones there are for walking, running and jumping,' he instructed, leaning toward Tess and pointing at her controls. 'Okay now, practice your controls with the character.'

'What's my character's name again?' Tess asked.

'What? Oh, um, I think it's Emerald. Yes, the green one is Emerald,' Jackson replied.

Tess and Jackson watched as they made their two characters walk along in the game. 'Where are they?' asked Tess, 'I can hardly see them.'

'They're in one of the dark desert caves,' Jackson said. 'They're in the first level, the Land of Mungo. Lots of desert. This level starts in the caves.'

'Oh yes, I remember reading about the Desert Lands. We have to find a red Burnstone. Easy,' she said confidently.

'Not so easy, Tess,' Jackson disagreed. 'There are many dangerous things along the way. Giant creatures will try to kill us. We'll have to use our weapons and all of our magic to get through. Mackenzie and I got owned heaped of times already when we tried to get through this level.' The siblings continued their electronic adventure, laughing and shrieking at times.

Mrs Taylor continued preparing tea in the kitchen and was in the middle of setting the table when a large clap of thunder startled her. Mr Taylor came in through the back door. 'The rain and wind are picking up out there,' he told her. 'Lucky you got that washing in.'

Mrs Taylor looked out the window. The sky was almost fully dark now, the sound of rain getting heavier. Lightning flickered, illuminating the outside area for a few seconds, showing the fence and the dog kennel. 'Where's the dog?' Mrs Taylor asked.

'Tess brought him in before,' Mr Taylor replied, taking his boots off.

'Yes, but I think he might have gone outside again when we were bringing in the washing,' Mrs Taylor pondered. She walked toward the lounge room and called out to the children. 'I need one of you to go outside and get the dog.' She walked back into the kitchen and pulled the blinds down.

A few minutes passed and there had been no movement from the children. Mrs Taylor walked back to the lounge. 'I asked one of you to go outside and get the dog before the storm's on top of us,' she said in a louder voice.

'You do it,' Jackson told Tess.

'No, you do it. I did it last time,' Tess argued.

'No, you do it. I have to hold the game on pause for us,' Jackson said with a cheeky grin.

Mr Taylor came into the lounge. 'Right, that's it from you two. Stop that game and you can both go out and find the dog!'

Jackson gave Tess an angry look as he pushed the pause button on his controller and got out of the bean bag. Tess ignored him and walked to the back door. She turned on the outside light, stepped out onto the back verandah and began calling the dog's name. 'Buddy, Buddy!'

Jackson stormed past her in a huff, walking outside and down the steps into the backyard, disappearing behind the corner of the house.

Tess heard barking from the front of the house. She turned and ran toward the front door. 'It sounds like he's in the front yard, Mum. I'll check out there and see if he got through the gate somehow.' Tess opened the newly installed front door, turning the front light on. She ran out into the driveway and yelled over the side gate to her brother, 'I think he's out the front, Jackson.'

The barking sounded again, this time from the park across the road. Jackson came back through the side gate. As he walked past the front porch, a strong gust of wind blew through the house and slammed the old door shut with a loud bang. In her haste, Tess had left it open. *Oh no,* Jackson thought to himself. *Mum will be furious about her new door slamming. I hope it hasn't broken.* Jackson didn't want to go inside and check. He continued down the driveway, out towards the street. He didn't notice the porch light flickering on and off, nor was he aware of the vibration that continued to reverberate in the old door long after the effect of the bang had subsided. In the lounge, the game console also vibrated.

Jackson ran to catch up with his sister, who was calling the dog's name again. 'He's over there somewhere.' Tess pointed toward a large group of trees barely visible from the street lights. The two children ran across the road, calling the dog. They pressed on, leaning into the wind as they reached the trees, but then heard barking even further back in the park. It was becoming more and more difficult to see as they ventured further in, away from the street lights. 'Maybe we should get a torch?' Tess suggested, feeling quite worried. Jackson nodded and fumbled with his phone, trying to get his torchlight app working.

At that moment, a tremendous lightning bolt lit up the whole park. The lightning had struck the television antenna on the roof of their home. In those few seconds, an enormous surge of power shot through the home's electrical circuits. The television and game console lost power. The front doorbell buzzed and then stopped as smoke began to wisp out from the ancient door knob. All the lights in the house and the street were extinguished. Everything was dark. The extremely loud crack of thunder that followed was deafening. The children had collapsed unconscious to the ground.

Back in the Land of Mungo, huddled together for warmth in the dark, cold cave, Jackson, Tess, and Buddy sat together, leaning against a wall. They had finally pieced together their memories of that fateful day, ending in the storm, and now they felt emotionally and physically exhausted. They did not understand how they came to be stuck in the game and they felt the gravity of what lay ahead. 'We were in the park,' Tess pondered, 'but how did we get here?'

'I have no idea,' Jackson replied.

The console in the Taylors' lounge room flickered intermittently and then the power light went out. Time stood still.

4

Suspicious Circumstances

SUNDAY (Cont.)

'Hello?' said a muffled voice through the front door. Mr Taylor recognised the voice. Mackenzie knocked as well, uncertain if he had been heard. The doorbell had not worked since the lightning strike. Mr Taylor rose from his chair and walked toward the door, wondering how he would have this conversation.

'Coming, Mackenzie,' he called as he turned the old metal door knob.

'Hi Mr Taylor,' Mackenzie greeted him cheerfully, stepping back as Mr Taylor pushed the screen door open. 'How are you?' Mackenzie continued politely.

'Hello Mackenzie,' Mr Taylor answered hesitantly. 'Come in.'

Mackenzie walked in, glanced into the lounge and couldn't see Jackson so continued into the kitchen. Mackenzie didn't notice the computer technician sitting at the family computer in a corner of the lounge. Mr Taylor closed the front door and turned. 'Where's Jackson?' Mackenzie asked, 'we've got a game to win.'

'Mackenzie, sit down for a minute,' Mr Taylor said softly, gesturing toward a chair. Mackenzie felt a little puzzled, but followed the instruction and looked up at Mr Taylor curiously.

'Oh, I see you've had a bit of a party,' Mackenzie commented, observing the leftover food on the table. 'I wondered what those two police cars were doing in the street. Noise complaints from the neighbours?' Mackenzie joked.

Mr Taylor sat down and looked across the table at the boy. He liked the lad. He wondered why Mrs Taylor disliked Mackenzie and why she worried so much about Jackson being friends with him. Mr Taylor had found him pleasant and polite, often more so than his own two children. The thought of Jackson and Tess brought him back to the task at hand. 'I'm really sorry to tell you this, but the children are missing.'

Mackenzie looked at him, blinking, uncertain about what had just been said. 'Missing?' he enquired.

'Yes, I'm afraid so. They went outside in the storm to look for the dog last night and we haven't seen them since.'

Mackenzie made a small chuckling noise, shaking his head. 'No,' he disagreed, 'that couldn't be true.' Mackenzie wondered if this was a joke and looked over his shoulder at the door leading to the back of the house. He expected Jackson and Tess to jump out laughing any minute. Mackenzie looked back at Mr Taylor, searching his face for some giveaway sign, but all he saw was a sad, serious expression. Now Mackenzie felt worried. It was hard to take in; he needed to know more.

A firm knock on the front door interrupted their conversation. A police sergeant let himself in and walked into the lounge to speak to the technician. Mackenzie was surprised. 'Who's he talking to?' Mackenzie asked Mr Taylor.

'Oh, there's a technician searching the computer to see if there's a clue anywhere of where they might be … anything,' Mr Taylor explained. Mackenzie found all this news very hard to comprehend. It didn't seem real, any of it. It felt like just a few minutes ago, he had been sitting in the lounge room, playing Jackson's new game with him. How could Jackson and Tess be missing? Where were they? What had happened? So many questions ran through his mind.

The sergeant came into the kitchen and Mr Taylor looked up hopefully. 'Nothing yet Sam,' the sergeant informed Mr Taylor, 'but our technician is now planning to search through all the telephone accounts to see if there are any phone calls to unknown numbers lately. How many phone accounts do you have?'

Mr Taylor thought for a moment. 'Three mobiles and one landline,' he answered.

'Good. Can you help him access those accounts, Sam? And who is this young man?' the sergeant enquired, nodding his head in the direction of Mackenzie.

'Oh sorry, this is Mackenzie, Jackson's best mate. He lives at the end of the street,' said Mr Taylor. Mackenzie stood up awkwardly, uncertain of how he should greet the policeman. 'Mackenzie, this is Sergeant Bourke. He's in charge of the investigation,' Mr Taylor continued. The policeman stretched his hand toward Mackenzie, who responded and shook his hand.

'Pleased to meet you, young man,' the sergeant responded. 'Must be a shock for you hearing all this?'

'Yes sir,' Mackenzie agreed. 'I can't really believe it.'

Sergeant Bourke began writing on his notepad. 'And what's your surname, Mackenzie?' he enquired.

'My name?' Mackenzie answered, feeling apprehensive.

'Yes, yes,' Sergeant Bourke continued, 'the more people we talk to, the better chance we have of finding clues that might lead us to the children's whereabouts. You, being the best mate, might know a lot more than some of the others, but I'll need to speak to your parents first,' he added.

'There is no father,' Mrs Taylor announced, standing at the doorway of the kitchen. She had been asleep for a few hours. Mackenzie was starting to feel very uncomfortable.

'Right,' Sergeant Bourke asked, 'what's your mum's name then?'

'Jones,' Mackenzie answered, 'Teri Jones.'

Mrs Taylor walked over to the policeman and held out an address book. 'Yes, and here is her phone number.'

Mr Taylor had gone into the lounge and could be heard speaking with the technician. Sergeant Bourke took down the details. 'I was surprised to hear they'd gone out so late in a storm,' Mackenzie shared with the sergeant.

'It wasn't that late, Mackenzie,' Mrs Taylor corrected, 'It was before tea, before 6 pm.'

Mackenzie looked puzzled. 'Oh, I thought it was much later than that.'

'I think I'd know when my own children went missing,' she told him bluntly.

'What made you think it was later?' the sergeant questioned him.

'Oh, um, well …' Mackenzie fumbled with his thoughts. 'Well, it was unusually dark yesterday … um, maybe I just made a mistake, you know, it sort of seemed a lot later.'

'Mm,' Sergeant Bourke murmured. 'Oh well, you best run along and let your mother know I'll be in touch. Then you can tell me all you know, heh?'

Mackenzie nodded toward the sergeant and glanced nervously in Mrs Taylor's direction. 'Yes sir,' he answered, walking toward the front door as quickly as he could. 'I'll let her know as soon as she gets home from work.' His mum had accepted a Sunday shift at the local supermarket. She'd be home about 4 pm.

Mackenzie couldn't get out of the house quick enough. Once he had made some distance between himself and the house, he located his mobile phone in his pocket and searched his messages. Mackenzie stopped walking, coming to a standstill as he stared down at his phone. He felt a strange sensation in his gut. The message from Jackson last night came to him at 10 pm. That was more than four hours after they had disappeared. He had sent a response to Jackson but then nothing. What was going on?

Mackenzie lay down on his bed, staring at the ceiling. The house was quiet. It always was when his mum was at work. His mum had taken a second job to make ends meet. It had been difficult since his father died two years ago. Before that, he remembered a normal life in a small country town. His dad, Simon, had been a musician in a band, working most weekends; his mum had worked in a childcare centre. It all changed when his dad got sick.

He remembered the first year of his dad's sickness. Mackenzie had been only twelve at the time, in his first year in secondary school. Everything had been new and exciting, so he hadn't noticed much change in his dad except he was home a lot more than usual. He would hear his mum and dad talking late at night and if he entered the room, they would stop and change the subject.

When he started second year at secondary school, he would come home after school and learn guitar with his dad. His father had stopped working completely and was home all the time, except for lots of appointments. In the end, his mum had to stop work as well to look after his father as he got sicker and sicker. That was when things got really tough.

Mackenzie started spending a lot of his time helping care for his father, so that his mum could go into town for shopping, appointments or just to see a friend. In the last six months of his father's life, Mackenzie felt so removed from who he'd been just a year and a half before. Secondary school had been an exciting new adventure back then, making new friends and joining music and sports clubs. Everything had changed. Now he felt older, different to his friends.

About three months before his father died, his parents had asked him to sit down with them. They explained that the specialist had told them there was no more treatment for his dad, and that he was going to die within a few months. Mackenzie found it very hard to believe. He got angry with his parents for not trying harder to find another doctor. He begged his father to go overseas for treatment. For a week, he refused to go to school and searched the internet for something or someone to save his father's life.

Eventually, his father called him to his side. 'I'm sorry mate,' he told Mackenzie, reaching out for his hand and pulling him over to sit on the bed beside him. 'We can't fix this.'

Mackenzie was shaking his head, looking at his thin, frail father. He had lost so much weight. 'Why?' Mackenzie pleaded, 'I can't do this without you. I need you to stay. Mum needs you.'

Simon had looked at his thirteen-year-old son. It was painful to see his family so distressed. It was painful to think about not being there for him as he grew up. 'Mackenzie, I need you to know that I've done all that I can to stay, but there's nothing else that can be done.' Mackenzie's head was bent low. 'It's okay to be sad, mate. It sucks,' his father reassured him.

'What's going to happen to you? Where will you be when you're dead?' Mackenzie asked with anguish.

Simon took a long breath and thought for a moment. 'Well mate, there are a lot of different ideas and beliefs about all that. A lot of people believe in an afterlife. You'll learn more about that as you go through life and you can decide for yourself what makes sense to you. I can't give you any guarantees, but what I can tell you is that I'll be with you in your heart and in your mind forever. You can carry everything I've taught you into the future. And if there's any way of connecting with you from an afterlife, I will. Listen for me. Look for me. I will really try, son.'

Tears ran down Mackenzie's face. His father pulled him into an embrace and they held on to each other for a very long time.

A few months after his dad died, they left their little house up in the country. They couldn't keep up the mortgage payments. His mum had shifted him to this new place in the city, 'Because it's a nice area and I can get more work.' Now his mum was paying a high rent and one job just wasn't enough to get by. She'd found a new childcare job during the day and was also working casually at the local supermarket in the evenings (and sometimes on weekends if she could get a shift). She was determined that Mackenzie would live in a quiet area with a good school, and she wanted him to continue with guitar lessons. This was their second year in the city.

Mackenzie hoped that this new situation with his missing friends wouldn't stress his mum out too much. She had already been through so much and he wanted to protect her, just like he promised his dad. He went over and over in his mind what had transpired yesterday. He just couldn't understand what had happened to Jackson and Tess. He looked at his phone again. *Maybe*, he thought, *I can send a message.* 'WHERE ARE YOU JACKSON?' he messaged. Of course, he received no reply. He wondered how he should tell his mum about this. Why did the police need him to go to the station? So many questions ran though his head.

Later that afternoon, Mackenzie and his mother were ushered into a private room at the police station. The policeman explained to Mrs Jones all that had transpired over the past twenty-four hours and informed her that they needed to ask Mackenzie more questions. 'We have a development in our investigation, Mrs Jones. Our technician has discovered phone messages between your son and the missing children after their disappearance. This is highly suspect behaviour and your son indicated to us that he knew nothing about their disappearance.'

Mrs Jones looked at her son, confused. Mackenzie felt helpless. The sergeant began questioning Mackenzie in earnest in front of his mum. Mackenzie could add nothing to the information they sought.

'I got a shock. I couldn't make sense of it all. I didn't know what to do. I really don't know anything else,' Mackenzie told them.

The sergeant spoke. 'Young man, this is a very serious situation. Those children may be in terrible danger. Their parents are grief-stricken. You are the last person to have communicated with them, yet you claim to know nothing. Let me tell you this,' he continued, 'If you are hiding something from us, from their parents, we will bring the law down on you and you will pay a huge price. You can be charged as being an accessory to the fact if they have been harmed.'

'Really Sergeant, my son is an honest boy,' Mrs Jones interjected, 'he would tell us if he knew anything about his friends.'

'I hope for his sake you are right, Mrs Jones,' the sergeant responded, shaking his head. He packed up his papers and stood up. 'You're free to go, Mackenzie,' he instructed in a stern voice, 'however, we will be watching you.'

Mackenzie and his mother left the room. As they were going past the administration desk at the front of the police station, the front door opened and Mr and Mrs Taylor walked in. Mackenzie and Mrs

Jones stopped to let them pass. 'Walking free, are you?' Mrs Taylor snapped at Mackenzie. 'You know where my children are,' she said accusingly. 'What type of human are you?' she continued in a high-pitched voice.

Mr Taylor waved his hand at his wife. 'That's not going to help, Margaret – leave them be.' He grabbed her hand and pulled her toward the waiting area.

'Come on,' Mrs Jones encouraged Mackenzie, putting her arm around him. 'Let's get you home.'

'I'm so sorry Mum,' Mackenzie told her as they sat side by side in the car. 'I wish you weren't going through this with me.'

Mrs Jones reached over and took hold of his hand. 'We go through everything together, remember?' she reassured him. 'I wouldn't want you to face this alone.'

'I just don't understand any of it, Mum. I can't explain the messages on my phone. I thought they were home. Jackson asked me to come around and help him because he was stuck in his new game. It doesn't make sense. Anyway, Mrs Taylor has never liked me anyway. She doesn't trust me. She thinks she's better than us,' he complained.

'Never mind, the truth will come out in the end. It always does. Don't take notice of Mrs Taylor. She's beside herself and can't make sense of it all either. She's desperate to find her children and not thinking straight.'

MONDAY

The police search intensified. Monday arrived and the news spread. The story of the disappearance appeared on the television news, on community posters and on Facebook. Mrs Jones worried deeply about her son's mental health. 'I think he's anxious and depressed,' she shared with Bronwyn, her manager and friend at the child care centre. 'I was already worried about all that he's had to cope with, and now this. He's just sitting alone in his room. He just can't manage going to school. He's not eating. I just feel so helpless.'

'Let's have a break,' Bronwyn suggested as she filled the kettle for a cup of tea. 'The little ones are napping and the older kids are having a ball out there in the sand pit. Mary is watching them.' The two sat down to a pot of Irish breakfast tea. 'You know, he's probably still grieving. He's lost his dad, his home and friends up in the country, and now is probably thinking the worst about his best friend.' Mrs Jones stared at her cup, unconsciously playing with the handle. Bronwyn saw the slight tremble in her hand. 'It's more stress for you too, Teri. This is taking a toll on you as well. I really don't know how you go on. I think you should take some time off work.'

'I haven't got a choice, Bron,' Mrs Jones explained, 'I can't afford to take time off work. I have to keep a roof over his head, no matter what's happening. I'll be alright. It's him I'm worried about.'

Bronwyn took a big breath. 'Well, your work mates are worried about you,' Bron began. 'We really care about you, Teri, and we feel helpless too. We watch how hard you work. We know what you've been through and we know how much you've struggled. But if you don't look after yourself, Mackenzie won't have any parents. So, we came up with an idea.' She took another breath. 'You know there's thirteen of us working here, and we have all decided to donate one day's annual leave to you, so that you can take a couple of weeks off and support your son. He needs you now and heaven knows what's still ahead. You need to be home.'

Mrs Jones tried to take it all in. She thought of her work colleagues' generosity. None of them were wealthy. Each had their own set of challenges in life, in their own families. Mrs Jones was overcome. 'I don't know ...'

'It's decided, Teri. We've organised it. Think of the boy. Anyway, we've changed all the shifts so we want you to take the leave from now. Go home, Teri.' Bronwyn knew she had won when she saw a small nod from her very tired friend.

Throughout the day, Mackenzie kept going over and over everything in his mind, searching for clues and answers. Sometimes he lay on his bed or paced his room. Other times he sat in the bean bag, sat outside or walked up and down the street. He even searched the park. He couldn't imagine going to school.

His mum understood. She knew he wouldn't be able to concentrate at school. It had taken a long time after his father's death to hear him laugh again with friends. She wondered if this latest stress might all be just too much for him. All she could do was be there, be available to talk if he wanted to. She'd watched him sitting in the same place, playing his electronic games so often since his dad died. It's a 'distraction', people told her. 'Time, just give him time.'

After picking up shopping supplies on the way home from work, she knocked on his door. 'Mackenzie, I'm home,' she called. She knocked again a bit louder this time.

'Yeah, come in,' he replied.

'How's your day going?' she asked.

'Yep,' he responded, his eyes glued to his game.

'Hey you. I'm talking to you,' she ruffled his hair.

'Yep, yep, I'll be with you in just a sec, Mum. I've just got to finish this bit,' he advised her as he deftly manoeuvred his game character on the screen via his controller.

'What are you playing?' Teri enquired, trying to connect in some way.

'Oh, it's just an old game I've had forever. I've been going through all the older games. I might sell some.' He was hoping to make some money to help his mum. Mrs Jones picked up the game cover and tried to be interested. 'It's okay Mum, you won't understand this game,' Mackenzie said good-naturedly.

'Well, I'll go and put the kettle on and think about tea,' she told him a little wearily. 'I guess you had better concentrate on what you're doing, otherwise you might get stuck forever,' she joked, trying to cheer him up.

'You can't get stuck in a game, Mum, you just keep going or die,' he said, shaking his head.

'I meant stuck in your room, silly,' she added.

A little while later, Mackenzie came out of his room. Mrs Jones noticed a strange look on his face. 'What's the matter?'

'I don't know, Mum. I'm feeling really weirded out about something.' Mrs Jones put her head to one side, waiting. 'That message Jackson sent me, you know, the one after they went missing. He said he was stuck in his new game and was asking me for help. It doesn't make sense.'

Mrs Jones shrugged her shoulders. 'Beyond me,' she told him. 'It's all too technological for me.'

'Mum, I know this is going to sound strange but what if he was actually stuck inside the game, like somehow he and Tess are in the game?'

'Mackenzie,' Mrs Jones started, 'Oh Mackenzie, I know this has been terrible for you and I know we want to believe we will find them, but really that's just not possible.' By this time, Mackenzie had taken a seat at the small kitchen table and was staring off toward the window, deep in thought. 'I think I'll order pizza tonight,' she announced, not really knowing what else to say.

Mackenzie's mind was racing, considering a thousand ideas. He just knew that he would have to rule out this persisting idea that somehow his friends were stuck in the game. He had no time to waste. He was on a mission. He had to get into the Taylors' house and get the Burnstone game.

He knew that Mrs Taylor would never let him in. He decided he would break in. He knew where they kept a spare front door key at the front steps. He waited for the dark of night and made his way up the street to their home. He had dressed in dark clothes and tried to keep out of the glow of street lights. It was 10 pm. He made himself as comfortable as he could, sitting quietly in the bushy garden where there were many small trees and shrubs to provide cover.

He waited and watched until the Taylors' bedroom light was turned off. He then waited another hour. He had learnt about sleep cycles at school and he wanted them to be in a deep sleep. With his small pen light, a leftover relic from his spying adventures in childhood, he made his way to the front door and quietly let himself in.

He quickly scanned the room. There it was, neatly packed alongside Jackson's other games. Mackenzie opened the case but found the disc was missing. He moved over to the game console and turned it on. After what seemed like forever, a small green power light flickered on and he was able to eject the disc. Within three minutes he was back on the footpath, running home.

Mackenzie couldn't wait to start the game. He had to be very quiet coming back into the house. His mum was used to him staying up late playing games, but she might wake with the sound of the front door. The last thing he wanted to do was wake her and waste time with her questioning him.

Soon, he was seated back in his bedroom waiting for the game to load. He needed to familiarise himself with the game rules. If Jackson and Tess were in there, this was no longer just a game.

It didn't take him long to reacquaint himself with the intricacies of the game. But in the back of his mind, he knew this game was not going to be normal. If Jackson and Tess were somehow stuck in *Burnstones*, then the game would not be operating like a standard console game. Were they even alive? So many questions. If they were alive, how would they interact with game characters? Could they use weapons? Could he use Hadwyn to find them and help them find their way home? Could he keep them safe? Was any of this possible? He had no time to lose.

Within ten minutes, Mackenzie had entered the first level of the game as Hadwyn. Mackenzie located his character on the map of Lake Garnpung, one of the three dried-out lakes in the Desert Lands. He couldn't see where his friends were located. All he could do was get in there and start searching.

Switching to close-up view, Mackenzie observed keenly as the interior of a cave came into view. He could see Hadwyn standing off to the side, waiting for direction from him. *Best to be ready and prepared for anything*, he thought to himself. He had chosen a character with high intelligence and dexterity, and a good measure of strength. After what he had read about *Burnstones*, he was going to need all the abilities he could find.

He got into a comfortable position in his bean bag, making Hadwyn walk further into the cave. He travelled in the direction of a faint light, rounding bends and crawling through low passages. After about twenty minutes, he saw light ahead becoming stronger. He kept walking to where the cave opened up into a larger space. Slowly, two bodies came into view. Mackenzie stopped Hadwyn in view of the two characters ahead. He had found them.

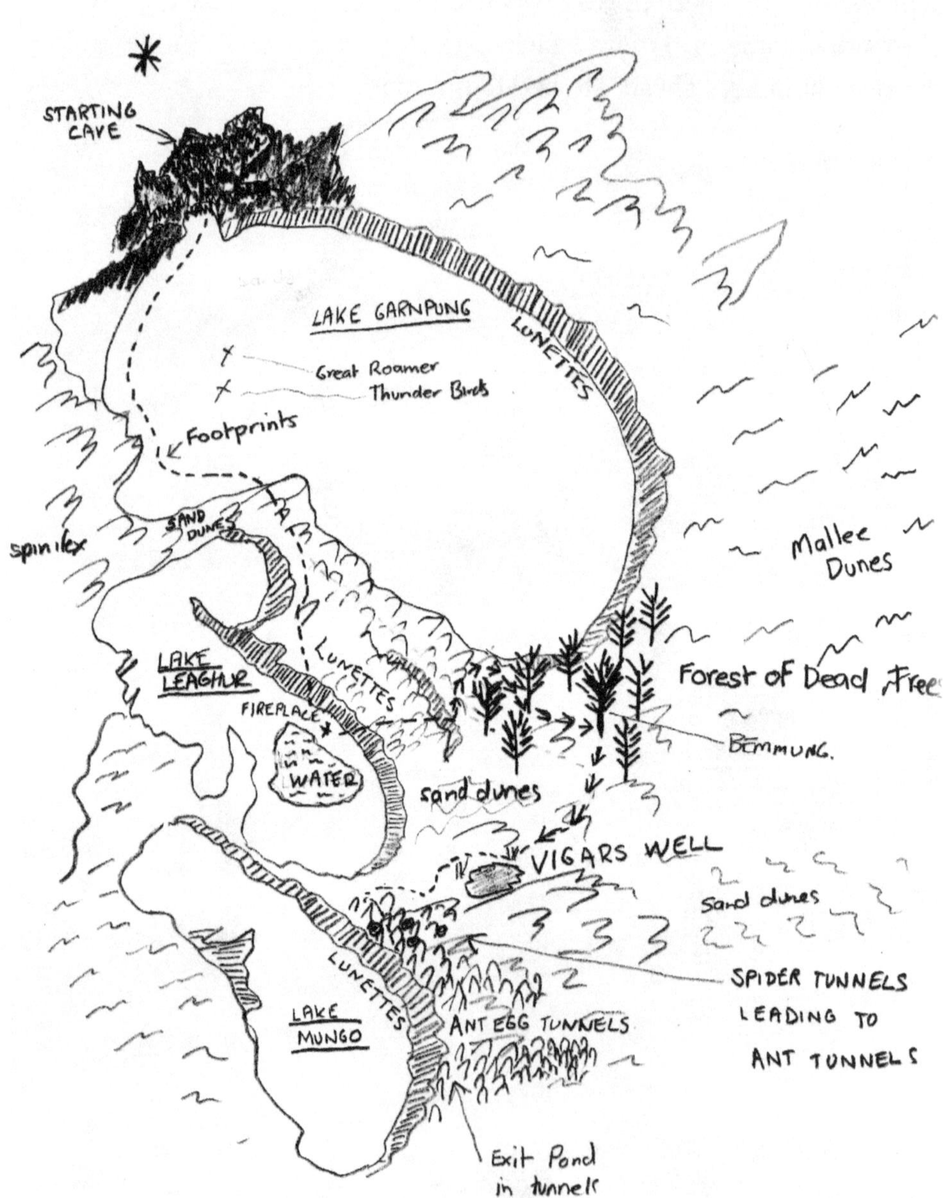

DESERT LANDS
Savannah open woodlands
STARTING CAVE
LAKE GARNPUNG
Great Roamer
Thunder Birds
Footprints
LUNETTES
Mallee Dunes
spinifex
SAND DUNES
LUNETTES
LAKE LEAGHUR
FIREPLACE
WATER
Forest of Dead Tree
BEMMUNG.
sand dunes
VIGARS WELL
sand dunes
SPIDER TUNNELS LEADING TO ANT TUNNELS
LUNETTES
LAKE MUNGO
ANT EGG TUNNELS
Exit Pond in tunnels

DESERT LANDS

5

Lake Garnpung

The character stood motionless, waiting. A tall, formidable picture, dressed fully in black with shoulder-length black hair. A huge sword was latched to his back. Buddy looked up and started barking. The two siblings awoke startled, scrambling to their feet, stepping backwards and bumping into each other. Jackson quickly recognised the character in front of him as Hadwyn, whom Mackenzie had chosen when they had played *Burnstones* together, but that made him no less afraid. He had no idea what this character would do, why it was here. He was alarmed.

He pulled Tess behind him, who started to cry. 'Go away, go away,' she sobbed. Mackenzie could see Tess was talking to the character but he couldn't hear Tess's voice. He kept the character still. Buddy was growling, sniffing and circling the cave intruder.

Mackenzie wondered what he could do. Using his controls, he raised Hadwyn's right arm in an attempt to greet them. Jackson and Tess stepped backwards. 'Don't move,' Jackson instructed Tess. The siblings looked toward the character, apprehensive and confused. The character raised his arm again several times.

'I think he's trying to communicate with us,' Tess guessed.

'I'm not so sure.' Jackson hesitated.

The character stepped toward Jackson with an arm outstretched. Jackson took a big breath and steeled himself. The hand came up again. Seeing very little choice, Jackson obliged and shook its hand. It wasn't quite human skin and a lot colder. The character nodded slowly at him. Jackson remained uncertain. They stood facing each other; Jackson didn't know what to do.

Tess peered around from behind her brother. It was definitely Hadwyn, the mercenary. He was so much taller than them and looked almost real. Hadwyn reached his hand toward Tess. She stepped out from behind Jackson and leaned forward. *He seems friendly*, she thought.

'Can you help us?' Tess asked. The character remained motionless. 'Can you talk to us?' Tess asked. There was no answer.

Mackenzie looked at his friends on the screen. He could see they were wearing the outfits of the characters Eadric and Emerald. *What did that mean?* he thought. He could see they also had weapons. *Were they still completely human? Were they now game characters?* he wondered. There was no way of telling – not yet, anyway. Although it was out of the ordinary. *Anything is worth a try*, he decided.

Hurriedly, Mackenzie opened the game settings and enabled in-game voice chat, then reached for his headset. 'Jackson, Tess, it's me, Mackenzie. Can you hear me? I'm here to help you.'

Jackson looked around in surprise when Mackenzie's voice reached his ears. He looked up. It seemed to have come from somewhere above him. A look of disbelief washed over his face.

Meanwhile, Tess let out a shriek of delight and ran over to Hadwyn, almost pushing him over as she gave him a huge hug. Mackenzie watched as Hadwyn managed to regain his balance after Tess's embrace and returned to his motionless standing position.

That was weird, Mackenzie thought, *Hadwyn moved and I wasn't making him move*. Mackenzie pondered this dilemma. If the character had independent control over itself, how was this going to impact on his efforts to rescue his friends? It now seemed certain to Mackenzie that he would not be able to depend on the usual game rules. It was an altered environment. The entry of humans had changed the game's operation.

Jackson felt an incredulous sense of relief when he heard his friend. 'I don't know how we got here mate, but I am so glad to hear your voice. We're in so much trouble. Where are you?' Jackson asked.

Mackenzie could now hear his friend speaking. Now they had a chance. 'I'm at my place. In my bedroom. I'm using the headset. I can hear you,' Mackenzie told them.

Tess looked over at Hadwyn, feeling a bit awkward that she had just hugged a game character.

'There's a lot to tell you. We've got a lot to work out.' For the next hour or so, Mackenzie relayed the events since their disappearance two nights ago. He told them about the police, their parents and how he had stolen the game from their house.

'Really? We've been missing for two nights? But we really only just arrived here,' Jackson queried.

'I don't know mate,' Mackenzie replied. 'I got your text the day you went missing, so maybe you were matching our time at first … but once you were properly in the game, I'm thinking there's been a time lapse while the game has been off. You went missing on Saturday night. It's Monday night now, nearly midnight. Maybe when I started the game, you both woke up? It's confusing, I know. Listen, I'm going to try to use Hadwyn to help you. I'm not a hundred per cent sure how it's going to work. I'm controlling his movements but I think he can move by himself as well. I just don't know how much I can control him yet.'

The siblings looked at Hadwyn.

'There are going to be many things in here that we don't understand,' Mackenzie told them. 'We're just going to have to learn as we go along.' Mackenzie shared his plan to help them find their way home. 'All we can do is try to get to the Last Door.'

'What happens to us at the Last Door?' Jackson asked.

'I don't know,' Mackenzie admitted, 'but we have to do something. You can't stay where you are. All I know is that you entered right at the start of the game, so I'm hoping that if you get to the end of the game, that will be the way out.'

An orange hue illuminated the cave as the sun began to set. Tess heard Buddy barking in the distance, coming from deeper into the cave. She called him to no avail. 'He must have found a mouse or something. I didn't even notice him leave,' Tess piped up. Mackenzie told the siblings to follow Hadwyn. They ventured towards the barking, travelling around a few bends. 'Wow, look, cave paintings,' Tess reported excitedly.

The rock walls and ceiling were covered in paintings depicting huge emu-like birds and lizards, kangaroos and fish, portrayed with orange, brown, red and white paint. A native man, smaller than the creatures, stood balancing on one leg and holding a spear. Footprints painted across the wall led to him. Tess stopped to admire them for a moment. 'Wow, I wouldn't want to run into those huge animals. They're the megafauna that used to live in Australia,' she declared.

Mackenzie said nothing but thought to himself that it was most likely they would be running into these creatures, given that level one was based in ancient Australia. Jackson raised his eyebrows while looking at his sister, the ever-present encyclopaedia.

Buddy barked again, which sent them on the move. As they rounded the next bend, they found Buddy standing his ground and barking towards a large dark shape. It was difficult to see anything in the shadows. Hadwyn raised his hand, indicating they should stop. His sight was far more advanced than his human companions and he could see a large creature, resembling a huge wombat. Its back was as high as a full-grown man. Buddy was freaking out. Tess picked him up, trying to reassure him with a good pat. Tess's fear of running into the megafauna had been realised in an instant.

'Welcome, travellers,' the creature began in a slow, deep, raspy voice. 'I am Bunyip, of the Land of Mungo. You have been expected for a long, long time.' Jackson recognised the creature from his time playing in the first level. 'This journey is your destiny. Our destiny is in your hands. Your mission is to restore the balance of our lands.' Bunyip paused, looking slowly at the group in front of him. His large brown eyes looked gentle but tired. 'Along the way, seek those who support you. They will do what they can to help you. You may receive special gifts, if it is believed that it is necessary to ensure the success of the mission. Such gifts involve sacrifice. Use these gifts wisely.'

'What does that mean?' Tess asked her companions. Hadwyn raised a hand to silence her.

Bunyip went on. 'In this land, you must travel for many days. The ice winds have come upon our land for many years now and our lakes are drying up. Water is scarce. There is much competition over diminishing food resources. On top of this, the land has been taken over by gigantic Whistling Spiders that hunt us down as prey. Listen for their hissing – when you hear it, you must take cover.' Bunyip shook his head despairingly. 'You must search for Bemmung, the grand ruler of the last tribe of Leliyn Lizards. His kin have been trapped in the Burnstone for thousands of years. He will give you information that you will need to find the Burnstone, to set his kin free so that they can resume their rightful place in our fragile ecosystem. Only when you have succeeded in this task will you be able to continue on.'

Jackson asked, 'What direction shall we travel?'

Bunyip looked around at the encroaching darkness. 'The sun sets. Rest now,' he encouraged. 'At dawn, you must climb down into the dry Garnpung lake, then head toward the rising sun and make your crossing. The ancient spirit creatures you have seen upon these walls will reveal your path – but beware the winds of change, or you may miss that which has been revealed.'

'Well, that's even more confusing,' Tess interjected. 'I'll never make it. I am so thirsty,' she added. It felt like forever since she'd had a drink.

Bunyip moved back a little further into the shadows of the cave. As he moved, a small wooden box came into view. The box faintly glowed. Hadwyn approached the box and stood in front of it. Back in Mackenzie's bedroom, the contents of the box come up on the TV screen. There was a leather bag of dried berries, dried meat and a water flask. He watched as Hadwyn reached forward and took the objects into his hand.

'Take the objects from Hadwyn, Tess,' Mackenzie's voice instructed. Tess did as instructed and returned to her brother's side. She opened the flask and drank to her fill, then poured some into the cup of her hand for Buddy.

'I gift you the last of Garnpung's water,' Bunyip's voice came from the shadows. 'The flask will not run dry,' he explained. Bunyip's voice slowly faded. 'Remember, fear will weaken you. Courage and hope will strengthen you.'

'Here, do you want some?' Tess asked Jackson, holding the flask up to him. Jackson took the water and also quenched his thirst, then tried to hand the flask back to Hadwyn, who shook his head and held his hand up. Jackson pondered the situation as he fixed the flask to his belt. Perhaps as a game character, Hadwyn didn't eat or drink.

'Where is Bunyip?' Tess asked, realising that the creature had disappeared. All three looked around; there was no sign of Bunyip. 'Bunyip, where are you?' she called. Bunyip did not answer.

Mackenzie spoke to his friends. 'You must go back to the cave entrance in preparation for the morning departure. Follow Hadwyn.' The siblings moved in behind Hadwyn as Mackenzie moved the character. 'Just remember I'm here,' he reassured them. 'I won't leave. Just follow Hadwyn. He has a lot of knowledge about his world and I'm reading up as much I can. I'll step in wherever I can,' he added. The group travelled back though the caves as they darkened. Buddy trotted along on their heels.

As they walked back past the cave paintings, Tess noticed something different. 'Hey, look. That wasn't there before.' A new figure had appeared amongst the painted creatures. A large wombat-looking creature just like Bunyip had appeared on the wall. 'I think it's Bunyip,' Tess exclaimed. 'He's gone to be with the others.'

Once they arrived back to just inside the cave entrance, the siblings looked around to find a comfortable spot to wait for morning. Hadwyn stood motionless nearby. Apart from dusty dirt and rocks, there wasn't much choice for comfort.

Tess took off her green cape and lay it on the ground. As she spread the cape out, she felt something hard underneath. Pulling back the cape, she found a long wooden stick partly buried in the dust. She picked it up and looked it over. It was quite long. She stood up and when she placed one end on the ground, she found that it was taller than her height. It was reasonably straight but gnarled. The top had several tiny wooden branches encircling a green stone.

'I think this is mine,' she announced, 'it looks like a druid's staff and I think that's an emerald stone.'

Jackson put up no argument. He didn't fancy fighting with a stick anyway.

Mackenzie decided to take the opportunity to read up about Hadwyn again, so that he understood the character's goals and abilities. He brought Hadwyn's bio up on the screen.

Hadwyn

As a young boy, Hadwyn befriended the daughter of a knight. He confided to her the secret relationship between his people and the Triado frogs. When the girl's father heard of this, he proclaimed it sorcery. The Amber Knights pillaged and burnt the village to the ground. Many villagers were killed. The rest fled. Hadwyn ran far, eventually becoming a beggar. A band of mercenary soldiers took him in as a servant. By adulthood he was one of them.

As a mercenary soldier he drifted, plagued with guilt for his people and full of revenge against the Knights. In one of his quests, he unknowingly burnt down a sacred forest to cover his tracks from enemies. This upset the druids. He hoped one day to return to his homeland to find his people, and put things right with the druids.

GENDER	STRENGTH	WEAPONS
Male	18	Longsword
		Dagger
	INTELLIGENCE	
RACE	12	
Human		SPELLS
	WISDOM	Furious Strike
	10	Statue
CLASS		Triple Jump
Mercenary	CONSTITUTION	
	10	5 amber
		gemstones
	DEXTERITY	
	15	
	CHARISMA	
	5	

Hadwyn was a mercenary soldier, clever and smart. Mackenzie relayed his understanding of Hadwyn's character to his friends.

'It appears you all have similar goals and common enemies,' Mackenzie continued to explain. 'Hadwyn needs to travel back to the land of his people. It doesn't sound like he is welcomed by the knights or the druids. I'm thinking he needs your characters as companions and by accompanying him on his mission, hopefully I can get you guys closer to where you need to be.'

'Can I just point out that we aren't actually the characters that can help him?' Jackson interjected. 'I might have these weapons but I don't actually know how to fight with them.'

'The thing is,' Mackenzie responded, 'whether we like it or not, you are the characters of Eadric and Emerald to other characters in the game, so we need to understand how you fit in. It's going to be dangerous and we need as much knowledge as we can get.' Mackenzie then brought up Eadric and Emerald's character bios on the screen. 'Now let me read this to you. Who knows what's ahead – you will need to have a good understanding of your characters.' Mackenzie proceed to explain each character's background and abilities.

'Jackson, your character is needed by Hadwyn to help him defeat the Knights of Amber. You are a perfect companion for him, as you're also seeking revenge on the knights. It seems Eadric is a Prince in Waiting going by that bio. Eadric is going to fight the knights and get his family crown back. You have loads of charisma so hopefully that might get us out of some sticky situations.'

Jackson interjected again, 'Okay, so stating the obvious again: I am not Eadric. I can't sword fight. I don't possess this character's abilities. This is all sounding worse by the minute.'

'Well, that's true,' Mackenzie acknowledged, 'but we still need to proceed forward to get you out of this. I need you to know about Eadric, even if you're just acting the character. At this stage, I don't know how other characters in the game will respond to both of you. I really think it best that you try to behave in a way that makes you seem to be the character.'

Prince Eadric

Eadric is of noble birth. His royal family were killed or exiled when the Knights of Amber took over his homeland.

Eadric is the rightful heir, and hopes to return to his homeland and restore his kingdom, freeing his people from the knights.

He no longer has his royal guards or soldiers and searches for those who can assist him in his quest to take back the Juodkrantė Crown.

GENDER Male	**STRENGTH** 12	**WEAPONS** Twin swords Dagger
RACE Human	**INTELLIGENCE** 14	**SPELLS** Fireball Skin shield Furious strike
CLASS Nobleman	**WISDOM** 6	5 amber gemstones
	CONSTITUTION 8	
	DEXTERITY 15	
	CHARISMA 15	

Makenzie then spoke to Tess. 'Tess, your character Emerald is probably meant to be a help for Hadwyn in resolving things with the druids.' Mackenzie pulled up Emerald's bio on the screen and read it to Tess.

'Wow, that's so awesome,' Tess responded. 'Well, I know a bit about druids and the environment already, and I can certainly act.'

Jackson looked at his younger sister incredulously. Apparently, she had lost focus on the danger ahead and was getting caught up in the fantasy.

'I'll do my best,' Tess declared.

'Tess, your character Emerald is a druid apprentice,' said Mackenzie. You're still developing skills. You're not as physically strong as your companions but you do have higher levels of wisdom, so that's probably relating to magic and the environment. You're travelling in the same direction as the others but for different reasons. And by the way, that long wooden staff you have – it's magic.'

Emerald

Emerald is a druid apprentice. She has never known who her parents were. All she remembers is growing up in a druid clan. Now in her sixteenth year, she has been sent away.

Destined to become a druid queen, she must first travel through many lands and develop druid wisdom, deepening her understanding of the natural world, and the relationship between nature and humans.

As a druid she must learn how to use this wisdom to maintain a balance between them.

On her journey, she is expected to develop ways of seeing the unseen, communicating with ancestral connections, strengthening her intuition, and become skilled in druid magic.

GENDER Female	**STRENGTH** 8	**WEAPONS** Bow and arrows Neart staff (magical power, physical strength)
RACE Human	**INTELLIGENCE** 14	
	WISDOM 14	
CLASS Druid apprentice	**CONSTITUTION** 8	**SPELLS** Invisibility spell Charm stare Replenish quiver
	DEXTERITY 14	
	CHARISMA 12	5 amber gemstones

'I knew it. I knew it was a druid's staff,' Tess said with satisfaction. 'Maybe I should practice with it?'

'I think you're both going to have to practice your skills and get familiar with your weapons. Hopefully sooner rather than later,' Mackenzie replied. 'There's no choice. We have to be as prepared as possible. Hopefully, I can use Hadwyn to handle most of the situations and find a way to keep you two out of danger as much as possible,' he added. 'So, my plan is that basically that you two just follow where Hadwyn goes and follow my directions at all times. Some things will happen in the game automatically and other times I'll have some control. Hadwyn should know how to interact in his world. I'll try to work out what's happening ahead wherever I can.'

As Monday night came to a close, Jackson and Tess lay down and entered an uncomfortable sleep. Hadwyn sat motionless beside them. Meanwhile, Mackenzie paused the game for a short time, put the controller down, sat back and stretched. He needed time to think. With the game paused, he could have a rest, a drink and some food himself without worrying about his friends still being in a live game. He knew that he would have to return and start the game to enable his friends to get sleep. Then he would watch over them for as many hours' rest that was needed.

He had worked out that their time was parallel to his own when the game was running. For now, they had lost two days compared to the outside world, between entering the game and Mackenzie turning the game back on. This was going to be a long ride.

TUESDAY

With first light, Tess decided it was a good time to eat. She tore the tough dried meat apart with her teeth and shared some with Buddy. Jackson sampled the dried fruit, which he normally hated, and concluded it tasted particularly good. His hunger had returned.

It was Tuesday morning. For Mackenzie, it had been three nights since their disappearance, but for the siblings, they had just survived their first night in the game. Mackenzie wondered how many days and nights this rescue would take.

Soon the companions left the safety of the cave; they emerged at one of the highest points in the Desert Lands. Below them, the land sloped down to the dried-out Garnpung Lake. They scrambled and stumbled downhill, traversing the windblown lunettes. These crystallised sand structures had the appearance of huge ripples stretching from the top ridges down toward the dry lake bed. Gradual sloping dirt and sand became looser underfoot and the land began to level out. Once they had descended to the dry lake floor below, they turned and saw many high lunettes stretching as far as they could see, lining the perimeter of the lake bed. Hadwyn headed off. Tess and Buddy followed with Jackson just behind.

The long trek continued under a hot sun. Sweat beaded on their foreheads. An occasional seashell poked its whiteness out of the sand, telling of the old sea bed long forgotten. The sand gave way to baked, crusted mud that cracked underfoot. Tess tripped and fell backward, grabbing Jackson's clothing to break her fall. 'Oh my God, what are you doing?' Jackson complained as he tried to maintain his balance. 'You're so clumsy!'

'I didn't mean it. You're so nasty, Jackson,' Tess retorted. Tess was feeling stressed and tired.

'Yeah well, you're not my favourite person either. You're always creating a drama. This is probably all your fault for spilling that juice on my game,' Jackson retorted. Jackson was also feeling weary and irritable.

Hadwyn moved and stood between the squabbling siblings, facing Jackson with his hand up in a halting position. Jackson rolled his eyes, threw his hands up in the air, shook his head and turned to walk away, feeling that Mackenzie was taking Tess's side over his. 'Whatever!' Jackson commented as he walked off in a huff.

Jackson reflected on his squabbles with his sister. He often felt that no one understood how difficult it could be. Mackenzie was his best friend but he had no idea what it was like to have an annoying younger sister. He didn't have to live forever with someone who interrupted all the time, butting in and ruining everything. Jackson envied Mackenzie. He had it so easy: never-ending peace and quiet living at his place just with his mum, not having to put up with constant chatter about absolutely nothing important. Never having to share everything from food treats to new presents – sharing every part of the house, every area of his life. He looked forward to the day he was old enough to move out.

The sun rose higher. After about an hour of walking Tess asked, 'Is that water?' pointing to the far-off horizon. The sun was almost overhead.

Jackson peered toward the haze. 'No silly, that's a mirage.' He laughed. 'It's a trick from the hot ground and the cold air. It's not real. It's an illusion, something like that,' Jackson told her. He was surprised by her question, given how much she had studied the environment and weather in her school projects. He couldn't remember her ever doing an assignment on anything else.

'And what's that dark shape way over there?' she continued, pointing further over to the left.

Jackson squinted in the bright light. 'Mm, I'm not sure about that. What do you think, Mackenzie?'

Hadwyn had stopped walking and stood facing the dark shape. Whatever it was, it was moving slowly but it was big – very big. Mackenzie selected the shape and an information box appeared on the screen. 'The Ancient Great Roamer,' he read to them. 'A spirit creature.'

Tess had a vague memory of reading about this enormous lizard creature in the game manual. The Great Roamer was king of the food chain in Mungo, about ten metres long and without equal. It was a very dangerous creature and capable of eating them.

'It's not close enough to be a problem yet,' Mackenzie concluded as he looked at the on-screen map. He estimated that it was at least a kilometre away. 'Let's keep pushing on along the edge of the lake bed and keep as far away from it as possible.'

'How do you know which way to go?' Tess asked.

'I'm not completely sure, Tess,' Mackenzie answered, 'but I figure it's safer to travel alongside the ridges rather than out there in the open.' The on-screen map displayed a zoomed-out view of Lake Garnpung. From this, he could see where Hadwyn was located and that they needed to keep traveling in their current direction to get to the far edge. Somewhere ahead would be a crossing to the second lake. However, he could not see any clues as to where they might cross. From time to time, there were strange sounds and flashes of movement, too far off to determine what they were.

After another couple of hours, the hot sun disappeared behind clouds. Arctic winds blew, biting cold into their skin. This was a time of great climatic change, the end of an ice age. Mackenzie encouraged them to continue. 'We don't want you out here in the dark, guys. Keep going. I think we can make the end of the lake by nightfall. We need to find a safe place for you to rest.' They put their heads down, pulled their capes around themselves and pressed onward.

Above the sound of the wind, the travellers became aware of a rumbling in the distance that slowly grew louder. A thick sandstorm appeared, growing rapidly as it approached them. The ground vibrated; the wind grew stronger, sand swirling faster, stinging their arms and faces, clouding their vision. Rapidly moving shapes began to materialise within the sandstorm. 'Okay guys, crouch down behind the saltbushes and keep still,' Mackenzie told them.

They held their breath. They recognised the Spirit Thunder Birds that had been painted on the cave walls. The giant flightless birds raced past, some coming so close that sticks and rocks flew from their leathery pronged feet. The siblings felt gusts of wind created by the flock. In a matter of minutes, it was over. The flock sped away. The dust cloud followed them. The group awaited further instruction.

'Jackson, come here.' Tess beckoned her brother. 'I've found something.' Jackson turned to look at her. He decided he was going to tell her off. This was a serious situation they were in and there wasn't time for showing off her discoveries. He felt like she had shown him every insect, every bird, every plant ever known to humankind whenever they went on the family nature hikes. No peace ever. Tess was pointing at the ground. 'Look Jackson, there are footprints.'

Jackson reluctantly went over and looked to where she was pointing. He turned his focus to the dried mud. A short time ago, the area had been covered by fine sand, but since the Thunder Birds passed, the sand had been blown away, uncovering the dry earth beneath. Now they could clearly see human footprints deeply embedded in the rock-hard earth.

'The Spirit creatures will reveal your path!' Tess repeated the words of Bunyip, feeling a restored sense of importance with her grumpy brother. 'Remember the man in the paintings with the footprints? Maybe it's him?' Jackson didn't answer her. Sometimes she secretly wished Mackenzie was her brother instead.

Jackson stood up and surveyed the line of footprints. He wasn't sure of their relevance. 'What's this all about?' he asked.

Mackenzie selected one of the footprints that had a pale red glow around it. A message appeared on the screen and he read it to his friends. 'Mungo Man walks before you. Follow in his footsteps if you want to survive.' It triggered a memory for Mackenzie. 'I remember learning about him from my dad,' Mackenzie went on. 'They found Mungo Man's bones in one of our deserts. You've probably heard about that, Tess? And there was Mungo Lady as well. It was proof that the Indigenous people had lived here for over sixty thousand years.'

'Yes, that's right. I did an assignment on that,' Tess agreed.

'Of course, you did,' Jackson interrupted.

'Shut up Jackson,' Tess retaliated. 'Anyway, Mackenzie,' she continued, 'my assignment looked at how the Aboriginals looked after this land until Europeans arrived, and then compared what happened after that. In the last two hundred years, we have destroyed about fifty animal species and about sixty plant species. Australia has the highest loss of mammal species in the world. If only we could talk to Mungo Man and Mungo Lady. They knew how to look after everything.'

Jackson decided to keep his mouth shut.

'Okay then, let's just follow the footprints,' Mackenzie decided. 'Going by the sundial on my screen, I think it's late afternoon. We need to keep moving.' The footprints led them away from the high ridges and a bit further into the lake bed. It seemed that they were following a very old path.

'I hope this is right,' Jackson wondered out loud. 'I feel like we might be getting off track?' Nevertheless, they followed the footprints for most of the afternoon. The lake bed was very dry, with dusty grey dirt and occasional patches of white salt and clumps of spinifex. The cold wind continued to press against their weary bodies. Tess was dragging her feet and falling behind, Buddy close by her side panting.

Mackenzie noticed movement on the edge of the map. He couldn't quite work out what it was. He stopped Hadwyn and told the siblings to stop. They looked up. It was the same dark shape they had seen earlier. 'Oh no, we're out on the open,' Tess said. She picked up Buddy. It was true; they were in the open and they had no cover. Mackenzie decided he would just have to trust that the ancient footprints would guide them to safety.

'Stand behind Hadwyn,' Mackenzie told them. 'Now be still and wait. Don't do anything unless I tell you to.'

Jackson's hand reached up to the handle of one of his swords. He hoped this wasn't going to be his first sword practice.

The Great Roamer came closer and closer, as it made its way across the lake bed. Its nostrils flared as its keen sense of smell picked up a new and unfamiliar scent. The Great Roamer looked around and then turned its head back in their direction, now only about a half a kilometre from the party. The enormous leathery predator lumbered closer to them, adjusting toward its target, its next meal. Tess and Jackson looked on with alarm. Hadwyn stood still in front of them. Time seemed to stand still. Their hearts were beating out of their chests.

A thunderous crack sounded overhead, followed by flashes of forked lightning and continued thunder cracks. The Great Roamer stopped and crouched, its belly flat to the ground in a stalking position. It was the Thunder Birds again. The flock ran at great speed, a blur of grey and brown feathers and thick muscular legs making their path between the terrified siblings and the Great Roamer. The swirling sandstorm became thicker, the Thunder Birds now barely visible. There seemed to be scores of them. A loud screech broke through the roaring wind and thunder. They held their breath and waited for what felt like forever. The icy winds continued and gradually swept the sandstorm away, leaving no trace of the Thunder Birds. As the sand dissipated and their view cleared, the Great Roamer could be seen heading back to where it came from, with a limp carcass of a Thunder Bird clamped in its sharp teeth. Blood dripped from its motionless orange beak.

Mackenzie waited a while before moving Hadwyn in the direction they needed to travel. He'd looked at the on-screen map and could see there was still a fair bit of distance to cover to reach the far perimeter of the lake. Tess was busying herself looking at small stones scattered at her feet. She had always loved collecting various stones. Jackson grabbed her arm and pulled her up with an exasperated frown on his face. 'It's time to move. Stop playing.'

'I'm not playing,' Tess protested, pulling her arm away and getting to her feet.

'You can be such a nincompoop, Tess!' Jackson scolded her.

Mackenzie interjected. 'Now's not the time for fighting, guys. Let's get moving. There's no time to waste.'

Tess scowled at Jackson. 'Tess,' Jackson said in a low voice, 'grow up! You're so loud you're going to attract danger. If you don't shut up and follow directions, you're going to be mauled to death.'

Tess screwed up her face at him and stuck her tongue out, but gave a quick nervous glance around her.

The party walked until the sun went down. Their footsteps trudged past saltbush and spinifex bushes with their needle-sharp leaves. To Tess's delight, she even got to see beautiful wildflowers, yellow and white daisies, and tiny bluebells.

The grey earth and timeless lunette rock formations took on an orange glow as the burnt skies bathed them with evening colour. They had almost walked the length of Lake Garnpung and were nearing the rising landscape between Lake Garnpung and Lake Leaghur. They scrambled up the uneven rising slopes dotted with rocky outcrops of dirt and saltbush, and even a few small stunted trees. Eventually the land underfoot became more level as the dry dirt was replaced by an arid sand dune rippled by the wind. They walked on and on.

As dusk descended, they had crossed the sand dunes and reached a ridge, where they had a clear view down to Lake Leaghur. The lunettes tapered down to the flat sands surrounding Lake Leaghur, which had become a receding waterhole, surrounded by dry, cracked mud. The moon was beginning to rise. 'Haste,' Mackenzie told them.

6

Lake Leaghur

Their final descent to Lake Leaghur coincided with the evening watering, when creatures of all kinds came for their life-saving drink. The sun was no longer visible and shadows lengthened with the fading light. The party sat amongst the deep crevices created between the lunettes, trying to keep out of sight. To their astonishment, a very large wombat, similar to Bunyip, plodded to the water's edge to drink its fill. Several different types of birds, individually and in flocks, descended to the water.

A thumping sound caused the birds to scatter as a family of strange-looking kangaroos appeared. They were about two metres high with forward-facing eyes and a flat face. Their feet and paws looked odd, with only one toe on each foot and two extra-long fingers with long claws on each paw. Tess let out a gasp and went to speak. She had recognised an extinct Australian kangaroo. Jackson put his hand over her mouth. 'Bookamurra,' Mackenzie informed them, 'ancient spirit kangaroo.'

The great wombat looked up and lumbered back into the Mallee dunes. Bookamurra, who was bent down drinking the water, also looked up quickly, as though it had heard something. It looked around and then bounded off with the other kangaroos. From the far side of the watering hole, a large lion-type creature quietly appeared. It was a marsupial lion. Mackenzie instructed the group not to move. The lion walked stealthily around the water's edge, minute by minute coming closer. 'Follow Hadwyn,' Mackenzie told them as he made Hadwyn move back, further in between the lunettes, for protection. The siblings squatted down, trying to keep as low as possible and out of sight.

Tess held on to Buddy tightly. Her heart was beating rapidly. This was another extinct creature, one that was so dangerous. She had seen its skeleton at the museum.

The wind picked up and blew sand over them. Jackson sneezed. The lion raised its head and turned its head toward them with a deadly stare. Its body moved to a crouch and it moved slowly toward them. Makenzie had to think quickly.

Hadwyn moved to stand at the entrance of the sandy crevice and pulled out his longsword. Hadwyn had two hands on the hilt, his feet spread apart in a strong stance; he raised the heavy sword in readiness for attack. The huge cat crept closer and then ran straight at Hadwyn. The earth shook. Snarling, the lion revealed large sharp incisors protruding from a muscular jaw. Mackenzie moved Hadwyn further back into the lunettes. The lion was at least three times larger than any other lion he had seen before. Hopefully retreating would work to their advantage. Surely it couldn't get into the lunette crevice.

Mackenzie manoeuvred Hadwyn back a bit further as the great cat stretched its thick paws with razor-sharp claws towards him, scratching around in an attempt to snatch its prey. The claws caught Hadwyn's clothing and started pulling him towards the entrance. Hadwyn's sword came down, missing the paw. Hadwyn was dragged further out. Tess started screaming. Buddy was barking ferociously.

Hadwyn's sword smashed down again and again at the lion's paws. Its head was half-way into the crevice but its wide shoulders were blocking it coming in any further. It was difficult to swing such a large sword in the confined space of the lunette. Hadwyn was struggling. He was pulled closer to the outside and then was gone from sight. The siblings yelled in terror. 'Mackenzie, Mackenzie, help!'

In that instance, Mackenzie paused the game. He needed time to think.

Looking at Hadwyn's stats on the screen, he could see that he had lost a lot of health. It was certain that Hadwyn would die if this battle proceeded much longer. He pulled up the map view and a large shape caught his eye. There was something rather huge not far away: it was the Great Roamer. It looked as though it was heading in the direction of the lion.

What to do? If he continued the game, the lion may kill Hadwyn off, but just maybe the Great Roamer would kill the lion first. Even then, Hadwyn may not be safe. If Hadwyn was killed off, what would happen to Jackson and Tess? Mackenzie felt sick. He knew he had no choice. He decided to take the chance and keep the game going. If worse came to worse, then he could restart the level – not that he knew what this would do to his friends.

The lion was dragging Hadwyn's body away. Mackenzie checked Hadwyn's stats. His health was down to ten per cent. He didn't have enough health left to resist the lion. The sand was left furrowed by Hadwyn's limp body, leaving drag lines. Mackenzie waited, holding his breath. The cat was probably taking Hadwyn to its lair. In what seemed like forever, Mackenzie finally saw the Great Roamer come into view. 'What's happening, Mackenzie?' Jackson called.

'Just keep still, guys. Wait until I get back to you,' he responded.

The massive lizard paused as it passed by where Jackson and Tess were hiding, sniffing at the entrance but unable to enter due to its size. The lizard moved on. While not as fast moving as the lion, the Great Roamer had a keen sense of smell and would not give up stalking its prey easily.

The lion was slowed down by the weight it pulled. It paused for a rest and then noticed The Great Roamer. The lion was hungry but did not want to be the Great Roamer's next meal. It arched its back and snarled, its tail moving angrily. It turned and made a hasty departure, leaving Hadwyn lying in the sand.

The Great Roamer approached Hadwyn; Mackenzie again struggled to decide what to do. By this stage, Jackson and Tess had crept toward the opening of the lunette crevice and were peeking out.

Tess caught sight of Hadwyn's body and could see the Great Roamer closing in on him. 'I can help him,' Tess called out to Mackenzie. 'Let me help him. I can use my spells. I'm a druid. Please let me help.'

Mackenzie paused the game again. *Was that even possible?* he wondered. He pulled up Emerald's bio again. Yes, she had spells. Perhaps the Invisibility spell could be used to save Hadwyn and Tess from the Great Roamer – if Emerald could just get to him. *Wait,* he thought, *Am I going crazy? It's not Emerald. It's Tess.*

He had no other ideas. What else could he do? There was no point sending Jackson out to fight something that big with his swords. Emerald was just an apprentice druid at this stage; maybe the magic wasn't strong enough yet? He had to think. Sooner or later he was going to have to find out if Tess and Jackson had any of their character's capabilities. What would he do if Tess went out and had no ability, no magic?

He decided there was nothing to lose. If he let Hadwyn be killed off, he would have to restart the level anyway and hope his friends would live through it. Maybe he could do the same if Tess was killed or just before she was attacked?

'Okay Tess. Listen to me,' Mackenzie started. 'If you can make yourself invisible and get past the Great Roamer, you might be able to make Hadwyn invisible.'

'How do I use the Invisibility spell?' Tess asked.

Mackenzie wasn't actually sure. If he was controlling the Emerald character it would be easy to activate a spell using the controls. This was a very different situation. 'It's your staff,' Mackenzie reminded her, 'it has magical power. Just hold on to it and try thinking "Invisibility". Time is running out.'

Tess nodded and stood up straight, holding the staff in both hands and closing her eyes. She imagined herself invisible as hard as she could. When she opened her eyes, she was disappointed to see her arms and hands in front of her; however, the green stone was glowing. 'It didn't work,' Tess called to Mackenzie.

Yes, it did. I can't see you,' Jackson interrupted. 'Run Tess, run as fast as you can!'

Tess was taken aback for a moment, but as the enormity of what had transpired dawned on her, she pushed Buddy into Jackson's arms and confidently ran out into the open. Daylight was gone and dusk had descended. The colours of red earth had been replaced by colourless greys, but she could still make out the moving shape of the Great Roamer. She ran as fast as she could, jumping rocks along the way. She soon caught up to and passed the Great Roamer, arriving at Hadwyn's side about fifteen metres in front of the lizard. She held his hand and closed her eyes, wishing for them both to be invisible. Hadwyn's body disappeared but she still held his hand.

The Great Roamer stopped, looking around and sniffing. Tess remained still. She held her breath. Minutes passed. The Great Roamer turned its gaze directly toward her and approached. Panicking, Tess looked down and saw that Hadwyn was visible again. Her magic was too weak. *Damn it*, she thought.

Mackenzie watched the screen helplessly. As he had feared, as an apprentice her magic was still underdeveloped. Jackson, seeing the danger, ran towards the end of the lake where Tess faced the lizard. He fumbled for a sword. Buddy was by his side, barking ferociously.

Tess lowered her head. *Oh no*, she thought, *I've loved lizards all my life and now a lizard is going to kill me.* With resignation, she raised her head and looked the Great Roamer in the eye. *If only he knew I had never meant to cause him harm.* The Great Roamer came right up to her, so close she could feel its breath. And then it just stood still, looking into her eyes. *Oh my goodness, I think he understands me.* Hesitantly, Tess reached out and touched his nose. The Great Roamer lowered his head further and closed its eyes. A tear rolled down Tess's cheek. 'I am a druid,' she rejoiced.

Jackson had stopped in his tracks halfway to Tess, as he had seen the lizard reach her. He had grabbed Buddy and now held the squirming, frantic dog tightly. He watched in the dim light as the lizard moved off, continuing its path in the direction of the lion. Jackson ran to Tess's side. Buddy, back on solid ground, beat him to her. 'Wow Tess, that was amazing.' He looked at her shaking hands. 'Come on. Let's get you both back to safety.'

With Tess and Jackson on each side, they managed to help Hadwyn stumble back. He was extremely weak. Mackenzie used the controls to help as much as he could.

Once back in the lunette crevices, the issue of Hadwyn's weak state needed to be addressed. Mackenzie selected a book symbol on his screen called 'The Book of Amber'. It was full of details about amber, including its properties and the forces it contained. 'Here's the thing,' he told Jackson and Tess, 'you get five pieces of amber each at the start of every level. Once you use them, they're gone until the next level.'

Mackenzie read about the properties of the amber. They could be used for many things. One purpose was to restore health. 'Okay. I'm going to lay Hadwyn down. I want you to find all your amber gems and put them on his body,' Mackenzie relayed. Soon Hadwyn lay flat with ten amber gems resting on his body. 'Now we wait,' he told them.

After a while, Jackson carefully ventured down towards the shoreline, where Buddy raced to the water's edge and began to drink. A full moon was rising and a silvery path of light shone across the still water. Tess stayed by Hadwyn's side, watching the amber gems glow and fade. She felt so different, and had a lot to think about. She kept her druid staff close by her side, looking at it every now and then with complete wonder.

As Jackson walked along, the light of the moon cast foreboding shadows across the landscape. Jackson tripped on the ashes of an old fireplace with what appeared to be very old seashells scattered around. 'Humans?' Jackson questioned. 'Who are these people, Mackenzie?'

Mackenzie selected the fireplace. Information appeared on his screen. 'Mungo Man walks before you. Follow in his footsteps if you want to survive.'

'What does that mean?' Jackson asked.

'I'm not sure,' Mackenzie responded, 'we followed those footprints to get here. They were human. Let me think for a minute.'

Mackenzie considered the fireplace. How could they follow in Mungo Man's footsteps here? Maybe it didn't mean actual footsteps.

He had to think outside the square. The people of Mungo were an ancient Indigenous tribe of Australia. Maybe the message meant they needed to follow their ways? What did they use fire for? It would have provided warmth and protected them from the predators of the night. After a few moments, Mackenzie decided a fire would help, but there didn't appear to be much wood around. He considered what they had with them that might burn – and then remembered that amber gems could be used as a heat source. They also provided protection for travellers. Maybe if he told them to put them at the entrance of the lunette crevice … *Oh, darn*, he thought, *we've used the gems on Hadwyn.*

Mackenzie checked Hadwyn's stats. His health had only improved to about half-way. He would have to leave the amber gems on Hadwyn longer. He considered Jackson's spells. Given that Tess had some of Emerald's powers, it seemed quite possible Jackson had some of Eadric's powers. 'Jackson, I need you to collect a pile of rocks and make a mound of them near the front of the lunette crevice.' Soon Jackson had completed the task. 'Now I want you to try to use your Fireball spell on the rocks.' Jackson looked surprised and a little uncertain of himself. 'Get the black coals out of your pouch. Just throw one at the rocks and yell "fireball",' Mackenzie suggested.

Jackson nodded, raised his hand and then flung the coal as hard as he could, yelling, 'Fireball!' Nothing happened.

'Do it again,' Mackenzie encouraged, 'louder. Like you mean it.'

'Fireball,' he yelled. Nothing happened. 'Fireball,' he yelled again, getting exasperated. He screamed at the rocks and threw more coal. 'FIREBALL!' A wisp of smoke made its way up between the rocks. 'FIREBALL!' he yelled again. The rocks began to glow red. 'I did it. I did it!' Jackson called to everyone, astounded by his ability. He'd started with five pieces of coal. He only had one left.

The night slowly ticked by. A strong smell of pine emanated from the warm amber gems laying upon Hadwyn's outstretched body. Somewhat reassured, the siblings lay down to rest behind the protective glowing coals at the entrance. Tess and Jackson slept. Hadwyn lay still. He didn't require sleep. All night, the hairy Whistling Spiders crept around on top of lunettes, the sound of hissing ever-present. Occasionally a dark shape passed overhead. Buddy gave a small whine and lay down close to Tess.

Meanwhile, Mackenzie dozed in his bean bag, headphones on so that he would hear any disturbance. It had been one long day. Tuesday ended as midnight passed. Mackenzie read as much as he could about where they were at in the game, in between dozing on and off as the early hours unfolded. Unfortunately, much of what was ahead would only be discovered as they ventured forward.

WEDNESDAY

As dawn broke over the watering hole, all that remained of the once great lake of Leaghur, the children were woken by snorting and the footsteps of animals starting their day. Tess and Jackson stirred, sat up blinking and looking around. They couldn't see Hadwyn. All that remained where he had lain were ten amber gems, now dark in colour and cold. They had transferred their magical energies and restored Hadwyn's health.

Tess stood up and scanned the area. They could see a procession of animals and birds visiting the water's edge. 'There he is, on the other side of the waterhole.' She pointed. 'What is he doing?'

Jackson followed the direction she had indicated and also saw Hadwyn. He appeared to be crouching high up on a lunette ridge. 'I don't know,' he said. 'It's really Mackenzie controlling him, don't forget. He's probably read something in the game manual and is following the instructions.'

Eventually they heard a distant *thump, thump* getting louder and louder. One of the flat-faced kangaroos appeared, bounding past Hadwyn. In a split second, Hadwyn jumped from the ridge and landed on its back. Startled, the kangaroo bounded erratically around the waterhole and amongst the lunettes. Hadwyn stayed astride the beast, which eventually slowed down and stopped jumping, coming to a standstill. 'That's one strange looking kangaroo,' Jackson pointed out. It didn't look like the kangaroos they were familiar with growing up in Australia. It was also much bigger, standing about twice the height of a big horse.

'It's Bookamurra,' Mackenzie told them after selecting the creature and reading about it. 'Apparently, it will take you to the Forest of Dead Trees.' The siblings watched and waited as Hadwyn rode the kangaroo towards them. It came to a thumping stop, raising a small cloud of dust in front of the group's hideout. The rocks that had kept them warm and safe through the night had cooled. The siblings jumped over the rocks to get closer to Hadwyn and Bookamurra. 'You need to climb on behind Hadwyn,' Mackenzie told them. Jackson pushed Tess up first and handed Buddy to her. He then grabbed Hadwyn's leg to help pull himself up. It took him several attempts until he finally had enough strength and momentum to climb aboard.

Once all three were on board, Bookamurra bounded up and across the lunette ridges, leaping in great strides, reaching the top of the lunettes very quickly. Bookamurra had a super-strong tail that he used like a third leg, helping him to maintain his balance on the uneven lunettes with their treacherous deep gaps. Jackson looked down and saw many spider burrows below, silk threads like silver wisps waving in the wind at the burrow entrances. Jackson felt alarmed at the size of the burrows. The spiders were very big.

As Bookamurra cleared the last of the lunettes, the journey continued along in the rippled golden sand dunes. After about half an hour of bounding, the blackened skeletons of trees came into view. Bookamurra came to a halt at the edge of a large flat white sand dune; in the centre stood the Forest of Dead Trees. The companions slid to the ground. Bookamurra shook his odd-shaped head, turned and bounded away. His great body leapt and leapt – and after a final great leap, he disappeared into the clouds, into a timeless spirit world.

Hadwyn walked toward the trees. Jackson and Tess followed him to the centre of about fifty trees, all black and lifeless. Every now and then they caught sight of a small darting movement on one of the trunks. It was a stark, barren environment. Tess, the ever-keen wildlife spotter, kept her eyes scanning her surroundings. 'I think there are baby lizards,' Tess exclaimed excitedly. 'They seem very shy,' she informed the others.

The largest tree was at the centre of the forest. Hadwyn began to circle the tree, Tess and Jackson following him. 'I saw it,' Tess announced, 'there's a huge frilled-neck lizard on the other side of the tree.' They kept circling the tree but the lizard also kept circling, so that they could not see it properly. Finally, Mackenzie told them to stop and wait. Tess fell back on the sand and watched the clouds. Jackson sat beside Hadwyn and then proceeded to ask Mackenzie questions about the game and what to expect in the days ahead.

Time passed. Tess felt impatient. She really wanted to look for baby lizards. Unnoticed by the group, Bemmung the Great Lizard had appeared on their side of the tree and was quietly watching and listening to them.

A loud hiss drew their attention to his presence. They looked up and saw the magnificent oranges and browns of his leathery body – and the great frill that circled his head, spread like a huge collar and making him look even bigger. His yellow mouth was open and motionless. Once he had their attention, he spoke. 'At last the foretelling comes to be, as it is told. I am Bemmung, Leader of the Leliyn Lizard tribe. We lost our lands in the North and have travelled south into the deserts in search of food and refuge. The spirit of my kin was trapped in the Red Amber Burnstone in the time of the Rising Seas. We have lost our place. The Whistling Spiders hunt us. We are on the brink of extinction. The creature spirit must be freed if our world is to have any chance of resurrection.'

'Oh my gosh, I know all about the balance of nature,' Tess responded, 'It's a big mistake to disrupt the balance. In our country there are rabbits and foxes and cats and camels that were introduced, and a lot of our mammals have been killed or had their habitat destroyed.'

Jackson screwed up his face in horror at his sister's lack of decorum. He looked to the ground in embarrassment and quickly pulled Tess aside. He could not believe she kept forgetting they were stuck in a game. She was talking to a game character as though it could understand talk of their world. 'Tess, you need to listen, no matter what you think you know,' he muttered, 'Mac and I barely understood last time we played this part and we got destroyed so I'm pretty sure his advice will help us!' Tess seemed to shrink away as embarrassment dawned upon her, turning with Jackson to face the mighty creature.

Jackson straightened up, looked Bemmung in the eye and then delivered a long, princely bow of respect. 'Your Excellency,' Jackson began apologetically. No doubt this creature thought of him as a Prince in Waiting, of noble birth. As Mackenzie had suggested, it was best to act the part and not raise suspicion.

Tess, somewhat puzzled by her brother's behaviour, but always wanting to be included, dropped into a royal curtsey and gave Bemmung a beaming smile.

Bemmung gave a deep, bemused laugh. 'Young human, you have much to learn, as it should be. On your quest, your fellow traveller Hadwyn will protect and teach you, but that other young one who follows you around will also teach you much.' Jackson looked around. Surely he wasn't referring to Tess? 'There is anger burning in you that will serve no purpose, but will impede your learning. You must learn tolerance, and forgive the weaknesses and mistakes of others. Show patience in their learning and take them into the future with you. There is no other way for all of us.'

Jackson decided Bemmung must have been talking about the Emerald character; after all, she was just an apprentice.

Bemmung pressed on. 'Anger is your enemy. You must listen and learn, and take this message into your world. This responsibility is entrusted to you.'

Jackson was speechless. Mackenzie sat upright in his bean bag. This was concerning. The creature Bemmung had just indicated an awareness that Jackson and Tess were from another world. This was not part of the game. Things had just become even more unpredictable – and with unpredictability came danger.

Bemmung then turned to Tess, who was still smiling excitedly at the magnificent Frilled-Neck Lizard King and holding her beloved dog in her arms. Tess loved lizards – and every other creature she ever ran into. 'Now, young one, you are indeed a heartfelt protector of all living creatures. I can see your soul. You have the heart and the blood of a druid. You have already done many things to help your creature friends in your short lifetime. Do not lose connection with your life purpose.'

Tess stood motionless, mouth agape.

'Order and balance between the natural world and humans in your own world must be maintained, or your world will be destroyed. You know this. What you must conquer is stillness. You are enthusiastic, passionate and compassionate – however, you are racing through life and missing some important lessons on your path. Listen carefully. You must learn to slow down, be still and observe. The answers are all around you. Learn all that you can, develop your skills, teach others and spread the message. Fight for them. This is your destiny.'

A fly flew into Tess's mouth, making her cough and splutter. In seconds she regained her composure, lifting her chin high with pride.

And finally, Bemmung addressed Hadwyn. 'You are of a twin soul. You are here and elsewhere.' Bemmung looked up toward the sky. Mackenzie flinched. Was Bemmung referring to him? 'You are bound to another who is not here, but together you will take the responsibility on your shoulders for our destiny in these fading lands. Here in the Land of Mungo, you are close to your goal. You must now travel to the Valley of Lunettes. You need to leave now and find Vigars Well. Rest there until noon. When the sun is directly overhead, you must move quickly in the direction of Lake Mungo. You will see many spider burrows, but do not fear. The spiders will not come out – they cannot survive in the midday sun. Find your way down through the lunettes and wait there until midnight. The spiders will emerge to hunt. Wait for them to pass. Move swiftly until you see a red glow emanating from the correct burrow. This is the Burrow of Imprisonment.'

'That leads to the ant tunnels,' Jackson piped up. He remembered the battle he and Mackenzie had fought.

Bemmung nodded. 'Yes, it does. Travel quickly through the burrows before the spiders return. When the spider webs are no more, you are entering the ant tunnels. Search for the Reddening. Then you will be entering the domain of the Trap-Jaw Ants. They are the guardians of the Burnstone. Find the Burnstone and guard it with your life. We thank you for the coming Awakening.'

Jackson looked over at Tess, feeling very uncertain.

Bemmung continued. 'You have a strong and courageous heart. You have all you need to succeed.' With that, Bemmung moved around to the back of the tree. Tess ran over to ask Bemmung a question and peered behind the tree.

'He's gone,' she announced with disappointment.

7

Lake Mungo

After examining the game map, Mackenzie located Vigars Well. The three figures walked briskly in that direction. The land was dry and cracked underfoot. Within an hour, they came across a dried-up waterhole. Mackenzie selected the waterhole. The description 'Vigars Well' appeared on his screen. 'This is it,' he told his companions.

There were no trees for shade, so they sat amongst the saltbushes and waited in the searing heat. Tess pulled her cape over her head for protection from the sun. To keep occupied, she plaited long grass stems into a dog lead. She had decided things were getting a bit too dangerous for Buddy to be running off anywhere. Buddy made bites in the air, trying to catch hundreds of flies that seemed to have appeared from nowhere. Jackson placed a stick in the sand and watched the shadow shorten as the sun moved overhead.

'Right, it's time to go,' Jackson announced. The companions moved again in usual single file – Hadwyn in the lead, followed by Tess and then Jackson protecting the rear of the party. Hadwyn walked at a fast pace. Soon they left the flat land behind and found their way across the top of the lunettes, leading down to the final lake. This was the Valley of Lunettes. Tess tripped and stumbled several times; at one point she almost fell into a crevice.

'Be careful,' Jackson admonished her.

'I didn't mean it,' Tess defended herself, 'I have shorter legs than you.'

Hadwyn stopped. Mackenzie's voice spoke. 'Right, stop with the arguing, you two. You need to be as silent as possible.'

Tess stuck her tongue out at Jackson and turned to follow Hadwyn.

Along the way, they observed many more large, circular holes surrounded by silvery-white thick cobwebs. They were Whistling Spider Burrows. Danger lurked within but nothing moved. Hadwyn manoeuvred into a deep crevice pathway between high lunettes. The siblings scrambled down after him. This was safer and cooler.

They came upon a fork in the pathway and Hadwyn halted. Mackenzie wasn't sure which way to go. He looked at the map again and saw there were pathways going in many directions. Given he didn't know where the Burrow of Imprisonment was located, he couldn't use the map to find it.

With the game on pause, Mackenzie went through all the character bios and stats again, looking for something to help him. Then he realised that there were still five amber gems in Hadwyn's pouch. He had forgotten all about them in the drama at Lake Leaghur. Exploring the amber properties, he discovered that amber could be used to help make decisions. 'Jackson, go to Hadwyn and take an amber gem from his pouch.' Jackson did as he was told. 'Hold it in your hand while crossing both hands over your heart. Now I want you to close your eyes and ask for direction.'

Jackson nodded and stood quietly for a moment with his eyes closed. 'We are going that way,' he announced confidently, pointing to his left. He slipped the gem into his pouch and they moved off.

A short time later, the companions came across an area of the lunettes where a natural bridge had formed overhead. 'This is where you can wait safely,' Mackenzie told them. 'You must wait here till midnight. We have some planning to do.' The companions sat down and rested. Mackenzie shared all the information he could of the next part of their journey. They needed to have their wits about them. They all rested and waited.

Mackenzie rested while the others rested. It had taken him hours to get them through to Lake Mungo. He knew that this final part of level one would decide if they could move to the next level. He didn't want to make a bad error of judgement. It was better to take a little longer, rather than rush and get this wrong. He felt an enormous weight of responsibility on his shoulders for Jackson and Tess's lives. There was no way but forward. He was as ready as he could be.

Mackenzie picked up the controller and began preparing Hadwyn. Avoidance was going to be his main strategy. He had two humans he needed to get through this safely. He may have the ability to renew Hadwyn's health, but nothing was certain for Jackson and Tess, or Buddy for that matter.

Hadwyn had a Statue spell, which would be able to freeze his opponents for a short time and give his friends time to get away. Like Jackson, Hadwyn also had Furious Strike, which would make him super-fast in battle. Hadwyn's final spell was Triple Jump.

He knew Tess had an Invisibility spell, but it remained uncertain how much they could depend on it or how long it lasted. She had used her Charm Stare successfully with the Great Roamer, so hopefully they could depend on that to disarm beasts and humans. Tess's Replenish Quiver meant she would never run out of arrows.

Jackson had Fireball, Skin Shield and Furious Strike. So far, they all knew the Fireball spell was working. The Skin Shield would be invaluable in protecting Jackson's body in battle. *Let's hope they all work*, Mackenzie thought. They were going to find out one way or the other.

THURSDAY

Midnight had passed. The companions stood ready to start their final dangerous venture in the Land of Mungo. They had reviewed their strength and weaknesses, their abilities and skills. They had discussed various scenarios that may lie ahead.

Suddenly, they heard a hissing sound, and then another from a different direction. The spiders made a noise as the stiff bristles around their mouths moved backwards and forwards against each other. Tess sucked in her breath. Jackson put his finger to his lips. In the moonlight they could see large shapes moving slowly from the burrows and climbing the lunettes. Tess was wide-eyed and stepped closer to Jackson. Soon there were at least a hundred large, dark spiders moving like an army, spreading out into the Land of Mungo. The hissing grew louder as many dark shapes crossed overhead. After what seemed forever, the shadows faded off into the night. It was time to move.

Very quietly, they moved off. Jackson had made a sling from part of his cape and carried Buddy safely out of harm's way. They soon came out of the protective lunette crevices into an exposed pathway between the lunettes. Many of the crevices were doorways into vacant spider burrows. They walked at a steady pace along the moonlit path. Cobwebs glinted in the moonlight. Hadwyn rubbed an amber gem between his hands, activating the electron light particles which provided illumination like a dull torch.

After they had walked for about ten minutes, the amber light began to fade. 'Oh no,' Tess whispered, 'remember we read that the amber will darken as a sign of an enemy approaching.' Hadwyn quickly steered the companions into a narrow lunette crevice. The hissing sounds became louder – and then, to their horror, a Whistling Spider lumbered up the pathway and came within two metres of them. The spider paused and turned toward them. Hadwyn held his sword in both hands. The spider came closer and reached with a large hairy leg toward the crevice, trying to manoeuvre its way in to reach the captives. The hissing increased. The hairy leg almost touched Hadwyn. He raised the sword and brought it down swiftly, dismembering the beast. The spider continued sending its hairy arms in, reaching and flailing about. Hadwyn kept fighting. Soon there were three long hairy spider legs wriggling in the sand near their feet. The spider recoiled and lumbered away, lopsided.

After some moments, Jackson and Tess stood still with shock; Hadwyn motioned for them to follow. 'That's gross,' Tess whispered, stepping over the wriggling legs. They headed out quietly onto the moonlit pathway and continued along the path between the lunettes on the edge of Lake Mungo. They crept quietly, keeping a lookout for unexpected visitors.

As they cornered a bend in the path, they came upon the largest burrow they had yet seen. A pale red glow emitted from the entrance. Hadwyn pointed to it and nodded, beckoning them to follow. It was the Burrow of Imprisonment. Tess took a big breath and entered right behind Hadwyn, almost on top of him.

Hadwyn slashed at sticky cobwebs with his sword, making their way clear. He slowed down and pointed to the ground. A large bird carcass and a lizard skull littered the burrow floor, evidence of the spiders' recent meals. Tess recognised that many of the bones had belonged to creatures like Bemmung, although many were smaller too. She hoped the Leliyn Lizards would not be wiped out. They just had to succeed.

Swiftly through the burrow they went. Jackson felt nervous being at the back of the group. The cobwebs lessened; soon they left the burrow and entered into a dirt tunnel. A faint red glow continued into the deep earth. Mackenzie instructed Jackson to begin their plan. A battle with the Trap-Jaw Ants lay ahead.

Jackson pulled a small vial from his pouch and drank an effervescent liquid. Jackson waited a minute or two and then began hitting his arm. It had worked. His arm felt like steel; he could not feel the impact of his punches. He was now protected by his Skin Shield spell. Mackenzie then reminded Tess about her part in the plan. If they ran into trouble, she was to use her Invisibility spell and try to get past the battle, but she had to stay close enough to the boys so they didn't lose her. It was time to complete the Land of Mungo quest.

After about two minutes, they came to a wider part in the tunnel. Jackson recognised the place from the game. 'The Burnstone is up there,' he whispered, pointing toward a stream of bright red light coming from a hole high up in the cave wall. 'I can't imagine why there are no Trap-Jaw Ants,' Jackson queried. Jackson and Tess were looking up at the ceiling.

'Actually, guys,' Mackenzie corrected, 'they are creeping up behind you right now, so turn around slowly. Jackson, stand next to Hadwyn. Tess, you go up those rocks and get the Burnstone, we will cover you. Put the Burnstone in your pouch and then make yourself invisible and come back to us. Grab Jackson on the arm so he knows when you are back with him.'

In the dim light, Jackson counted seven Trap-Jaw Ants. They moved with intention toward the intruders. Hadwyn and Jackson stood side by side with their backs to the wall. It was now or never.

Bedlam ensued. The giant ants split up. Some came straight on, spreading their straight mandibles wide open to 180 degrees. Four of them kept striking out at the intruders, trying to slam their mandibles against them. Hadwyn and Jackson fought using Furious Strike, defending the attacks and causing some injury. Jackson was amazed at his own skill. The other three ants had slammed their mandibles against the floor and used this to catapult themselves past the intruders, landing on the opposite side. Now they had two fronts to fight. 'Fireball!' Mackenzie called.

Jackson's last piece of coal was quickly ripped from his pouch and thrown on the ground near the four menacing ants. 'Fireball,' Jackson yelled confidently. The ants erupted in flames and disintegrated into a messy pile of goo and twitching legs.

Meanwhile, Hadwyn turned to fight three ants that were about to pounce from the other direction. Jackson got knocked over by an ant's swinging head. Hadwyn threw his Statue spell at them, covering them with a fine silver dust. Within seconds they were frozen in time.

Jackson stood up. He checked himself. No injury. His Skin Shield had protected him. Jackson felt a pull on his arm. It was Tess. He felt for her hand and nodded. 'Great, Tess. Let's get out of here.'

They ran further and further down the tunnel, getting as much distance between them and the ant chamber as possible. The red glow faded and they were surrounded by darkness. Hadwyn pulled another amber gem from his pouch to light their way. The amber sparkled with the golden light particles, previously captured from sunlight. They kept running.

Tess's hand became visible in Hadwyn's hand and then the rest of her body materialised. This time her Invisibility spell had lasted longer. 'I'm getting puffed,' she called. Mackenzie stopped Hadwyn and told Tess to climb on to his back. They kept running.

Finally, the tunnel opened up into a vast area with high rock walls. Before their eyes, they discovered a blue saltwater pond surrounded by white sand.

'The Burnstone, Tess?' Mackenzie requested. Tess carefully located the precious Burnstone from her pouch and held it out for the others to see to see. There it was. An immaculately preserved lizard, a miniature version of Bemmung, suspended lifelessly inside the red stone. Hadwyn reached forward and took it from her.

'Oh no, this is a dead end,' Tess called to Mackenzie. Jackson and Tess searched their surrounds for an escape route. 'What if the ants come? I think we need to go back and find another way!'

Mackenzie tried to calm them down. On the screen, he could see at least two ants approaching. So far, his friends were unaware of the danger. They didn't have much time but he didn't want to panic them. 'This is the end of level one, guys. We just have to find the door. Keep looking. Look for anything.' Mackenzie moved Hadwyn to stand in between his friends and the approaching ants.

The amber gem Hadwyn had been using for light began to blacken. Amber had been used for centuries to warn of enemies approaching. The pool cave became dark. 'Jackson, go and stand next to Hadwyn. Tess, get right back over to the rear wall.'

'I'm scared. It's getting darker,' Tess called to the others. Jackson wasn't feeling any braver. He stood beside Hadwyn as instructed but he felt sick. He didn't feel confident at all.

Seconds passed. A Trap-Jaw Ant appeared, heading straight for Hadwyn and Jackson, closely followed by another. Their swords swung rapidly, keeping the first ant at bay. Hadwyn lunged forward and stabbed it between the eyes. His longsword became stuck. Jackson continued fighting the second ant, which had clambered over the body of the dead ant. Both of Jackson's swords were knocked from his grasp. Tess screamed. 'Get back Jackson,' Mackenzie called.

At the same time the battling ant made a screeching sound as black liquid sprayed from a wound in its side. Someone had speared it.

Everything went quiet. Hadwyn pulled another amber gem out of his pouch for light. Tess's eyes opened wide. She pointed to a figure standing on a large rock off to their side. It was the native man in the cave painting: Mungo Man. They stood silently, not knowing what to do.

Mungo Man walked over and retrieved his spear from the twitching ant. Then he walked up to Hadwyn and stretched out his hand. Hadwyn handed him the Burnstone. Mungo Man nodded and handed it back, then proceeded to walk towards the pool. He continued walking into the water until he disappeared from sight. All that was left were his footprints. The pool began to glow from a light source deep down.

'Okay, that's it guys. That's the door. You need to follow his footprints. Are we ready for this?' Mackenzie checked in.

'We'll drown. What about Buddy?' Tess asked Mackenzie.

'I don't know, Tess. I don't know about any of you, but we were told to follow in the footsteps of the ancients. If you stay here, more ants will come. They want that Burnstone. We don't have a choice.'

'Can we have a hug first?' Tess asked, looking wide-eyed and very young.

'Sure,' Jackson replied, holding out both hands for her.

Tess hugged her brother then walked to Hadwyn. 'I don't know if you can feel this, but I want to hug you too. Just in case we never meet again.' Tess embraced Hadwyn's motionless figure. His hand came up and touched Tess on the head. Tess smiled at Hadwyn. 'I like you,' she told the character.

Jackson looked at his sister. Obviously, the stress was getting to her.

Meanwhile, Mackenzie contemplated what had just happened. He hadn't had control of Hadwyn when Hadwyn touched Tess's head. This was getting interesting. He decided to keep the developments to himself. No point arousing any more anxiety and uncertainty for his friends.

'I need you both to go over next to Hadwyn,' he instructed. 'Now hold on to him. Jackson, you've still got Buddy in the sling?' Jackson nodded. 'Just hold your breath, guys. We need to get out of here.' Using Hadwyn's superhuman strength, he catapulted them all into the pool and swam with them, down toward the light.

Waiting patiently in the Forest of Dead Trees, high above the scorching sand, an old lizard raised his weary head. The magnificent frill that circled his neck, like a regal collar of orange glory, glowed brighter. Through his soft leathery feet, Bemmung sensed vibrations, signalling a long-awaited change beginning in his land.

Mackenzie paused the game. He needed a break. He headed down to the kitchen to get a drink. Over the kitchen bench, he could see through to the lounge where his mum sat watching the news. He walked around to greet her and found she was asleep in the old armchair. The room felt a bit cool. He grabbed a knee rug and gently covered her legs, then took her empty coffee mug to the kitchen. Then he heard something on the TV news behind him. 'The Department of Meteorology has predicted a once-in-a-thousand-year weather event in the south-western deserts of New South Wales. Over the next three days, the region is expected to receive the equivalent of two years' average rainfall. This will mean that the Willandra Lakes in Mungo National Park will fill for the first time in thousands of years and the dying rivers of the Murray Darling system will be bursting their banks.'

Mackenzie felt shivers down his back. He needed to get back to the game. So many unexplainable things were happening around him. The sound of the news continued as he walked away. 'In other news, police remain baffled by the disappearance of the Taylor children. It has now been five nights since they were last seen. Distraught parents were unable to be interviewed while police report there have been no credible leads ...'

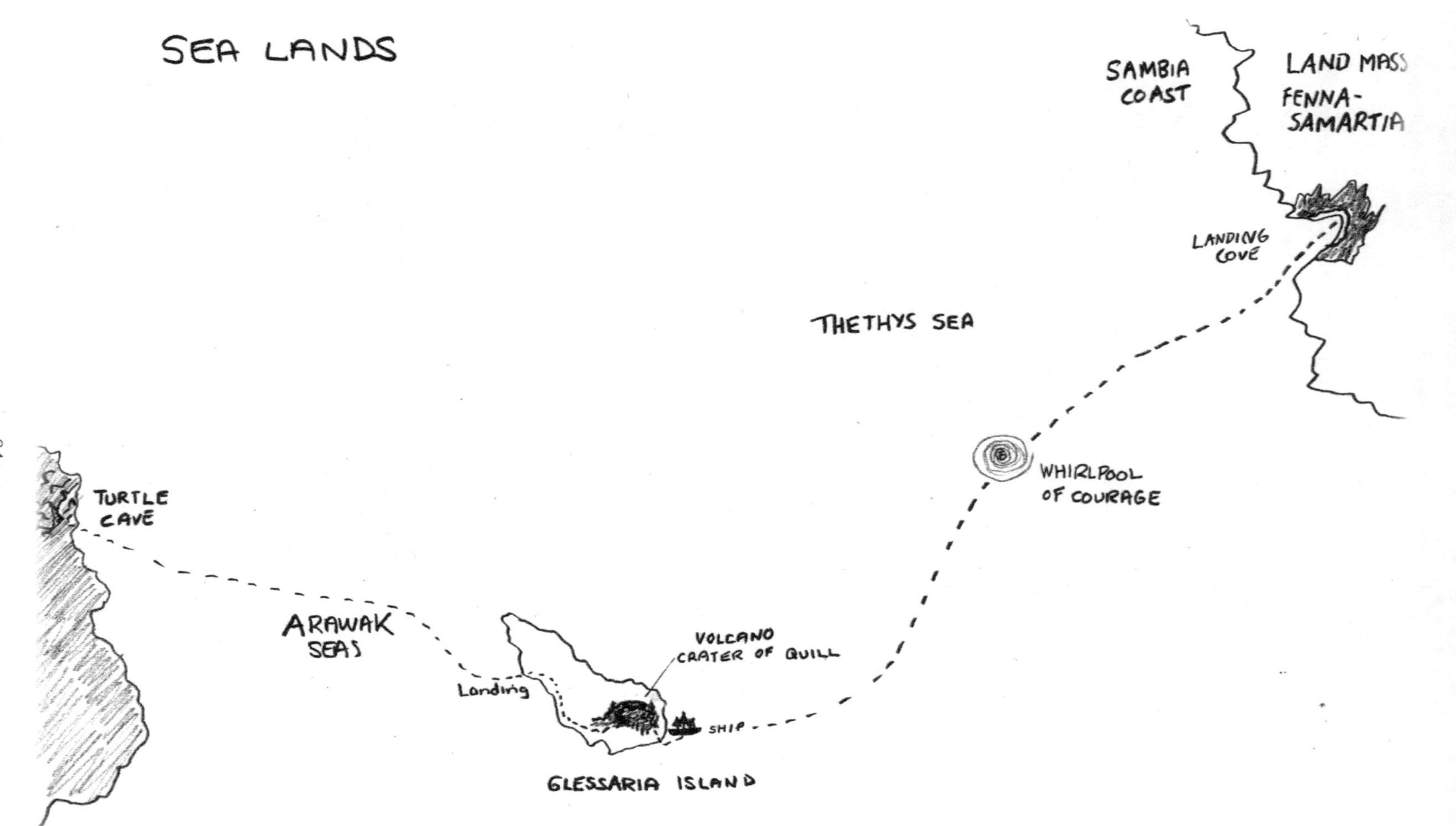

SEA LANDS
SAMBIA COAST
LAND MASS FENNA-SAMARTIA
LANDING COVE
THETHYS SEA
WHIRLPOOL OF COURAGE
TURTLE CAVE
ARAWAK SEAS
VOLCANO CRATER OF QUILL
Landing
SHIP
GLESSARIA ISLAND

SEA LANDS

8

Queen Kulibari

Hadwyn swam fast underwater. He steered them swiftly through an underwater archway of light, and within seconds they had surfaced on the other side. Hadwyn pushed Jackson and Tess toward the edge of a pool. As he let them go, they found themselves knee-deep in a warm saltwater pool inside a large seaside cave, which opened out to the ocean. Jackson and Tess looked around the cave. The ceiling of the cave was very high. 'Where do you think we are?' Tess asked Jackson.

'The next level. The Sea Lands,' Jackson replied. 'We made it.'

Jackson quickly released Buddy from the sling and checked him out. Buddy appeared no worse for wear apart from being completely wet and looking like a drowned rat. Buddy shook his body and head vigorously, sneezing water out of his nostrils.

Tess, who had been sitting on the pristine white sand since emerging from the water, crawled over to his side and ruffled him. 'Oh no, we nearly killed him,' she exclaimed. 'Here Buddy,' she called, patting the sand beside her. Buddy ignored her and began to roll around on his back, trying to dry himself.

'Your friend will survive,' came a voice from the shadows. They looked around at the large rocks and, after a moment, realised that one rock was in fact a very large sea turtle, as large as an average sized car. 'Yes, I am speaking to you,' the turtle confirmed.

Jackson stepped forward. 'Excuse me, we have just come from the land of Mungo ...'

'We know why you are here. We have been expecting you. It was written long ago.' The companions came closer to the turtle in anticipation. 'I am Kulibari, Queen of the Leatherback Turtles. Our population is being decimated and in danger of extinction. The spirit of the Leatherback has been imprisoned in the Burnstone from the time of the rising seas.

'Long ago we swam freely and we feasted on the Cannonball Jellyfish, but since our spirit became trapped in the Burnstone we have been weakened. The Cannonballs have grown large and powerful. They hunt us. They have taken over the Arawak Seas that surround our islands. Our food supplies have almost been destroyed. Soon, even the Cannonballs will not have enough food to survive. Our land is in peril. You are our last hope.'

'Thank you, Kulibari,' Jackson responded, 'we await your guidance.'

'Yes of course,' Kulibari answered. 'In our land, you must get past the Cannonballs to get to Glessaria Island. The Arawak sea is saturated with these giant creatures and they are very dangerous. There are also Spider Crabs. They are the scavengers of the dead. You will encounter them on the beaches, feasting on the remains of our kin who have been killed by the Cannonballs. They will also be on Glessaria Island, for it is the Spider Crabs who guard the Blue Burnstone. They will fight you to the death if you try to take it from them.'

The companions listened intently as Kulibari continued. 'If you make it to the island, you must climb to the top of the volcano and then down into the Crater of Quill. You will travel through a jungle and down at the bottom of the crater is a saltwater lake. Deep in the lake you must locate the Burnstone. Once safe in your possession, you must make your way to the treacherous Tethys Sea.'

'How will we ever survive this danger?' Tess asked. 'We are just humans in a game.' Jackson nudged Tess sharply.

'This is no game, child,' Kulibari answered. 'Everything is connected. Your world, our world – the past, the present and the future. The animal kingdom will do all in its power to help you. There will be those who guide you along the way. Listen for them. We must all maintain courage and hope.'

The companions were transfixed, absorbing the story and their place in it. Buddy wandered around the sea cave, sniffing behind rocks. He disturbed a few baby Leatherback Turtles, who waddled quickly to the water's edge and began swimming in the pool. 'Oh my,' Tess piped up, 'I love baby turtles.'

Kulibari nodded her head slowly. 'Yes, young one, I see you. You are a guardian of nature – a descendant of the ancient druids, no doubt. Welcome to our world and thank you, in anticipation of your life's work ahead fighting for the survival of our worlds.'

Tess beamed with pride. 'How do you know about my wildlife work?' she asked.

'The animal kingdom watches and they know. Your ongoing efforts to save wildlife, even at a very young age, has made you known to us.'

Jackson looked over at his sister as someone he'd not met before. From his point of view, she had brought injured and neglected creatures into their home forever and a day, making a lot of work for everyone in the family. Most of them had died. He had considered it a waste of time.

Meanwhile, Mackenzie shifted uncomfortably in his bean bag. Kulibari was speaking of the human world. This was hard to comprehend. He had no idea how this interplay between two worlds would impact on his friend's survival chances.

'And you, Wungarra,' Kulibari continued.

'My name is Jackson, actually,' Jackson volunteered.

'Yes, that may be so,' Kulibari patiently explained, 'but you are Wungarra to me.'

'Why do you call me that?' Jackson asked.

'"Wungarra" means "boy", but I am here to tell you that when you have completed this quest, you will no longer be "wungarra". You will then be "mula", a man like this one.' Kulibari used her great bobbing head to indicate toward Hadwyn. Jackson was a little put out to be called a boy, but was pleased to hear he was soon to be a man. 'As you grow into a man, you will come to know your courage and great heart,' Kulibari added.

Tess smiled, looking at Jackson with admiration. 'He does have a great heart,' she confirmed. 'He's a great brother,' she added. Kulibari nodded.

Mackenzie paused the game and got up for a stretch. All the excitement and fear had made him tense beyond belief, and now he was feeling very sore and stiff. He checked the clock: 2 am Thursday morning. They all needed to rest.

First, he would get some food. He headed out to the kitchen to forage for something. He needed to get back quickly and tell the others to rest before the next day's venturing. He wanted to read more about level two, the Sea Lands. He now knew that when he paused the game, no time passed for his friends, so he hurried, grabbing an apple, some biscuits and a glass of water. He checked Hadwyn's health and was relieved to see that it had been fully restored, which was what he had hoped for at the beginning of another level. He discussed with the others the need to try to sleep and he then did the same with headphones on, just to keep at the ready for the unexpected.

About five hours passed with no interruptions. It was still dark. Getting up, Mackenzie moved his bedroom blind to one side and saw the break of dawn showing behind the dark silhouetted garden shrubs.

He needed to prepare his friends. He hoped to get them through the Sea Lands level before the end of the day. Five nights had passed since their disappearance. Perhaps tonight he would then be able to move on through to the Low Lands. Maybe tomorrow, he would get them through the final two levels and they would be home. He must retain hope. He would just take short breaks for rest and food. He now had a huge bottle of water beside him and plenty of snacks. He was as ready as he could be.

Back in the sea cave, Jackson and Tess were still sleeping. There were now two large turtles, off a short distance from the children. Mackenzie called to his friends. Buddy's ears pricked up and then his head went to one side quizzically. Mackenzie's voice was coming from above him. The dog looked around for the voice's owner to no avail. Slowly they sat up and stretched. Hadwyn was in the same standing position Mackenzie had left him in all night.

'Yep, we're getting up,' Jackson responded. Jackson and Tess ate and drank again. Buddy joined in. They stood up and shook the sand from their clothes.

'You have company,' Mackenzie told them.

They looked around and saw the two great turtles. Kulibari acknowledged them. 'This is my sister Waru,' she introduced. 'We will help you to the island.'

'How will we do that?' Jackson enquired.

'You and the small creature that you carry will ride with Waru. The other two will ride on my back,' she explained.

'Oh, my goodness, that's amazing,' exclaimed Tess.

'Well, if you like being attacked by giant jellyfish, I guess it is,' Jackson piped up. Tess turned her head toward her big brother with a frown. 'So, what should we do if things go wrong?' he asked. 'For example, you Leatherback Turtles can stay underwater if need be, but we cannot.'

'Yes, this is very dangerous and we understand your limitations. We will endeavour to avoid such a situation. We are familiar with the ways of the Cannonball. Normally they hunt in swarms at night, so we will travel in the midday sun. They also are normally in more shallow waters, so we plan to travel through where there is a deep channel underneath us. We can also swim much faster than the Cannonballs.'

'Right.' Jackson nodded.

Kulibari addressed Hadwyn. 'Of course, you are not limited like these two, so if anything does go amiss, you must get them to safety. We would try to hold the Jellyfish back.'

Tess looked longingly at the baby turtles swimming and diving around in the pool. She was going to miss those babies. 'They are safe in here,' Kulibari told Tess. 'And when you succeed in releasing the turtle spirit from the Burnstone, these babies will get the chance to grow up and survive.'

They were learning that many creatures avoided the midday sun and hunted at night, or when there was less light in the mornings and evenings. This was the type of learning that might keep them safe.

Kulibari and Waru began their slow progress out of the protective cave. Their bodies were bulky and their movement laborious. 'Look a bit clumsy, don't they?' Tess whispered to Jackson. Jackson shook his head furiously at her. 'I wanted to tell you that I studied them at school,' she continued. 'Once they're in the water, they can go really fast. Their flippers are like bird wings.'

'Good to know,' Jackson replied.

'And they can stay underwater for hours,' she continued.

'Okay, thanks for that,' Jackson replied again, waving his hand at her as a signal that she could stop now.

The group moved off, following Kulibari and Waru. They moved out through the opening of the cave to the outside. Before them stretched a pale blue-green sea, with bright sunshine and clear blue skies. 'There's phytoplankton in that water, see the green? It's just as well 'cos the zooplankton feed off that and jellyfish eat zooplankton, so maybe they won't need to eat any more baby turtles,' Tess chatted.

Jackson looked upwards for support. He'd had enough biology lessons for the day and it had only just started.

'Tess, it's great that you know a lot about the environment, but right now we need to really concentrate on moving along and keeping safe,' Mackenzie suggested. 'How about when we next rest, you tell me more about that?' he offered.

Tess smiled. 'Of course I will,' she agreed.

The group made their way across the sands. As far as their eyes could see, great turtle carcass shells littered the beaches while hundreds of crabs could be seen swarming over the skeletons. The Spider Crabs were larger than usual; their backs about as high as Hadwyn's shoulders, but thankfully they were preoccupied with their feasting. Their bodies were a greenish brown, contrasting with long white claws. Their rough-looking backs were covered in protruding spines. At the front of them was a tapered snout and short eyestalks. 'Creepy critters,' Jackson declared, 'I don't fancy fighting them.'

'Me either,' Tess concurred, 'they're so much bigger than they should be.'

Soon they had reached the water's edge. Kulibari spoke. 'Once we are afloat, you must climb on our backs and hold on to the front of our shells. We will travel as fast as we can, so don't let go. We will aim for dark blue water further out. That's the deep channel, where we will be safer – but first, we need to get through the shallows where the Cannonballs await their prey.'

Together they moved into the shallow water, Buddy safely secured in Jackson's sling. The warm waves lapped against their legs. The sea was crystal clear and the sand below clean and white. Kulibari instructed them to climb aboard. Slowly, the Leatherback Turtles pushed themselves forward with their flippers, heaving their bodies and their riders along. Eventually, the water became deep enough for their bodies to float. 'Now hang on,' Kulibari told them. 'If we run into trouble, we may have to dive for short periods. If that happens, hold your breath. It won't be for long, just long enough for us to swim under the Cannonballs.'

With that, the turtles began to glide through the water, their flippers becoming graceful underwater wings.

9

Battle on the Arawak Sea

The sea was very calm. Small rhythmic waves lapped the shore. The midday sun was hot on their backs. There was barely a breeze. They glided along for about ten minutes, heading for a few islands they could see off in the distance. One of the islands had a volcano at one end and the top of the volcano was enveloped by a low cloud. That was Glessaria Island.

After a while, Tess noticed a dark area in the water some distance away and assumed it was the deep channel. Kulibari warned the companions, 'Unfortunately there is a swarm of Cannonballs ahead. Pull your legs up. We will try to outswim them.'

At that moment, another dark patch of water began to build a circle around them. Kulibari and Waru changed direction several times as they manoeuvred this way and that way, trying desperately to avoid a collision with the swarm. The unnaturally large Cannonballs had depleted their own environment of most of the food resources, so they were now hunting all day long to satisfy their hunger. The Cannonballs were as big as the old Leatherback Turtles. The children were terrified. The Cannonballs seemed to be closing in on them, creating a trap.

Suddenly, several Cannonballs emerged right beside them. They turned over on their backs, reaching out with long arms that protruded from their mouths, trying to attach to the children. 'Fight, Tess!' Jackson called, swinging a sword left and right with one arm, cutting off jellyfish arms that extended towards his legs. Using his Furious Strike, Jackson managed to dismember many of the jellyfish arms.

Mackenzie felt helpless. None of Tess's spells would help in this situation. Jackson's Fireball was useless in the water and he was using Furious Strike and Skin Shield continuously. It was all they had.

Kulibari and Waru pressed on, pushing their way through the swarm as Jackson and Hadwyn fought on. Jackson looked up. They were getting very close to the deep channel, which was now clearly visible. *We should be there any minute*, he thought. He looked over at Hadwyn, who, like him, was swinging his sword furiously at the Cannonball arms. Tess was laying as flat as she could on Kulibari's back, hanging on to the great shell tightly with both hands.

'Hold your breath,' Kulibari called, 'we are going to dive.' Within seconds, Kulibari and Waru had dipped their heads underwater and began a rapid dive, trying to find a way under the thick swarm of jellyfish. Tess, who still had her eyes open, saw a mass of brown and purple dome-shaped bodies with long white menacing arms extending beneath their bodies. Kulibari was struggling as heavy collision after collision occurred, battering her body.

Abruptly, Kulibari shook her body so violently that Hadwyn and Tess became detached. One of the jellyfish arms wrapped around Tess's leg and began to pull her down. Hadwyn quickly grabbed Tess's arm and pulled against the Cannonball. At the same time, he swung his sword to cut the creature's arm from Tess's leg. As soon as she was freed, Hadwyn swam swiftly beneath the Cannonball swarm, following Waru as she continued with Jackson on her back towards Glessaria Island.

The last they saw of Kulibari was her body sinking down. Hundreds of Cannonballs swarmed her body and she faded from their sight. Waru swam strongly on, not looking back. Hadwyn held on to Tess tightly as he kept pace. Waru dove at high speed into the deep channel and then they glided silently in the direction of the island. Overwhelmed with the need for air, Tess gasped but realised immediately that somehow, she could now breathe underwater. Jackson also found this to be true. It slowly dawned on them that Kulibari had given them this gift to survive underwater, ensuring that they could succeed in their quest to save her kin. Kulibari was no more.

Eventually, Waru came in close enough to the shore of Glessaria Island for the children to alight without sinking beneath the waves. 'I can help you no further,' she told them sadly.

'I am so sorry,' Tess said quietly.

'The price we have paid is high,' Waru shared, 'but we had no choice. Now I must return to the young and protect them. Go forward with our blessing and our hope.' Waru turned and, within no time, had disappeared under the water.

'I can't believe that just happened,' Tess said. 'We didn't drown. Kulibari let herself drown. She made herself into a decoy so we could escape.' For a moment the companions were quiet as they processed what had happened. 'Are we safe now?' Tess asked Hadwyn.

Hadwyn stood still, looking in Tess's direction, but did not answer. Mackenzie responded, 'Yes, I believe you are for now. Just rest for a while. Have some food and drink. You have a big hill to climb.' They looked toward the volcano towering above them. 'I'm hoping you can get to the top before nightfall.'

Tess was listening to Mackenzie but looking at Hadwyn. 'Mackenzie, was that you or Hadwyn who saved me from the Cannonballs – you know, cutting them off my leg underwater?' Tess was having trouble distinguishing Hadwyn from Mackenzie. Hadwyn seemed so real.

Mackenzie hesitated. It hadn't been him at all. It had all happened so quickly and Hadwyn had stepped in independently before Mackenzie could respond. He really didn't want to scare them by telling them he wasn't in control. There was more than enough to be stressed about.

'Let's just say it was a joint effort,' Mackenzie told Tess. 'There are some parts of the game that happen automatically – you know, like walkthroughs.'

Tess wasn't completely sure what Mackenzie was talking about, but she had great faith in him as a knowledgeable gamer; so, for the time being, she was satisfied with the answer. Mackenzie himself, however, remained unconvinced of his ability in this game.

Jackson was ready for a rest. He looked a little paler than usual. 'Why is your hand bleeding, Jackson?' Tess asked. Jackson looked down. A purple line ran across the back of his hand and was bleeding. 'I think you've been stung by a Cannonball. Let me see that,' Tess asked, reaching for Jackson's hand. 'Don't worry, Jackson. They're not supposed to be poisonous,' she reassured him.

Mackenzie spoke. 'Nevertheless, these are not normal Cannonballs. You best sit down for a while, Jackson. Tess, take an amber gem from Hadwyn's pouch and put the gem on his wound. It'll draw any negative energy out of his wound.'

The midday sun slowly crossed the sky and the shadows of the tropical trees lengthened across the beach. The shade had been a welcome relief from the heat. The air was thick with humidity; both Tess and Jackson had beads of sweat on their foreheads. They rested for about an hour while Hadwyn sat and kept watch. Tess awoke before Jackson and sat chatting to Mackenzie about her many wildlife adventures back at home. As promised, Mackenzie listened patiently to her enthusiastic portrayals. 'I think they are coconuts?' Tess said, looking up into a palm tree. 'Can Hadwyn knock one down?' she asked Mackenzie.

'Sure, why not. Let's give it a go,' he replied. With that, Hadwyn climbed effortlessly up the palm trunk and hit a coconut down with his dagger, dropping it into the sand. With a sharp stab of his dagger, Hadwyn broke a hole in the top. Tess was delighted and drank the cool milk. Buddy came up and sniffed the coconut hopefully.

'No, you won't like that,' she told him. 'Here, have some of this,' she said, handing him a little piece of meat. Mackenzie called to Jackson, wanting to investigate his wellbeing. Jackson began to stir and as he moved, the amber gem slid off his hand. Mackenzie was very satisfied with what he saw. Jackson's hand was completely healed.

'There you are, people. The magic works,' Mackenzie reassured them.

It took the group several hours to ascend the mountainside of the volcano. As they climbed, the air became more humid. The sun had dropped lower and the perspiration stayed wet on their faces. The higher they climbed, the cloudier it became.

By the time they reached the crater ridge, the sun was close to setting. They paused to view the crater beneath them. It was the size of a small town but overgrown by a tropical jungle. A cloudy mist wisped amongst the tops of tall trees. They could hear birds calling as they roosted for the night. They decided to press on and begin their descent before darkness overtook them. They need to find a safe refuge for the night.

The descent into the crater was steep and slippery. The group found their way amongst mountain palms and tree ferns. Slowly, the jungle became denser with gigantic silk cotton trees spreading out like giant canopies. Competing for space were the colossal kapok trees, whose large gnarly root systems were partially exposed above ground. Mountain mahogany trees, somewhat shorter, were decorated with great looping vines. Below the canopy, an array of plant life grew lusciously. Elephant ears provided a green backdrop for colourful orchids and begonias. It was a sight to be seen. 'The Jungle of Quill,' announced Mackenzie.

'It's a tropical rainforest,' Tess declared. 'Did you know …' she began.

'Hold that thought, Tess, you can tell me later,' Mackenzie reminded her.

'Where are we going?' Tess asked.

'You'll be heading down to the bottom of the crater to the blue lake. That's where the Blue Burnstone is,' Mackenzie informed them.

'That sounds a bit too simple,' Jackson interjected.

'Yes, well, there is a bit more to it, but we can talk more about that later,' Mackenzie replied. 'What I want you to do is find a place to camp before it gets dark. You'll have to build some type of shelter. But equally important: I need both of you to practice your skills and weapons. We've been lucky so far – let's not push our luck.'

It was almost twilight, making it quite dark under the trees. 'Let's camp here,' Jackson suggested. 'We can make a bit of a shelter from those palm fronds, just in case it rains.' Jackson had learnt how to build bush shelters on his army cadet bivouacs. Jackson removed his sling and set Buddy free.

'Can I help?' Tess pleaded.

'Sure, why not? 'Jackson agreed. 'Maybe gather up as much dry leaves as you can and make us some comfy bedding. I'll make the shelter.'

Once the shelter had been constructed, Jackson and Tess started practicing with their weapons. Mackenzie had Jackson sparring with Hadwyn. They worked with one sword, then two, then one sword combined with the dagger. Jackson preferred using two swords; one to defend and one to attack. He showed skill in switching between the two as he lunged forward, striking Hadwyn's sword and blocking attacks. 'Check this out,' Jackson called to Mackenzie.

'Really great, Jackson,' Mackenzie replied. 'You're definitely improving fast. You must be absorbing your character's sword-fighting expertise. As a royal, Eadric has been trained as an expert swordsman from a young age. That's really promising,' Mackenzie added, feeling a bit more confident about their survival chances ahead.

Meanwhile, Tess practiced shooting her arrows. As fast as she pulled the arrows from her quiver, stretched the bow and shot them into the log, within seconds, arrows re-appeared in the quiver with a never-ending supply. To begin with, she missed the log quite a bit – but gradually her aim improved until most of her arrows were hitting the log right in the middle. Cheekily, she tapped Jackson on the head, having some fun with her practice of being invisible. Startled, Jackson spun around with his swords raised, ready to block an attack.

'No Jackson, it's me,' Tess yelled, jumping to the side.

'Seriously, Tess. You might be invisible but I could've killed you. That's not funny.'

'Okay, okay … sorry,' Tess answered. She was feeling more confident about her Invisibility lasting longer now. She decided to play tricks on Buddy instead, who was trotting around sniffing, listening for cracking twigs and trying to find her. Mackenzie tried out Hadwyn's Triple Jump up and down trees to get familiar with the action. He then repeated the jumps with Tess and Jackson on Hadwyn's back. He decided they were as prepared as they could be.

As darkness descended, Tess, Jackson and Buddy lay down to sleep in the shelter. The sounds of the night jungle interrupted their sleep: cracking twigs in the bushes, frogs, cicadas, bird calls, an unknown animal snorting, and leaves moving in the wind overhead. A light rain fell, trickling down the palm fronds like tiny rivers. Bats darted through the high branches. Mackenzie moved Hadwyn to a sentry position between his friends and whatever existed deeper in the jungle crater. Mackenzie then fell asleep.

FRIDAY

As daybreak arrived, the jungle awoke. Birds flitted and greeted the morning with their songs. Water dripped from branch to branch, making its way slowly down from the high canopy to the moist undergrowth. Tess looked up into the giant reaches of the kapok tree. Some of the pink and white blossoms had been knocked off and fallen to the jungle floor in the night as bats had feasted upon their nectar.

Jackson was stirring and Buddy emerged from the shelter, making his way over to a low-lying elephant ear leaf. He lapped at the water pooled in the leaf. Jackson arose and after a good stretch, he sat down on a moss-covered log near Hadwyn. 'Morning,' he greeted his companions. 'It's so weird you don't have to sleep,' he commented to Hadwyn. There was no response from the stationary character.

In the middle of the night, Mackenzie had paused the game for about fifteen minutes to have a quick shower and grab some food and drink supplies. Chocolate bars and orange juice were perched on a coffee table next to his bean bag. When the companions were resting, he also took the opportunity to do a few stretches, sit-ups and push-ups. It had been a hectic four days so far; he needed to maintain his concentration and stamina.

As Mackenzie completed his exercise routine, he noticed his friends moving about on the screen. He returned to his bean bag and put his headset back on. 'Hey guys,' he called to them. 'Time to plan the day.' They went over what Kulibari had told them. 'We don't have any other information yet. We'll have to pick up stuff along the way,' Mackenzie informed them. 'Keep your eyes and ears open.'

Tess was looking over the shelter Jackson had built the night before. 'Great shelter, Jackson,' Tess piped up. 'Look, it's been raining and I didn't even get wet.'

'My cadet survival skills,' Jackson reported, 'whoever would have thought building lean-tos with the cadets would have been needed for something like this?'

'I'm hungry,' Tess announced, 'and I'm getting a bit sick of dried berries and dried meat.'

Jackson offered Tess a solution. 'Keep your eye out for fruit and nuts that birds eat. Bound to be fruit growing in here somewhere. That's something else we learnt in cadets.'

Tess smiled. 'You're very clever.'

Tess threw some dried meat in Buddy's direction, which he quickly snatched and began to chew. She looked around their surroundings in the hope of finding something edible. Tree trunks were covered in liverworts in all shades of green, and colourful orchids and bromeliads provided splashes of bright pink, orange, red and yellow. 'Oh, this place is so beautiful,' Tess acknowledged. 'You know, in my environmental science class I learnt that tropical rainforests have been logged so much that now they don't even cover six per cent of the land … and that's really bad because the rainforests make forty per cent of our oxygen. And more than half of our plant and animal species live in these forests,' she added.

Jackson looked up. He believed he had heard all of Tess's science information ten times over. Mackenzie jumped in, 'Yes, Tess it's a serious problem humans have on their hands.'

The conversation was interrupted by Buddy starting to growl. He was looking in the direction of a bright green moss-covered tree stump. 'What is it, Buddy?' Tess asked. Tess squinted through the shafts of sunlight filtering through the branches and leaves from above. She could see nothing out of the ordinary. Hadwyn stood up and walked toward the stump, stopping about a metre away. He held up his hand to indicate to the others not to move. Part of the stump moved. Gradually, Tess could make out some type of bright green lizard now sitting atop the stump.

'Greetings,' the lizard spoke. 'My name is Antillean. I am of the Iguana race. This is the last home we have left on earth.'

Hadwyn put his hand down and the others moved forward to his side.

'The young apprentice speaks wisely. Our forests disappear and we are hunted by the hungry Spider Crabs that have taken over our home. When you meet the Spider Crabs, remember that they travel forwards, not sideways like other crabs. You must take the Blue Burnstone from them.' And as quick as that, Antillean was gone from sight.

10

The Crater

The companions sat and considered their foes, and how they could use spells to conquer them. 'I say we get as close as we can, and at first sight of them, we climb into the safety of the trees and await nightfall,' Jackson suggested, 'then we'll have an advantage because the crabs have poor sight.'

'And we can drop small pieces of dried meat all over the place to confuse them,' Tess added, 'they have sensors on the bottom of their feet to taste and locate food.' This time Jackson was a little more impressed with Tess's learning.

'Both good ideas,' Mackenzie agreed. 'And you'll be able to tell if they've seen you because they'll start waving their pincers up high in the air to scare you off. Watch out, especially for the larger ones. They're the males and they have stronger claws. Although they're bigger than you, you'll be faster. Let's remember what Antillean said: these crabs walk forwards instead of sideways. We need to use that to our advantage. Make sure you throw the bait to their side to make them turn and change direction.'

Eventually, they could plan no more. They began their descent further down into the crater, pushing their way through the jungle foliage. Exotic birds preened themselves high in the treetops while butterflies darted in and out of the ferns. Tess saw berries dropping to the jungle floor from birds feasting above. She grabbed a few handfuls of them and stashed them into her pouch.

Splashes of sunlight glistened on waterdrops. Brightly coloured fungi skirted the base of trees. As they journeyed deeper, the sunlight struggled to find its way through the thickening mist. Jackson and Tess perspired in the humidity.

Finally, they approached the bottom of the crater. Running water could be heard to their left. 'That's a small river draining down into the lake,' Mackenzie advised. 'You're getting close.' The undergrowth thinned out and visibility ahead improved.

'I think I saw the lake,' Tess whispered. The group slowed down and crept quietly forward. Jackson had Buddy safely secured in his sling.

'Get ready to climb,' Mackenzie warned. Patches of blue water could be seen through the trees. The group heard rustling around them. 'Okay guys. Get up those trees.'

Jackson looked up. Quickly Hadwyn climbed up a trunk and reached down to pull the others up to the lower branches. They continued up until they felt a safe distance from the ground. From higher up in the trees, above the undergrowth, the blue lake came in to view. As predicted, hundreds of crabs circled the lake, waving their white-tipped pincers above their heads.

'They've spotted us,' Jackson confirmed. From their high vantage point, the companions could see the brown crab shells, covered in algae and barnacles. They were not an attractive creature. On the far side of the lake, a rock wall rose high, much of it covered in green vines and shrubbery. The group stayed put and waited for darkness to descend. Occasionally, a dark shape moved in the undergrowth below.

'I think they're looking for us,' Tess whispered.

The bird noises settled down. Cicadas and frogs provided humming and occasional croaking. The jungle was almost asleep for the night. A full moon overhead provided an eerie blue glow to their surroundings.

'Okay,' Mackenzie instructed, 'It's time to put our plan into action. The Spider Crabs have retreated to the edge of the lake. Jackson, get your Skin Shield spell ready. We don't know how long it will last, so take care if it wears off. Remember, you have Furious Strike so your sword fighting should be super-fast. You have Fireball in your pouch and we are going to need that. Tess, you're going to need your druid staff at the ready for your Invisibility spell soon. I want you to start using your bow and arrows as soon as Jackson and Hadwyn start the battle. Aim for the crabs at the rear. Jackson, stay with Hadwyn. I'm going to get you both to make your way over to the left side of the lake so that the crabs follow you – hopefully it will clear a path for Tess. When you see the Spider Crabs moving far enough out of your way, Tess, make yourself invisible and head for the lake. We need you to go into the water and find the Burnstone. I'm hoping you can still stay underwater for long periods. Jackson and Hadwyn will help you as soon as they can. Right, any questions?' Both shook their heads. 'Okay, let's go.'

The companions crept toward the edge of the foliage. Buddy was secured safely in Jackson's sling. Hadwyn motioned to Tess to stay behind a large rock. She grasped her bow tightly with arrows at the ready. Hadwyn and Jackson moved forward. Jackson's foot snapped a twig. The Spider Crabs, alerted to intruders, began waving their pincers again and moving towards them. The crabs were slow and clumsy.

The boys tossed handfuls of tiny meat pieces off to the side of the marching monstrosities. Many of the near-sighted crabs became confused, turning away to face the bait; they felt around on the sand with their feet, trying to determine what was happening. Hadwyn nodded at Jackson and the two weaved their way over to the left of the lake. Once they were some distance from the confused crabs, they began banging their swords on the sand. The crabs felt the vibration and moved toward them. Tess raised her bow and began firing arrows. Before long there were at least thirty crabs motionless, with arrows piercing through the shells on their backs.

Jackson and Hadwyn used their swords to defend themselves as crab after crab came at them, waving their front pincers closer and closer. Hadwyn and Jackson fought strongly. Their blades glinted in the moonlight, and repeatedly their swords dismantled the persistent creatures. Above the clanging din, Buddy's bark ran out relentlessly. He was very anxious. The crabs kept coming, climbing over carcasses to get at Hadwyn and Jackson. Crab claws flew through the air while ooze gushed over steel blades. The prime target was to cut into the soft, feathery mouth parts. From a safer position, Tess had been shooting arrows endlessly.

The crabs began to reduce in numbers as they closed in, circling Jackson and Hadwyn, who were standing back to back. Tess saw a clear path to the lake. She knew this was her opportunity. She grasped her druid staff hard, closed her eyes and commanded her Invisibility.

Tess ran as fast as she could across the sand, passing dead and dying crabs, pincers and legs waving in the air. Her staff and bow rattled in their holdings. Hadwyn and Jackson could not see her, so they wouldn't know if she had made it.

She slowed down at the edge of the lake and took a deep breath. She'd never felt so terrified. The blue lake had deep, dark areas. Behind her, she could hear the continued clanging of sword against shell. *Courage and hope*, she thought and strode in. Once up to her neck in the water, she took a big breath, submerged herself completely and dove down. To her great relief, Kulibari's gift of water-breathing was still with her.

Deep down below, in the dark waters, she became aware of a fluorescent blue glow, getting brighter as she descended. The floor of the lake came into view, as did a mountain of crabs all piled on top of one another. The blue glow was coming from under the pile of crabs. *Oh, what can I do?* she wondered.

At that moment, a flash of orange darted past. Tess spun around and saw a strange little creature about a metre away from her, swimming on the spot. It was the cutest thing she had ever seen. It came up in front of her face. 'Hello,' said a high-pitched little voice. The creature was about the size of a basketball and orange, with two big black eyes and tiny fins fluttering where ears could have been.

'Are you talking to me?' Tess asked, bubbles coming out of her mouth. She looked below and noticed the crabs shuffling around on their pile.

The little creature blinked. 'Yes, I am talking to you. I am the Queen of Quill.'

'Yes, well … Queen of Quill, I'm in a spot of trouble right now and don't have time to meet new friends,' she apologised, glancing below again.

'Ah yes, you are in a predicament,' the Queen of Quill agreed, 'but I am here to help you.'

'Really? Oh, thank goodness,' Tess replied, feeling a bit doubtful about this possibility.

'You must approach the Spider Crabs and use your Charm Stare to disarm them. The Burnstone is underneath them. Grab the Burnstone and return to me as fast as you can. I will lead you to safety.'

At the surface, Jackson was tiring. The Furious Strike spell was very effective in keeping the crabs at bay, but the pace was taking a toll. Mackenzie was unable to read Jackson's health as he could read Hadwyn's, but it was clear Jackson was tiring. Hadwyn had lost at least sixty per cent of his health but had succeeded in demolishing the crabs on his side of the battle.

Mackenzie moved Hadwyn over to Jackson's side. There remained about twenty-five of the stronger, larger male crabs. 'Let's finish this,' Mackenzie told Jackson. 'Use Fireball.'

Jackson had to put one sword back in its scabbard, while he fumbled in his pouch for the black coals. Jackson then dropped his other sword. At the same time, the largest Spider Crab seized a hold of Jackson's leg. Jackson let out a yell, dropping the coals. Although he had Skin Shield activated and he couldn't feel pain, he was being pulled toward the crab's mouth.

Hadwyn responded in an instant, using Triple Jump; he pounced onto the back of the crab and stabbed it in the soft gap between its armoured plates. Hadwyn's longsword was buried deep into the crab's soft tissue. The crab reared up, letting go of Jackson, its claws bending backwards trying to grab Hadwyn. Black bile spurted out from the wound in a torrent, covering Hadwyn in a sticky mess.

Jackson crawled away from the crab, reclaimed his sword and got up quickly. Seeing two of the black coals that he had dropped on the ground, Jackson reached down and flung them at the remaining crabs, yelling 'Fireball!' Soon the hoard of crabs had been halved.

Hadwyn used his Triple Jump ability to leap high over the top of groups of crabs, yelling 'Statue!' Most of the crabs became motionless and rock hard. A few on the outskirts of the group were still viable. 'Finish them off,' Mackenzie told Jackson.

Reaching into his pouch, Jackson took the remaining three black coals and hurled them. Crabs lit up in flames; shells crackled and cracked. And then all was still.

'Great work,' Mackenzie commented. 'Now let's get to Tess.'

Side by side, Jackson and Hadwyn ran through the moonlight toward the lake. In the rush of battle and danger, Mackenzie had no time to think through the fact that Hadwyn had just saved Jackson without Mackenzie controlling his actions. Whatever was going on with Hadwyn, it was working in their favour for now.

As they arrived at the lake, they saw the blue glow lighting up the lake floor. The water was crystal clear. Hadwyn put his hand against Jackson's chest and halted him. They could see Tess on the lake floor, standing very still in front of countless crabs. What was she doing?

Before they could work out what was going on, the crabs spread themselves out in a wide circle. The blue fluorescent light strengthened. Tess moved forward, in between the great lumbering crab bodies. She quickly emerged, holding the blue light. It was the Burnstone.

Several crabs became restless and moved towards her with raised pincers. Tess turned, looked in their direction – and they stopped in their tracks. Tess then swam upwards. Jackson and Mackenzie were astonished to see something bright orange leading Tess up from the depths of the lake towards the surface.

As she neared the surface, the Queen of Quill stopped and turned to Tess. 'Now you must climb to the top before the moon is high. Make haste. When the sun rises, look for a pink flower. It is very rare. It grows nowhere else in the world. This will lead you where you must go.' Then there was a flash of orange and the Queen of Quill vanished.

Tess emerged from the lake, holding the glowing blue Burnstone. She quickly repeated the instructions to the others. Buddy, now free of his sling, jumped excitedly at her feet. They decided to let him run free for a while, now that the main battle seemed to be over. Once they started climbing in earnest, Buddy was back safely in the sling.

The companions pulled their bodies up the steep cliff by hanging onto vines and finding footholds of protruding rock. After hours of climbing in the moonlight, and with hands full of splinters and blisters, they made it to the top of the crater. The Queen of Quill had watched the blue light slowly make it all the way. With a delighted giggle, the little octopus darted back into the deep.

Back in the Taylors' home, an emotionally drained mother sat still on her daughter's bed, surrounded by pictures of wildlife on the walls. On the bookshelf, school environment awards stood framed amongst cute little stuffed toys, kangaroos, wombats and possums. She remembered her daughter's passion and energy. She remembered her voice, explaining to the family over the dinner table all her latest discoveries about nature. How she longed to hear that voice again. She sat for a long time.

The quiet was interrupted by the phone ringing. She rose from the bed and headed out to answer the phone. Unknowingly, as she stood, she had knocked one of Tess's magazines off the bedside table. It fell to the floor behind her, falling open to two blank pages. A story began to materialize on the pages. The heading read, 'Scientists report Leatherback Turtle population recovering in the Caribbean.'

The companions reached the crater ridge and located a rest area between a clump of trees that would protect from the wind. The undergrowth was drier up here near the ridge as a result of ocean winds. They raked up the dry leaf litter with their hands and made makeshift beds. They emptied their pouches of most of their amber stones and made a circle around the camp for protection. They knew by now that amber contained many amazing properties, including warding off enemies and keeping them warm. Hadwyn had the red and blue Burnstones safely hidden in a pocket of his tunic.

As they settled down for another night, they reflected on their adventure at the lake. Jackson listened intently to Tess's tale. She was as amazed as he was but somehow exuding a calmness and confidence he hadn't seen in her before. She seemed to be growing up a lot. Every now and then she stopped talking and just sat still, reflecting on things. Jackson would prompt her to continue, to tell him what it was like underwater, facing the mountains of crabs, communicating with the Queen of Quill. She told him that her encounter with the crabs had been like her telepathic communication with the great Roamer. It seemed that they had been disarmed by her Charm Stare.

Tess herself was still trying to believe what had happened. She didn't want to share how she felt inside: a growing excitement and awareness that she was changing. The game was changing her. She felt stronger and wiser. A little part of her was daring to hope that she was becoming a druid.

Eventually their talk came to an end. It was now the wee hours of the morning. They would rest before descending the mountainside.

SATURDAY

The rising sun appeared slowly and the companions stirred. Buddy gave a little bark for attention. He had been tethered overnight by the plaited lead Tess had made and was now keen for his freedom to explore. Soon the companions were on their way again.

Tess was first to spot the pink flowers, creating a trail down the mountainside. They were few and far between. 'This way,' Tess called, heading off, Buddy close on her heels.

Today would not be humid. The vegetation was far less moist than inside the crater. The sun was high and the air was dry. The earth too was dry, so there was less slipping. They spent the morning winding their way down the side of the volcano.

The steady descent was interrupted by Tess. She had recognised a plant that could be helpful on their travels. 'Wait guys, I need to get some of this.' Jackson and Hadwyn stopped. 'Look, it's a bashful plant. See it retracting its leaves as we walk past. It's trying to hide. That's really good medicine. I need to get some leaves and roots for my medicinal herbs.'

Jackson felt puzzled. It just looked like another pink flowering bush to him. He knew she was a wildlife enthusiast – but medicinal plants? He hadn't heard that before. He watched as she gathered parts of the plant and placed them carefully in her pouch. Then it dawned on him. Tess wasn't experienced in medicinal herbs, but a druid apprentice was.

11

Kastytis and the Mermaid

Onward they travelled. Occasionally they caught glimpses of an ocean between gaps in the tree branches. When they were about halfway down, they caught sight of a small sailing ship moored a little way off the beach. Tess tried to take what she thought was a shorter route and veered off onto another path. Her attempt was thwarted as she came up against an invisible barrier. 'There's something in my way,' Tess told Jackson as she pushed her hands up against something.

'You can't go there, Tess,' Jackson explained, 'that path isn't part of the game. This isn't an open world. There's only one direction.'

Tess found that confusing and frustrating.

The descent continued and eventually they walked clear of the trees, onto the beach of black volcanic sand. It was now almost midday. They could see a rowboat with a solitary man aboard. He waved a greeting so they headed over.

'Greetings,' the burly looking man said, standing up and stepping out of the boat into the knee-high water. 'I am Kastytis, the captain of this ship, and I am here to transport you across the Tethys Sea. Please come aboard.'

Hadwyn led the way, nodding his head in greeting as he shook Kastytis's hand. Kastytis looked down at the small dog on Jackson's back but made no comment. Soon they were all sitting on the boat as Kastytis pulled on the oars through gentle waves toward the sailing ship. The distance between the travelling party and the island of Glessaria widened. They were definitely relieved that that part of their journey was over, but they had no idea what lay ahead.

'Climb aboard!' Kastytis gestured toward the rope ladder reaching up the side of the ship. Tess and Jackson followed Hadwyn up the rope. Kastytis secured the empty rowboat to his ship with well-worn thick rope. 'This way please,' Kastytis continued. His heavy footsteps made creaking sounds on the wooden deck. 'Please, join me for refreshments before we set sail.' They followed Kastytis down steep wooden steps into the captain's quarters. Laid out on a wooden table, they saw a silver jug and several silver mugs. 'Ale?' he asked.

Hadwyn nodded and took a mug. 'Yes, thanks,' Jackson followed suit.

Tess frowned. She really didn't want ale, and she was fairly sure Jackson shouldn't be having ale. 'Jackson, maybe you should have water?' she ventured.

'Perhaps the apprentice doesn't know her place?' Kastytis interrupted. 'It is not wise to tell the Prince what to do, young druid. Perhaps orange water for you?' Kastytis smiled, picking up an orange in his big brown hands, cutting it in half with his dagger and squeezing juice into one of the mugs. 'Now that drink is your business,' he suggested.

Tess took the mug and stayed quiet. She had forgotten they were in character to most other characters in the game. She would have to remember to use her acting skills so she wouldn't get them into trouble. Kastytis unwrapped a piece of material, revealing some plain rough-looking biscuits that tasted sweet and divine to Jackson and Tess. Mackenzie wondered if Hadwyn could eat like the others and decided it was worth a try. To his surprise, Hadwyn was able to eat the biscuits. Mackenzie knew that accepting hospitality in unknown places would be a good idea rather than offending anyone.

'Please make yourself at home,' Kastytis encouraged. 'There is more food in here,' he said, pointing to a cupboard. 'Dried fish, cheese, fruit, bread … please help yourself.' Kastytis turned towards the stairs. 'I have a job to do before we set sail, I shall return shortly.'

The companions decided to make the best of the situation – and soon were making meat and cheese sandwiches and crunching on delicious apples.

'I wonder what he had to do,' Tess queried.

'Who knows, but let's get up on deck and enjoy the view and fresh air,' Jackson suggested. They scrambled up the steps into the bright sunshine. The sound of their boots echoed on the wooden deck. White sails flapped in the breeze.

'Look, a telescope,' Tess exclaimed, excitedly grabbing the instrument from its holder on the ship's wheel. 'I want to go up there. I'll be able to see forever,' she announced, pointing to the crow's nest.

'I'm not sure that's a good idea,' Mackenzie cautioned.

'I think she'll be fine,' Jackson interjected, 'after what she did at the lake, she's got this.' Tess's heart almost exploded with pride.

Mackenzie smiled. This was a positive turnabout for his two favourite siblings. 'You may be right.'

Tess proceeded to climb the ropes to the highest point on the ship with the telescope tucked in her belt. Finally perched in the swaying crow's nest, she could see many islands, the closest being Glessaria Island with its familiar volcano protruding from one end. Tess noticed Kastytis's rowboat moored beside some rocks close to the shore. *I wonder what he's doing*, Tess thought, squinting in the bright sunlight.

She remembered the telescope and raised it to her eye. It took a while to focus the lens and then find the boat. Tess screwed up her face, frowning intently. She could see Kastytis on the rock. He was talking to someone; a woman with long, auburn hair and a long blue dress. *Wait, what?* Tess looked harder. That wasn't a dress. That was a fin. He was talking to a mermaid.

Was she seeing things? Tess was dumbstruck. She saw Kastytis lean in toward the mermaid and watched as they embraced for a long time. Then Kastytis stood up and the mermaid slipped into the water and under the waves. Tess climbed down the masts as fast as she could. 'Boys, you are never going to believe this,' she began. 'I just saw Captain Kastytis with a mermaid way over there on the rocks.'

Hadwyn and Jackson looked in the direction Tess was indicating. 'It's just Kastytis on his own in his boat,' Jackson clarified. 'It's very hard to see that far even with a telescope. You know, rocks and seaweed have been mistaken for mermaids before. Besides, maybe he's got a lady friend and that's none of our business.' Jackson saw the upset look on Tess's face. 'Maybe you're really tired, Tess. You've been through a lot and … you know, sometimes we just see what we want to see.'

'I know what I saw, Jackson,' she insisted, shaking her head with frustration.

Kastytis retuned to the ship and began preparations to set sail. He gave them lessons on how to help position the sails to make good their course. At the beginning of every new journey, the captain engaged a new crew. He called out instructions to this new lot. 'We'll be getting underway now, the wind direction is perfect. I need one of you at a time to take turns on the watch up there,' he said, pointing to the crow's nest. Hadwyn nodded and climbed up. 'Doesn't talk much, that one,' Kastytis commented. Soon the ship was moving away from Glessaria and heading out into the wide ocean.

'Did you see the fish scales on his jacket?' Tess whispered to Jackson.

'Tess, he is a fisherman. He has been out in his fishing boat. There are fish scales on the deck. Look,' Jackson countered, pointing to the deck for Tess to see. Tess could not believe how close-minded Jackson was being.

'Never mind,' Tess declared, 'I'll prove there is a mermaid out there, sooner or later.'

Kastytis manoeuvred the sailing ship, negotiating between the wind and waves. The ship heaved forward, riding the waves as they grew higher and stronger further out to sea. Tess started to feel a bit queasy. 'Let's get you laying down and resting,' Jackson offered, 'you're seasick.'

Kastytis approached, 'Ah, no sea legs,' he commented. 'I'll get some amber stones from my healing chest. You must place them on your stomach. Your warm skin will pull the healing oil into your body. This is good for an upset stomach.' Tess went below deck with Jackson steadying her down the steep steps, and was soon sleeping peacefully as the amber healing took place.

A few hours passed as the ship made its way through the rolling waves. Seagulls perched atop the three tall masts. Jackson had replaced Hadwyn on the watch; he sat comfortably in the crow's nest, enjoying the sun. There was no land to be seen anywhere on the horizon. Down below he could see a pod of dolphins, leaping out of the water, one after the other, alongside the ship.

Tess had resurfaced and made her way over to Kastytis at the rear of the ship, where the steering wheel was located. 'Wow, these amber gems are magic,' she declared, 'I've never felt so good.'

'Yes, yes, that is good,' Kastytis agreed, 'the amber is a powerful gem. It is wise to learn of its magic and then keep it close, always.'

'You have a beautiful ship,' Tess told him.

'Yes, yes, indeed she is beautiful,' Kastytis agreed proudly.

'Does it have a name?' Tess enquired.

'She does, of course,' Kastytis told her. 'She is called *Jurate*, after the love of my life, keeper of my heart.'

'Jurate?' Tess asked. 'I've never heard that name before. Where does it come from?'

Kastytis was quiet for a moment. 'There is a legend in these parts,' he began. 'There is a mermaid named Jurate. She rules and protects the seas. The legend tells us that we must not damage her home or she will bring about our death.'

Tess looked away, thinking. This must have been whom she saw him with earlier. 'So, you've seen this mermaid?' she asked.

Kastytis chuckled. 'Yes, indeed. At first, in my dreams, then in the waves I caught glimpses of her hair. Sometimes I could hear her song in the wind.'

Tess looked at Kastytis intently, her head to one side but staying silent. She didn't want to mention seeing them together through the telescope. Jackson was right. It wasn't polite to pry. Maybe he would bring it up himself at some point, she hoped.

'Ahoy down there,' called Jackson, interrupting their conversation, 'there's a change in the weather ahead.' Kastytis and Tess looked to the north, where a darkened sky loomed.

'We are heading north-west, perhaps we can outrun this storm?' Kastytis told them. 'All hands on deck,' he commanded as Jackson skimmed down the mast. Hadwyn appeared from the front of the ship, where he had been waiting and watching. For an hour there was a flurry as Kastytis barked orders and the crew raced to keep the ship on path. The waves were getting much stronger. The wind was whipping the sails. Waves crashed over the decks and all were soon drenched. Black clouds collided overhead, creating lightning and thunder.

Tess was frightened. Buddy was barking below deck where she had put him, safely out of harm's way. She decided to go down below and reassure him. As she sat in the captain's great wooden chair, she held Buddy close. She couldn't wait for this to be over. Would they ever make it? The sound of water lashing the sides of the boat became deafening. Then Tess heard another sound. What was it? She could hear a type of singing, way off somewhere in the storm. A haunting sound. Where had she heard that before?

The ship tilted to one side. The chair skidded across the floor, coming to rest beside the captain's bunk. Tess moved herself and Buddy onto the stable bunk and found herself up close to a porthole. Through the circular glass, Tess could see mountains of blue waves rising and falling. Sea spray battered the glass, making it difficult to see. Another great tilt of the ship and the porthole was completely submerged under water. Within seconds the ship corrected and she could see waves and sky again. For what seemed an eternity, the ship rolled from this side to that. Tess held onto the wooden bunk post, transfixed by seeing underwater through the porthole again and again. *I think we might die,* Tess thought.

The sound of distant singing over the waves came again. As Tess sat staring at the porthole, she saw a face, just for a few seconds. It was a woman's face. Tess couldn't believe her eyes. The woman was under the water. Auburn hair swirled around the angelic face. For a moment she looked deeply into Tess's eyes. Her hand was resting against the glass. She gave Tess a small smile and then she was gone.

Tess was frozen to the spot. 'That's a mermaid,' she said out loud to Buddy. 'That was Jurate. I think she is following our ship.'

Up on deck, the others hung on tightly. The sails had been shortened and they did all they could to keep afloat until the storm passed. Kastytis had tied a safety rope around Jackson. Both Jackson and Hadwyn held on to wooden masts close to the great ship's wheel that Kastytis wrestled to keep on course. Jackson was very tired.

Kastytis pointed ahead and yelled through the sea spray, 'Gap in the clouds!' They all looked at the horizon and saw the break in the stormy sky. 'Heading there!' Kastytis yelled again as he wrenched the wheel around to change direction. His muscular brown arms worked hard. The ship turned away from the storm; gradually the waves began to lessen in height. Eventually, they left the thunder and lightning behind them. Hopefully, their exhausting fight would soon be over.

Before long, they knew they had broken from the worst of the storm. Jackson was untying his safety rope when Kastytis called to him, 'No, not yet.' Hadwyn and Jackson looked at Kastytis, somewhat confused. Kastytis had begun wrestling the ship's wheel again with all his might. It didn't make sense. The ship seemed to be going around in a large circle.

'What's going on?' Jackson called out.

'Lodestones!' Kastytis bellowed.

Mackenzie paused the game; he needed time to work this out. He selected the game manual and found the section on the Sea Lands. He skimmed down though the list of challenges. '*Ah, there it is, the lodestones*'. He continued to read. Lodestones were a naturally occurring magnetic rock that attracted iron. A legend told of ships disappearing into the Whirlpool of Courage, so named because sailors had naught but courage left when faced with this. The whirlpool took the sailors and their courage down with them. Mackenzie found nothing in the manual that indicated how to escape this. All he could do was hope they'd find a way. Mackenzie resumed the game.

The ship was being pulled around in circles, faster and faster. Jackson had yelled at Tess to stay down below with Buddy when she had appeared at the top of the stairs, alarmed at what was going on.

'What can we do?' Jackson called to Kastytis.

'We must get the ship's compass to point in the direction of the lodestones so that they repel each other,' Kastytis yelled back. Jackson felt some hope. He understood enough about the repelling action of magnetic forces that Kastytis's plan made some sense to him. 'Right. You two must hold this compass in the one position and don't let it move,' Kastytis instructed. The ship was pulled faster around the whirlpool circle as they moved closer to the centre. Hadwyn and Jackson each took hold of one end of the iron compass. Their hands grabbed the needle, which was about ten centimetres thick and about forty-five centimetres long. Kastytis leaned his whole body into the ship wheel, forcing it to move in the direction he needed. The ship strained. Wooden boards cracked.

Above all the sound, both boys heard a distant singing. They looked at each other, puzzled, but there was no time to query anything right now. The ship began tilting precariously over to one side. Tess appeared at the top of the cabin steps. 'What's happening?' she yelled in terror.

'Go back, Tess,' Jackson ordered.

Kastytis had almost turned the boat all the way around to face the centre of the whirlpool. Without warning, the bow of the boat nose-dived into the whirlpool. The ship was hurled backwards with such force that Kastytis, Hadwyn and Jackson went sprawling onto the deck, smashing up against the cabin wall. It took them a moment to pull themselves up.

Kastytis dashed back to the ship's wheel and gripped it with all his might. 'Set the sails,' he ordered. Hadwyn and Jackson raced to the task. The magnetic force had been broken and they were clear of the whirlpool. It was time to make haste before any further disaster could strike them.

Soon, they were sailing in calmer waters with grey skies overhead. According to Mackenzie's phone, it was around 6 pm. Despite their troubles, it appeared they had not been blown too far off course. 'Soon you will arrive at your destination,' Kastytis told the companions. Mackenzie was relieved to hear that. There had been more than enough adventure for one day.

'I can see land,' Tess called from the crow's nest. Buddy looked up and barked.

'That is the Sambia Coast of the great land Fenno-Sarmatia. I will anchor off-shore and row you in by the dinghy,' Kastytis explained to them. A short time later, the companions were taking in the sight of a mountainous coastline. As they came closer to the shore, Kastytis navigated around a large rocky outcrop and a small sandy cove came into view. 'This is where I must leave you,' Kastytis announced.

Six feet clambered out of the boat into the knee-deep water. 'Thank you for everything,' Jackson said, shaking Kastytis's hand. 'We really appreciate your help. All the best now.'

'I must return to be with my beloved Jurate,' he told them.

Tess looked at Kastytis knowingly. 'I saw her through the porthole. She looked at me. She's beautiful.'

Kastytis looked at Tess with raised eyebrows. 'Indeed, she is,' he agreed. 'Not many humans have contact with mermaids. She must have sensed your good intentions if she allowed you to see her.'

Jackson and Mackenzie looked surprised. 'Well, you'll have to hurry,' Jackson pointed out, 'because look, there's another storm coming.'

Kastytis smiled. 'Tis' the life of a fisherman.' Soon the small boat bobbed its way toward the waiting ship.

'I don't like the look of that storm,' Jackson stated apprehensively. A massive storm moved towards them. The setting sun was hidden behind the black clouds. At the same time, in Mackenzie's bedroom he noticed everything darken outside his window.

'Maybe we should find cover,' Tess suggested, looking around the cove. There didn't appear to be a way out. The sandstone cliffs were too high to climb and there was no dry land to enable them to walk out around the edge of the cove.

'No, not yet. I want to wait and see how Kastytis goes getting to the ship,' Jackson replied.

The companions stood silently on the small beach. Many tales spoke of how quickly a storm could appear on the seas. They had never seen anything like this, though. The sky had taken on a red glow. Rising waves appeared, tinged red and orange as they reflected the burning sky. The sea was getting very rough. The small fisherman's boat disappeared behind rolling waves and then reappeared again.

'What's that sound?' Jackson asked, straining his ears against the wind. 'That sounds like what we heard in the whirlpool storm.'

Tess was standing open-mouthed by his side. 'It's Jurate the mermaid,' she whispered, 'she's come for him.'

Loud cracks of thunder startled them all. To their horror, they saw the ship struck by several huge bolts of lightning, followed by further thunder. The ship exploded into flames. Kastytis and his little boat were nowhere to be seen. The ship disintegrated, slowly sinking below the waves. It was gone.

Mackenzie was also startled by the sound of thunder because it was not only in the game, but outside his home at the same time. Was that a coincidence? He had no way of knowing. He just had to stay focused. 'There's nothing we can do,' Mackenzie told them. 'I'm sorry guys, but you need to keep going.'

In shock, they turned and walked along the small beach.

'Where are we and where are we going?' Tess asked.

'You're almost into the next level, guys. You just have to find the door,' Mackenzie advised.

'There's no door here and there's no way out of this place,' Tess announced, looking around the walled cove again.

'There has to be a door,' Mackenzie reassured them. 'Just keep looking.'

The storm was on top of them. Rain pelted down. Wind whipped sand up into their eyes. The three of them trudged around the small area of beach, looking for any sign of a door on the ground or on the cliff. They were cold and saturated. Small waterfalls streamed down the cliff face.

'Oh great. Now we're going to get flooded,' Tess exclaimed.

'No, we aren't,' Jackson replied. 'Look Tess, there's the door.'

Under a gushing waterfall, sand had been washed away, revealing a wooden door. Hadwyn moved forward, reached through the water and grasped two long handles. He wrenched the double doors open. They could see nothing but darkness inside, a bottomless pit.

'You'll have to jump. Hold on to Hadwyn,' Mackenzie commanded. 'Now jump!' he yelled as they disappeared down into a dark abyss.

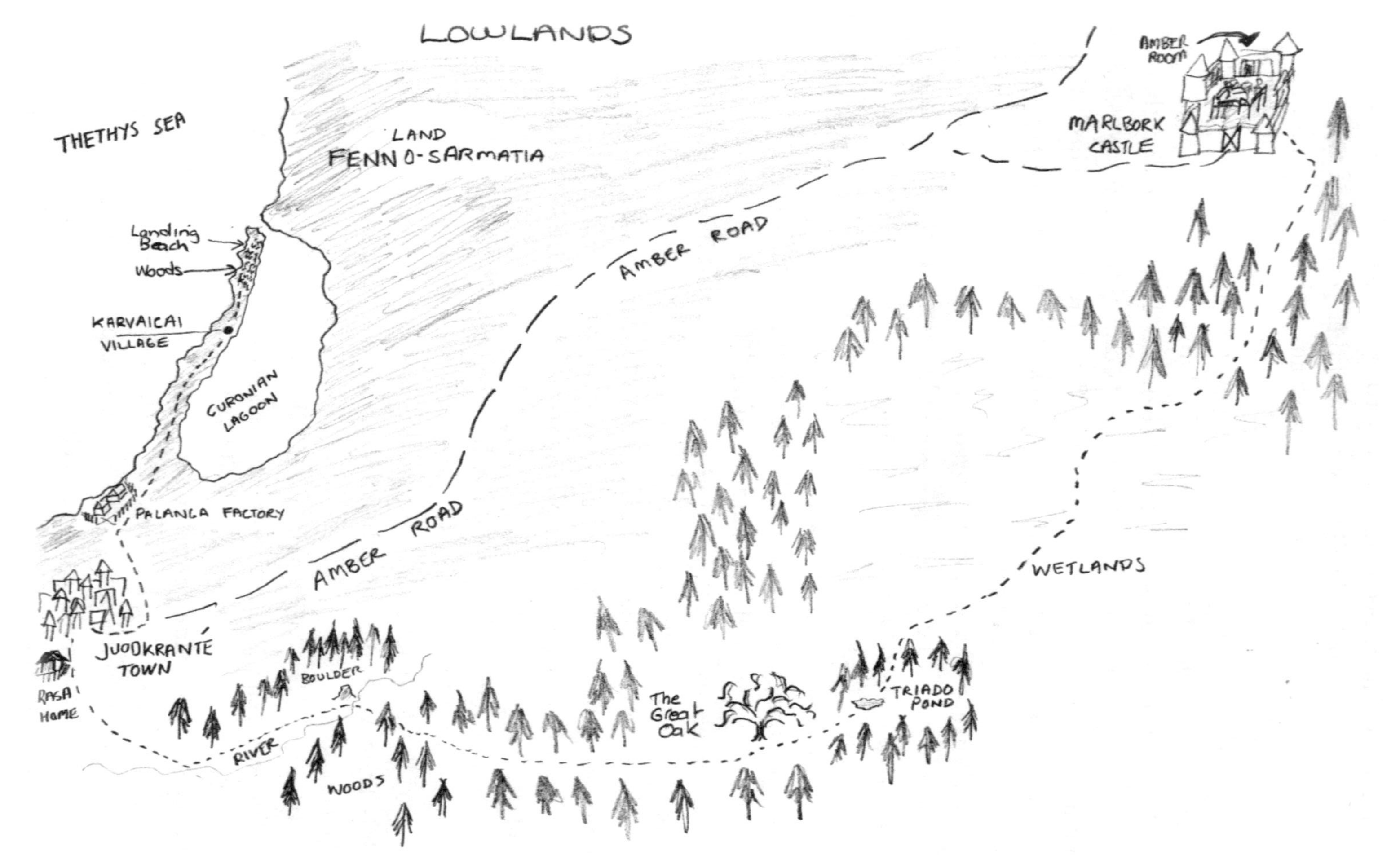

LOWLANDS
THETHYS SEA
LAND
FENN O-SARMATIA
Landing Beach
Woods
KARVAICAI VILLAGE
CURONIAN LAGOON
PALANGA FACTORY
AMBER ROAD
AMBER ROAD
AMBER ROOM
MARLBORK CASTLE
WETLANDS
JUODKRANTÉ TOWN
RASA HOME
BOULDER
RIVER
WOODS
The Great Oak
TRIADO POND

THE LOW LANDS

12

Curonian Lagoon

Mackenzie paused the game. He was feeling tired, and needed to take stock of where they were at and what was ahead. It was Saturday evening. It had been a long and exhausting day. A whole week had passed since Jackson and Tess had disappeared. How much longer would this take? Could they really survive? It was so dangerous. Jackson and Tess were definitely building up in skill and experience, but would it be enough? Could they keep this up?

There had been little rest. They were both exhausted. So far, they had passed through two of the levels of the game. They had two of the Burnstones in their possession, but there were still three levels to get through. There was so much to take in and so much of what was happening was hard to understand or predict. As an experienced gamer, he could usually outsmart and outwit his opponents – but this was so different. None of the normal rules applied. His gaming knowledge was out the window. These were real lives. It was overwhelming and felt impossible at the moment, but he knew he was their only hope.

'Mackenzie,' Mrs Jones called, knocking on the bedroom door, 'Mackenzie, are you awake?'

'What? Oh, yeah, sort of,' he replied, sitting up in the bean bag where he had almost dozed off.

'Can I come in?' she asked.

'Yeah, sure,' he answered.

Mrs Jones opened the door and came over. 'I've been worried about you,' she started.

'I'm fine Mum. I'm fine.'

'Are you eating and drinking?' she continued with a frown. Her hands were clasped tightly.

Mackenzie reached out and put his hand over hers. 'Mum. Really, I'm okay. Yes, I've been eating and drinking and sleeping,' he emphasised, 'but I am just finding it easier to cope at the moment by playing some games. It takes my mind off things,' he tried to convince her.

'Yes,' she nodded, 'I understand. You can't be thinking about your friends all the time. Is there anything I can do to help?'

Mackenzie thought for a moment. 'No, not really Mum, just look after yourself. I know where you are if I need anything,' he said reassuringly.

'I'm making a lasagne. It'll be in the fridge for when you want it,' she volunteered. 'It's your favourite.'

'Thanks Mum, that's great,' Mackenzie replied. 'I'm just going to have a quick shower and I'll come down and have some.'

Mrs Jones looked a little more satisfied at that and left the room. She hoped for news of the children soon. Good or bad. Her son couldn't remain in his room forever. At some point, he would have to deal with whatever had happened.

Mackenzie returned to reading and preparing for the next level, the Low Lands. The on-screen map showed a land of small medieval villages, larger towns, forests, roads and swamps. From what he could gather looking at the screen, Hadwyn's character was currently located on an area of shoreline off the Sambia Coast, where they had recently come to shore. Mackenzie couldn't find any other information to help them on their quest. It was clear that they would have to proceed regardless. With a click of a button, he was transported back to the travel party. They needed to rest somewhere safe.

Jackson sat up and looked around. After jumping through the door, they had passed through to the next level, arriving on a secluded beach. It seemed to still be sunset; the sky was a magnificent pink and orange. They were lying on dry sand between the water's edge and a very high, sandy cliff that rose up towards green shrubbery and small trees.

Tess began to stir. 'Where are we?' she asked, twisting around from where she sat to take in her surroundings.

'Low Lands?' Jackson questioned, looking up to Mackenzie for confirmation.

'Yep, that's where you are,' Mackenzie confirmed.

'This is really hard,' Tess confessed, 'I am so tired.'

Jackson nodded in agreement. 'Yeah, I know how you feel, it's been full on.'

Mackenzie instructed the companions to make their way up to the trees. 'Go up there and rest. Looks like it might be a safe place to have a rest out of sight.'

'Its strange sand, isn't it?' she noticed. 'It's very yellow.'

'Look over there,' Jackson told the others, nodding towards the water's edge where many small pebbles had washed up. The setting sun created a glittering effect on the tiny golden stones. 'There's amber everywhere.' The three of them strode over and examined the sparkling amber amongst the rocks and pebbles.

'I didn't know you found it at the beach,' Tess admitted. 'It's just like the amber gems in our pouches.' Tess proceeded to collect a few handfuls. Her pouch was getting full, so she found a few pockets in her tunic to fill. 'You never know when we might need these.' Jackson agreed and grabbed some for himself.

'You had better get up there before dark, and before anyone or anything finds you,' Mackenzie reminded them. 'I need you all to rest.'

They quickly pulled themselves up the sloping sand cliff, grabbing on to tufts of grass. Once atop the rise, they moved under the cover of the trees and bushes, affording them protection from prying eyes. 'You should be safe here,' Mackenzie reassured them. 'You two lay down in the grass and have a sleep. Hadwyn will keep watch.'

There didn't appear to be any sign of humans or animals around. Soon the other two were napping, with Buddy snuggled up against Tess.

Mackenzie checked the close-up map of the area. He could see that they were on a long narrow piece of land, like a small peninsula between two bodies of water, the sea and a lagoon. A few kilometres away, he could see what looked like a small village on the edge of the lagoon, smoke rising from several huts. He could also see several small boats on the lagoon. *Fisherman, perhaps?* he thought. He concluded that the companions must head toward the village. He wondered how they might approach the village or who to ask for. *Time will tell, I guess.*

With that, he rushed off for a quick shower, grabbed a plate of lasagne and returned to his room; within no time, he was napping with a full stomach. Mackenzie was far more tired from all the stress than he had imagined. He fell into a deep sleep and didn't hear the companions stirring in the morning, despite having the headset on.

SUNDAY

Tess and Jackson also slept deeply through the night. They had become accustomed to feeling safe with Mackenzie watching over them. Their early morning breakfast was interrupted by Buddy barking. 'Where is he this time?' Tess enquired, looking around the clearing. Buddy barked again.

'I'll get him,' Jackson offered. 'You keep eating. I'm finished.' Jackson headed in the direction where he had last heard the barking. He was going downhill amongst the trees for several minutes. He came across a small flowing stream of copper-coloured water. Jackson stopped in his tracks. There ahead of him was a peasant girl, squatting down by the edge of the stream with a wooden bucket. She was patting Buddy. She looked about the same age as Jackson. Buddy saw Jackson and wagged his tail. The girl looked up, startled.

Jackson was not sure if he had ever seen a girl so beautiful.

'Eadric?' she asked, 'Eadric?' The girl stood up. 'Is it you, Eadric?' The girl was looking at him expectantly. She walked over closer. 'I'm not going to bite, you know?' she reassured him.

She wore simple clothes, a long brown skirt and a beige shirt. Her face was clean and natural. Her eyes were a deep blue and her long, wavy, auburn coloured hair was held in place by a garland headband of tiny purple flowers. Jackson was having trouble thinking. Was she talking to him? Why was she calling him Eadric? Why did that name sound familiar?

Say something, you fool, he told himself. 'Hi,' he blurted out. 'Um, hi. Um, actually I'm Jackson.'

'Are you then?' she responded with a smile. 'Would you be new here then?' Jackson saw the sunlight catching in her hair like tiny sparkles of fire. 'Cat got your tongue, I see,' she laughed.

'No, no,' Jackson reacted hastily. 'Yes, yes I am new here. Um, that's my dog,' he stumbled over his words.

The girl walked closer and looked into Jackson's eyes. 'Mm … that's a shame. I was expecting an Eadric. You haven't seen an Eadric, have you? He would be wearing clothes just like you. And those bejewelled swords? They look like they belong to a Prince, do they not?' She looked him up and down. 'Yes, clothes just like you and very, very charming.' The girl raised her eyebrows quizzically.

Jackson put two and two together. 'Actually, I am Eadric,' he began to explain.

'Oh, so you are Eadric?' the girl responded, amused.

'Well sort of,' he replied.

'Sort of?' the girl continued playfully. 'Now is it Jackson Eadric or Eadric Jackson?'

Jackson blushed bright red. He took a big breath. 'Okay, I'll try to explain. I'm sorry. I just wasn't expecting this. It's a long story and I'm not sure you will believe it.'

The girl put her head to one side. 'Well, I have been expecting you and I am listening,' she added.

Tess had become alarmed when many minutes had passed and Jackson hadn't returned. 'I'm going to find Jackson,' she announced.

'Is that okay, Mackenzie?' There was no answer. *Maybe he had left the game for a moment,* she thought. *He wouldn't leave us for long,* she reassured herself. Tess made her way down through the thick bushes and soon heard voices. She slowed down and peered through the bushes. She could see Jackson talking to a girl. She was very relieved to see Buddy with them. She overheard some of their conversation.

Then Hadwyn came from behind, moved around Tess and walked forward. 'Perhaps I can help?' Hadwyn interrupted as he came through the trees with Tess following close behind him. 'I am Hadwyn from Karvaicai village.'

The girl did not appear frightened as she looked upon Hadwyn's tall imposing figure, his dark clothes and longsword. Tess and Jackson looked at Hadwyn, then looked at each other. This was the first time they had heard Hadwyn speak. Where was Mackenzie?

Back in his room, Mackenzie awoke with a start and sat up quickly. He could see the group talking to a girl. How long had he been dozing? Hadwyn was with them, operating independently. They didn't appear to be in danger. He decided to stay quiet for a while and try to work out what was happening with Hadwyn. Was it going to be an advantage to give him free reign or could it create more danger for his friends? Now seemed a good time to watch him and get some clues.

'Hadwyn, is it really you?' Lorna asked. 'I have heard of you. The villagers have spoken of you. They said you ran away as a boy. They never expected to see you again.'

'Yes, I am Hadwyn,' he confirmed. 'I have returned to complete unfinished business with the knights.' Hadwyn nodded toward Jackson. 'You were right though, he is Eadric but he is known to us as Jackson.'

'So, it is you I seek?' she acknowledged, giving Jackson a teasing grin. Jackson blushed again. 'A Spaewife passed through our village and told my family to expect wayfarers on an important quest. We were warned that if we did not aid you, we would suffer greatly. Life has been very difficult under the cruel rule of the Amber Knights. My family awaits your arrival.' The girl looked at Jackson again. 'And I was told that Eadric, our rightful Prince, would return and reclaim the throne. I am betrothed to the Prince. Isn't it so, Eadric Jackson?'

Jackson was speechless. He wished Mackenzie would step in. He had come looking for a dog and now appeared to have a fiancé. Hadwyn had taken charge. What was going on?

'Well,' Hadwyn interjected, looking just a bit entertained by Jackson's discomfort, 'it's complicated. Let me try to explain what is happening and what we need to do next. May we please know your name?'

'Of course. My name is Lorna. I am also from the village Karvaicai,' she revealed.

Hadwyn then spoke at length to Lorna, telling her of his plan of revenge against the Amber Knights for killing many of the people in the village years ago. He then told her that he also needed to put things right with the druids. 'My destiny is tied to these companions. If I help them achieve their quest in restoring the sacred balance of nature, then the druids will forgive me for my past transgressions … and I need to work with Prince Eadric against the knights. We have far to travel yet. For now, we are passing through.'

Lorna was confused. 'Passing though? Why can you not stay?' She looked directly at Jackson.

Hadwyn answered, 'You must not reveal what I am about to tell you to anyone or we will all be in great danger. There is a wizard that puts spells on me and can control me. They call him Makansee. I can hear him speaking to them but when he is controlling my body, I cannot speak. I have been fighting to break free from the spell, but it is so strong.' Jackson and Tess looked astonished. Where was Mackenzie now? 'When I met these two, I heard them speak of being from another world. I have heard them speaking with the wizard Makansee. This one calls himself Jackson,' he said, pointing in Jackson's direction, 'and this one is his sister, Tess.'

Back in his room, Mackenzie listened intently to Hadwyn's explanation. The scene before him unfolded like a game walkthrough. He didn't need to control anything, just watch and learn. The character knew much more than he had realized. Hadwyn could hear his conversations with Jackson and Tess. Now he also understood the times when Hadwyn had done something independently; he was fighting against being controlled. Mackenzie wondered if Hadwyn would gain enough strength to completely resist being controlled; after all, it was clear the game was having a progressive effect on the development of Jackson and Tess's character skills.

'But this is Prince Eadric,' Lorna protested, 'and she is clearly a druid. Look at her clothes.'

'Yes,' Hadwyn agreed. 'It is strange magic. All I can tell you is that somehow, two worlds have collided and now our destiny is entwined. The longer I spend with them, the more they become a part of us, as though they are losing who they were and becoming who they are meant to be in our land.'

'Is that true, Jackson? Is it true that I'll never be Tess again?' she asked her big brother anxiously.

'Look everyone,' Jackson began, 'it's true that we're from another world, and it's true that we, in part, aren't who you think we are. We don't understand why this has happened any better than you can. What we know is that the longer we are here, the more we seem to be Prince Eadric and Emerald. It's our intention to pass through these lands until we complete the quest, so that we may return to our own world. Yes, we do receive guidance from the one you call a wizard. He is our friend; he is helping us through the lands and trying to get us home. He brought Hadwyn to us, to help us get home safely.'

'This wizard friend of yours. Why does he control me? Does he think he knows more than I do? This is my land. Does he not know I am a mercenary with superior fighting skills? You would be safer with me protecting you. This spell of Makansee weakens me. He makes me move in directions that are not best.'

Hadwyn and Lorna were looking at the siblings. Jackson was trying to think fast and wondering why Mackenzie wasn't doing something. Tess jumped in. 'Hadwyn. Yes, our friend knows how skilled you are, but this all happened so fast there wasn't time to work out a better plan. We couldn't be sure of anything. We found ourselves lost in these strange lands, and our friend quickly decided to put a spell on you to save us. He picked you from many others because of your amazing skills.'

Hadwyn raised his chin in a defiant but proud expression. 'I do not need to be bewitched to help you,' he told Tess. 'Did I not save you from the Cannonballs? This Makansee of yours was not so strong then, was he?' How could she forget? She had wondered that day if it had been Hadwyn rescuing her. 'Can this friend of yours match my fighting skills? I think not.'

'Well, he does have fighting skills. It's a bit hard to explain …' Tess began.

At that moment, Mackenzie decided to step in. 'Tess, Jackson, leave this to me,' he instructed. Jackson and Tess looked relieved.

Hadwyn looked up towards the direction of Mackenzie's voice. He leaned over towards Lorna and stated quietly, 'The wizard.' Lorna looked around the treetops a little anxiously. She too had heard the voice from above.

'Hadwyn,' Mackenzie began, 'I apologize for the confusion. Jackson and Tess speak the truth. We did not come to your land to cause harm. We too do not understand what magic is at play or how this has happened. Somehow, our world and your world have become mixed up. The main thing we know is that we need each other's help to get through this. You cannot achieve your goals without our help. We need your help.'

'This I understand,' Hadwyn agreed. 'Why are you putting a spell on me?'

'I can't explain everything that is at work, Hadwyn. Up until now we've been unable to communicate with you. Now that we can, we must work together,' Mackenzie replied.

'I know this land. I know where we must travel. What do you know of this?' Hadwyn challenged.

'What I can tell you,' Mackenzie continued, 'is that from my world, I can see many lands. I can see your path and many challenges ahead. Yes, you are a skilled fighter but your companions are not. I can help you avoid as many dangers as possible rather than face every fight. It is too dangerous for my friends.'

'You must take this spell off me,' Hadwyn demanded. 'I am a mercenary. I need none of your magic. Your spell weakens, anyway. I am getting stronger. Perhaps I shall go my own way soon and your friends will be alone. What say you?' he challenged again.

Mackenzie feared Hadwyn's claims were true. He felt he had no choice but to negotiate with him. 'Very well, Hadwyn. It seems we can work together. We will have to trust each other. I will remove the spell you speak of, if you agree to work with me to get my friends through to the Last Door. I will only intervene if I think it is absolutely necessary and I will not speak near others in your world, as it may create suspicion and danger. I believe your goals will be achieved upon completion of the journey. What say you?' Mackenzie queried.

'What is this Last Door you speak of?' Hadwyn asked.

'The final destination of my friends. This is the way through to their world. You cannot see what I see, Hadwyn.'

'Very well, Makansee. I agree with your terms. We will work together. I will help your friends return to their world. They will help me restore order in my world.'

Lorna glanced at Hadwyn. 'And so, if you help them back to the other world, what will happen to Emerald and Prince Eadric?'

'I am sorry. We do not know the answer to this,' Mackenzie spoke. 'We believe that if we complete the quest in each land, then there will be restoration in your lands.'

The group were quiet for a moment, digesting the circumstances. 'Perhaps, they are Emerald and Eadric,' Lorna suggested, 'and this is magic confusing us all.' Tess and Jackson looked at each other. 'Perhaps they are here to stay?' Lorna paused in thought for a moment. 'I must take you to our home and help you prepare for your journey. As for my betrothed,' she added, looking directly at Jackson again, 'my future has been foretold and I will have courage and hope.' Jackson remained somewhat entranced by a different type of magic.

Well, this is not a problem I had anticipated, Mackenzie thought.

As they walked towards the village, Tess chatted to Lorna, who listened patiently and answered questions whenever she could. 'We saw amber all over your beach,' Tess exclaimed.

'Amber is well known to us,' Lorna explained. 'There is an old legend that has been passed down the generations that tells us about the amber that washes up on our beaches after a storm. The legend says the amber gems on the beach are the tears of Jurate the mermaid.

Her father was Perkunas, the God of Thunder. When he found out that his daughter had fallen in love with a fisherman, Perkunas sent lightning down and killed the fisherman. Whenever there is a storm at sea, Jurate cries for her lost love.'

Tess let out a gasp. 'I told you guys! I told you I saw Kastytis with a mermaid. I knew I heard her singing to him. Jurate is broken-hearted forever.' Tess's eyes brimmed with tears.

Jackson hastened over to Tess and put his arm around her. 'I am so sorry, Tess. I should've believed you. I'm really sorry.' He'd never felt quite this grown up and big brotherly before. He had to admit to himself he'd been very hard on her. Tess was a smart girl and she had managed better than most her age, being in this really scary situation. Actually, he was feeling a bit proud of his little sister.

Hadwyn reached out and put a comforting hand on her shoulder. 'I'm sorry too, Tess.'

Lorna then went on to explain her world to them. 'Our lives revolve around amber. We villagers collect the amber from the lagoon and transport it up the road to the Palanga factory, where artisans will make jewellery and ornaments ready for the travelling trade merchants. It is considered very valuable.'

Tess was now recovered from her upset and listening intently to Lorna. 'Can you learn to be one of the artisans and make jewellery?' she asked innocently.

'No Emerald,' Lorna explained, 'the artisans are all prisoners. Like us, they are forbidden to keep any amber. If anyone is caught with amber, they will be imprisoned, or worse, hanged at the gallows. We must hand it all over to the Knights of Amber. They keep a record of all amber in the Great Book of Amber. It is transported in its own carriage. The knights control everything here. You will need to be very careful around them.'

'Where would we encounter them?' Jackson asked.

'They could be anywhere. Their base is at Marlbork Castle but they patrol all along the Amber Road, and the smaller tracks between the villages and the factory,' Lorna told them.

'What's the Amber Road?' Tess queried.

'It's the only road we have connecting us from Juodkrantė to the far-off lands to the south. It veers east to Marlbork Castle first. It's the main trade route with many merchants coming from other lands to buy amber and sell their wares. It is not safe. There are many thieves and murderers,' she explained.

Lorna led the travellers down through the trees toward the village. As they left the cover of the woods, they walked along a track created by two cart wheels. Eventually they came to the village, about twenty-five buildings of various sizes. Several men could be seen ploughing a field with oxen. 'That is my father Jonas and my brother Andrius,' Lorna informed them. As they came closer to the buildings, they could see the homes were made of clay and straw with thatched rooves. Each building was surrounded by stick fences, with pens housing pigs, sheep, goats and vegetable gardens. Chooks and geese roamed freely, scratching and pecking the dirt. Straw bundles, pitchforks and wheels leaned against buildings. Several women stopped gardening and watched them pass. Halfway through the village, Lorna beckoned them into her home. 'Mother,' Lorna called, 'I found the wayfarers.'

They entered the hut. A short woman with long black hair stood from her spinning wheel and greeted them. 'I see,' she commented, 'you have arrived. Come in.' She waved her hand toward a few short wooden stools, surrounding a simple wooden table with several candles in their holders.

'Mother, this is Hadwyn, Emerald and Eadric. Everyone, this is my mother Deora.'

Deora walked over to Jackson and looked closely into his face. 'Your Royal Highness. Welcome back. We look forward to the reinstatement of your family … and the wedding,' she added, smiling in Lorna's direction. 'No doubt there is a battle ahead, but you have the support of your people. We wish to be rid of these ruthless and cruel knights.' She then walked over to Hadwyn, touching him on the arm. 'I remember you. You were lost to us when you were such a small boy. We heard rumours of your survival but we were unsure. I knew your parents. They would have been happy to know you were found. Welcome home. It has been too long.'

'My parents?' Hadwyn ventured.

Deora shook her head. 'I am sorry. We were rounded up when they came to the village. We were taken prisoner. Some resisted and were killed. Some escaped. Many of us were taken to the factories. Eventually, those of us who are here now were returned to the village to harvest the amber in the waterways. We do not know what became of many. It's been more than a decade, Hadwyn.'

The companions sat down. The one-room hut had a fireplace in the centre of the room surrounded by rocks, with a large black pot hanging above. The smoke climbed up into the thatched roof. The hut floor was well swept, hardened earth. At one end, beds were made up on wooden benches, covered with straw and animal skins. A rough wooden shelf was attached to the wall and held clay bowls, mugs, and jugs. Bundles of herbs hung from the walls. A basket in the corner appeared full of grain. The windows had no glass or flywire, but slatted wooden shutters opened out to let the light in. 'Don't worry,' Lorna reassured them as if reading their minds, 'we close them at night to keep the cold out, and the smoke will keep the insects away.'

Deora busied herself breaking some bread on the table and then ladling hot soup full of turnip, parsnip and beans into ceramic mugs for each of them. 'Well then, lads and lassies. We have been expecting your arrival. Here is some food. We will be helping you to continue on your quest tomorrow. We'll be needing to dress you before we depart.'

Jackson looked at Hadwyn, somewhat alarmed.

Lorna stepped in and explained. 'We need to make you look less conspicuous. Emerald, you're wearing green. That's against the law. Only nobles are allowed to wear colour. You would be jailed if you were caught. And Hadwyn, I don't know what type of clothes you are wearing but they certainly don't look anything like a peasant. And Eadric,' she smiled, 'well, it may be a little more difficult to make you look like a peasant. We just need to make sure you are all dressed in browns, greys and creams. Emerald, you can wear a white headscarf like me. We will give you all long woollen capes with hoods. They will keep you warm and dry because the wool still has oil in it. Oh, and no weapons,' she added.

Now Hadwyn looked alarmed. 'I am concerned about us not having our weapons. We will be defenceless.' Mackenzie also felt a sense of trepidation.

Deora shook her head, 'No weapons. Peasants cannot have weapons. You would be imprisoned. You can keep your stick,' she added, pointing to Tess's staff. 'We can have such things to defend ourselves from wolves and bears or robbers. And no amber. You must remove all amber.'

Mackenzie knew they must keep the Burnstones. He'd have to think of a way they could hide them.

'The Spaewife has visited upon us,' Deora explained, 'the prophecy was declared to us. Divination demands our attention to your needs. We do not question or expect to understand all that is. You must trust us,' Deora continued, 'as we must trust you. Tomorrow we will take you to the town of Juodkrantė. It is market day, so we will take the cart. There you can get supplies and further directions.' The companions felt nervous. 'Lorna, after they have eaten, take them to the outbuilding and make bedding for them. We can smoke manure in a coal pot to keep the insects from them. Now get some milk from the goat. Lads, bring in some firewood. It will be dark soon and we have an early start.'

Lorna's brother and father returned from the field. Andrius had dark hair like his mother. Jonas had wavy, copper-coloured hair growing down to his shoulders, identical in colouring to his daughter Lorna. After introductions, Jonas confirmed the plan of taking the travellers to the market in the morning and added that the week's gathering of amber needed to be delivered to the Palanga factory on the way. 'This thing you're doing,' Jonas acknowledged, 'we know it must be. We are grateful and we will do whatever we can to help you succeed.' Jonas reached for his mug of soup, fumbled and dropped the mug back on to the table. 'Damnation,' he growled.

Deora rushed to his side. 'Never mind, can't be helped. Did you burn yourself?' she asked, lifting his hand toward her. Jackson noticed Jonas was missing the best part of three fingers.

Jonas saw Jackson staring at his hand. 'Anchor chain,' he explained, 'caught in the anchor chain … a storm hit when we were out amber gathering. Ripped them off.'

Deora continuing mopping up the spillage on the table. 'Never mind. Maybe soon the frogs will return and you will get your fingers back,' she spoke reassuringly.

'What have frogs got to do with his hand?' Tess enquired.

Deora sat down on a stool and put her cleaning cloth on the table. 'I will tell you about the Triado frogs, young druid. It is important that you know,' she said.

Lorna had just finished lighting the candles and closing the window shutters. Buddy lay sprawled on the earthen floor by the crackling fire. All eyes were on Deora. 'Well,' she began, 'from the beginning of time, as we know of it, all life in our world, all creatures and plants, have needed one another. We call it "The Entwining". We have learnt much from The Entwining. As humans, we have learnt to use nature's gifts – plants for medicine, for cooking, for magic – but we have also learnt that if we do not honour the creatures and plants, the Entwining will be lost and we will all suffer.'

Jonas, Andrius and Lorna all murmured in agreement.

'Long ago,' Deora continued, 'the spirit of the ancient Triado Frogs became trapped in an amber prison. It is said that the knights have that Burnstone. Since that time, the entwining has weakened. We no longer hear the frogs. We no longer have their milk.'

Tess interrupted, 'Do frogs have milk?'

Deora nodded. 'Yes, in the skin on their backs. We did them no harm but we were able to use their milk for many things, like growing back limbs.' She pointed to Jonas's hand. 'Frogs can re-grow their own legs, you know. And they can survive through the coldest winters buried in the snow, so we were able to use their milk to heal frostbite in our fingers and toes. The village healers used the milk for chest pains, stomach pains and infections. We even used it on our skin to repel insects. But our people now suffer. The frogs are no longer amongst us. You must find the Royal White Amber to release the sacred spirit of the Triado frogs.'

Tess looked puzzled. 'So where have the frogs gone?'

Jonas put his mug down on the table, 'We do not know. That is why you are here, young druid. You must use your ways to help them. We are all connected by the entwining. We cannot survive without each other,' he concluded.

Later that night, the three companions rested on straw in the outbuilding which housed many of the farm animals. Mackenzie spoke to them, out of earshot of the others. He instructed Tess to wrap the two Burnstones in a small piece of material and fasten them under her long hair. Once her scarf was in place on her head, they would be hidden.

Jackson fell asleep quickly. Buddy was stretched out by his side, taking advantage of the body warmth. Mackenzie dozed in his bean bag with his headset on. Tess, however, was having trouble falling asleep after all the excitement of the day and started to chat to Hadwyn.

'It's just terrible what the knights have done to your village. I hope you find your parents one day. I miss my parents.' It had been more than a week since she had seen them, but to Tess it felt like months.

Hadwyn gazed upon the young human in the twilight. He had felt very angry, being forced into this situation with these strangers, but he was beginning to grasp that it was the same for his companions – and after all, he had years of experience becoming a mercenary. This one before him was but a frightened young girl. 'Tell me of your parents, Tess. Tell me of your world.'

Tess needed no more encouragement. For hours she spoke. For hours he listened. By the time the moon had risen directly overhead, Tess had drifted off to sleep.

Hadwyn sat thinking about all that he had heard. What a strange world she had described. So different to his own, yet some things like family and friends remained very important. She had also described troubles between her people and the natural world. This problem seemed to exist in both worlds. He wondered if he would succeed in returning her to her home. Could they even leave this land, now they were here? He had also seen her druid magic becoming stronger, and Jackson was definitely developing into Prince Eadric with superb sword skills. Was this reversible? Like Makansee, he had no answers.

Then he remembered how Tess had put her life at risk to save him from the lion and the Great Roamer back in the Desert Lands. She had been incredibly brave. He owed her his life. This he knew for sure. He was bound by duty to help her. He resolved to do his best.

13

The Knights of Amber

MONDAY

The morning air was cold. They had changed into their new clothes by the fire; their old clothes and weapons were nowhere to be seen.

Tess's staff lay inconspicuously on the floor of the cart. Hadwyn, Jackson and Andrius balanced on the back of the rattling wooden cart. The sides of the cart were wooden planks. The ladies sat inside the cart on top of straw bundles. In amongst their feet were baskets of vegetables and herbs, two sacks of grain and a wooden chest containing the precious amber. Tess had Buddy secured by some twine she had found. Jonas sat at the front end of the cart, driving the two oxen forward as the countryside became lighter with the dawn.

The oxen were slow-moving so it took several hours to reach Palanga. The companions had been warned to keep their heads down and not speak to anyone. The factory came into view and Jonas stopped the cart at the front gates, lifting the heavy chest out of the cart. When he reached the gate, a guard let him in. Jonas disappeared into the factory. The sound of horse's hooves came up behind them. It was the Knights of Amber. Mackenzie sat quietly, watching and ready to act.

'Who goes there?' a strong voice demanded.

'Deora Rudat and family, sir,' Deora replied, 'from Karvaicai, sir.'

'And your business?' The strong powerful horses pranced around restlessly.

'My husband delivers the gathered amber, sir,' Deora responded.

The two knights circled the oxen and cart. They wore white surcoats over their chainmail and full plate armour displaying a black cross on their chest. Helmets covered their heads so that only their eyes were visible. A sword and shield hung at their sides. The horses also wore face armour and coats that matched the knight's attire. Everyone kept still and quiet.

'Good morning to you, sirs,' Jonas called, returning through the gate carrying the empty chest.

The knights' attention turned to Jonas. 'And what have you delivered today?'

'Six pounds, sir. It was all we could get due to the storms of late. Stopping us getting out in the boats, sir,' he answered.

'Karvaicai village, you say?' the other knight interjected. 'Perhaps we need to visit upon you and teach you how to handle the boats. It is when the storms bring the amber to shore that we need you all out there. Take heed now. Don't let this happen again. We will be watching you.'

Jonas bowed slightly. 'Yes sir, I will do better.'

The knights pulled their horses' reins to one side, wheeling around, and rode off through the factory gates. The Rudat family's cart turned and moved off towards the town of Juodkrantė.

From a distance, the town could be recognised by the hundreds of orange turrets that made up most of the roofing. The town was bustling with activity. People and animals navigated through narrow streets and overhead archways. Men on horseback ducked under low-lying banners, street performers danced and sang, market stalls were laden with colourful fare and traders argued their prices.

Jonas had secured his oxen and cart with a trusted caretaker and carried the bags of grain to the market. The boys carried the baskets and straw bundles. Jonas weaved his way through stalls with the rest of the group following single file, finally coming to a stop outside the blacksmith. Jonas beckoned them all to follow him in. 'Ah, Jonas,' the blacksmith greeted him, 'your plough is ready.'

Jonas picked up the metal plough and inspected the blacksmith's work, nodding approvingly. 'This is good, Donatus, thank you. Here are your goods,' he said, putting down the sacks of grain and indicating to the others to put down what they carried. They shook hands and said goodbye. Jonas picked up the plough and they headed back to the street. 'I will take the cart and meet you all at Elena's.'

Deora led them further through the market until they came to a small shop with rugs hanging from the ceiling. They went inside, where many more rugs were rolled up and others were hanging from the eaves. Deep reds, bright blues and shades of green, all with cream and black patterns, surrounded them.

'Elena is out back,' a man called out.

'Thank you, Leonas,' Deora answered to her brother-in-law. 'Come,' she beckoned the others. They pushed their way past the hanging rugs and through a door leading to a small back room. (Mackenzie could see on his screen that the door frame was glowing, so he reassured himself that the party were on the right track.) In the small room, a woman sat sewing a garment. She looked a lot like Deora but with wisps of grey in her dark hair.

'So, they have come,' spoke the older woman.

'Yes, Elena. Yesterday,' Deora confirmed to her sister.

'Very well then, we must proceed,' Elena acknowledged. 'I will take them to the Spaewife.'

Deora turned to Andrius and Lorna. 'We will wait here for your father.'

'Please Mother, can't I show them the way?' Lorna protested.

'It is too dangerous,' Deora declared, shaking her head, 'say your goodbyes now.'

The suddenness of the parting took them all by surprise. Lorna approached the three travellers. She knew her parents would never tolerate her arguing with them. They had raised her in preparation for marriage into the royal family – arguing was not becoming. She resigned herself to the parting. Tess gave both Andrius and Lorna a hug and thanked them for their help. 'I will never forget you, Lorna.'

'Nor I you,' Lorna responded. Andrius shook both Hadwyn and Jackson's hands and wished them well.

Jackson stepped forward almost regally, took Lorna's hand and said in the most charming manner, 'May we meet again. Courage and hope,' he whispered, and then kissed her hand. (Mackenzie wondered: was that Jackson or Prince Eadric speaking?)

'Come,' Elena interrupted, 'make haste.'

Elena led them out a back gate and down many alleyways until they came to the edge of the town. 'This way,' she said, leading them through a gate which Mackenzie could see had a glowing latch. They stepped through an overgrown garden. She knocked on the door of a whitish clay hut. A woman, veiled from head to toe in red, answered the door. 'Rasa,' Elena spoke, 'these are the travellers.' Rasa opened the door wider and stood back to allow them in. 'Farewell, take care,' Elena whispered to them and left.

The companions tried to enter the hut but came up against an invisible barrier. The woman stood still, waiting in the doorway. 'How can we get through?' Tess called out to Mackenzie.

'There must be something around you that you have to locate,' he replied. 'So far I've been able to see you passing through gateways that glow. That tells me you're on the right track. Normally when you're playing a game, you would have to locate something that allowed you to pass through a gateway. You haven't had to do this when you've been accompanied by the game characters, but now you'll have to find the key to this gateway. I can't see anything glowing around you.'

The companions began to search. They looked under shrubs and felt along the walls of the garden fences to no avail. Mackenzie also searched the surroundings, selecting anything and everything, hoping to find a message or clue. He looked at the woman. She had one hand stretched out as though she was waiting to be given something. Maybe she had the answer. He selected her hand and a message appeared on the screen. 'The ancestors have bean waiting for your arrival.'

That's odd, Mackenzie thought. Since when do the game developers get spelling wrong? He quickly shared the hint with his friends, whom could make no sense of it either.

'The Spaewife makes no mistakes,' Hadwyn told them. 'You must trust the message.' Not knowing what else to do, they all recommenced the search.

Tess pushed her way through the overgrown shrubs and dangling tree branches towards a corner of the garden. Something green flew in her direction and landed on the top of her staff. The green crystal glowed. It was a luna moth with bright luminescent green wings; its beauty was captivating. Tess stood still, mesmerised. The moth fluttered up toward her face and hovered for a moment, then to a small bush about two metres away from Tess. She followed the moth and looked at the bush. It appeared to have some type of bean growing. Suddenly, a druid knowing came over her. She picked a few of the beans and returned to her companions.

'I have what we need,' she announced, holding out her hand, showing the beans in her palm. 'This is the Celtic Bean. This is what the ancestors have BEAN waiting for,' she told them, emphasising the word loudly.

'What do they want them for?' Jackson asked, puzzled.

'I'm not sure, but I know that the Celtic Bean can be used by druids to connect to ancestors.'

'Okay, give it a try,' Mackenzie agreed. Jackson was feeling really astonished at his sister's growing knowledge of Druidry. It was definitely helpful. The companions moved toward the hut and Tess dropped the beans into the old lady's hand.

'You sit and wait,' Rasa ordered, pointing to a bench against the wall. They couldn't see anything except her eyes and her hands, which were patterned with decorative black paint. Pine incense wafted through. The room was intriguing, with strange maps and charts on the walls. She brought a tall pot of fragrant tea and poured them each a drink in small matching cups. Then she sat quietly, watching them. They didn't know what to do or what to say, so they stayed quiet and drank their tea.

After what seemed forever, she stood up. 'I am Rasa, Spaewife of Juodkrantė, sought by nobles and knights for guidance. For you, I am serving of free will,' she explained regally. 'You come,' she instructed Hadwyn. He looked at the others briefly and then followed her through a bejewelled curtain doorway.

She took a turn to the left and went through another curtained doorway. They had arrived in the smallest room he had ever seen; just enough room for two chairs and a table, and a space to squeeze around to the other side. The room was bathed in red light. There were no windows. Rasa sat down on the far side of the table and waved her hand toward the other chair. Hadwyn sat and waited as she reached under the table and pulled out a white drawstring bag. She turned the bag upside down and emptied a handful of glowing White Amber gems onto the table. She gazed at them for some time. Then she placed her hands on them and closed her eyes.

She turned her head slightly as though she was listening to something. 'Someone wants to speak with you,' she began, 'someone not of this world. You wait.' Hadwyn sat motionless. Rasa's voice became deeper. 'Listen for me. Look for me,' she uttered. 'Listen for me. Look for me,' she repeated.

Mackenzie sat bolt upright. He knew those words. They were the words his father had said to him just before he died.

Rasa continued to speak in a deep voice. 'Your father wants to tell you that he cannot speak to you in your world, but he is always beside you. He will help you. You are not alone.' Mackenzie could barely breathe. She continued, 'Your father says he is sorry he left you, but please know he is proud of the man you have become. He is at peace knowing you are protecting your mother.'

Mackenzie's throat constricted with emotion and his eyes filled with tears. 'Dad ...' he sobbed.

Rasa continued. 'You are afraid, son. That is normal. I am here to tell you that if you follow your guides, you will succeed.' She paused for a moment. 'Everything the enemy least expects will succeed the best.' She paused again. Mackenzie was freaking out. A thousand emotions tore through his body. What was happening? Rasa straightened up and opened her eyes. 'I must now direct you to Bandruí.' Hadwyn had remained motionless throughout the communication. 'Come, it is time,' Rasa prodded. 'Your companions are waiting.'

Mackenzie grabbed the controller, calling out, 'Wait, wait.'

Rasa looked up, hesitated and waved her hand dismissively. 'That is all.'

'What happened?' Tess asked Hadwyn as he returned to them.

'We have received instruction for our travels,' he told her.

Rasa came into the room carrying a scroll and a small bag. She unrolled the scroll, revealing a map, and then showed them where they were. 'See this road. You avoid it. That is the Amber Road. The river follows its direction for some time. Do not be seen. Stay in close to the trees. Follow this river downstream until you see a big rock. Find the small path and follow it through the woodlands, maybe several hours, until you get to the Great Oak. You can't miss it. When you get to the Great Oak, stay under it. You can't be harmed there. That tree is sacred. You just stay there and wait.'

Rasa pushed the bag towards Hadwyn. 'Take this bag. It contains three vials. One is medicine. One is courage. One is hope. Use them wisely. And these,' she added, handing each of them five amber gems for their pouches, 'their power is needed. Throw them away if you are captured. Now follow me.' Rasa headed out through the back door of the hut and then made her way on a narrow dirt path between trees and bushes. 'See this path on the map, follow it. It will take you to the river.'

Ten minutes later, they came upon a coppery-coloured stream. They began their trek downstream, not knowing what lay ahead. Most of the time, they were well camouflaged by trees and bushes. Occasionally they saw the Amber Road far off to the east, but they were careful not to cross any cleared areas on their path unless the road appeared uninhabited. They didn't want to be seen by the knights.

One time when they stopped to rest, they peered through the foliage and had a good view of the road coming from Juodkrantė in the east and bending down towards the south. They could see horse-drawn caravans, groups of riders, camel trains and then what looked like about ten Knights of Amber on horseback, herding people along on foot in a southerly direction. Some knights had metal horns attached to their helmets to make them seem even more terrifying.

'Where do you think they're taking those people?' Tess asked.

'I think they're prisoners,' Hadwyn replied. 'Most likely they are being transported to the knight's castle to be imprisoned.' Hadwyn unrolled the map.

'How much further?' Jackson asked, coming over and peering over Hadwyn's shoulder.

'Shouldn't be much further to that rock,' Hadwyn estimated, 'then we go west, heading away from the Amber Road, so that's one good thing, and then through those woods … but I can't tell how far to the Great Oak, because the map stops at the edge of the woods.'

Tess joined in. 'Rasa said the path would take us all the way to the tree.'

They continued alongside the river, with Buddy scampering and sniffing around behind them.

The sun was directly overhead when a little way ahead, Tess spotted the rock. 'Wow, it's huge,' she exclaimed. It was on the far side of the river. Hadwyn utilised his Triple Jump to transport his companions across the river. One at a time, Tess and Jackson climbed onto Hadwyn's back and flew through the air to the far side of the river.

'Surprisingly cool,' Jackson admitted.

'Come on Buddy,' Tess called to her dog, who was by now paddling across to join them. He reached the other side easily and was soon shaking himself dry.

'Well, here is the path,' Hadwyn announced from behind the rock. The little path was not even a metre wide and wound its way into the woodland. The companions trekked on for many hours, occasionally stopping for a rest. It was all downhill. It was getting dark, so they had to keep an eye on where they were placing their feet.

'I'm getting tired,' Tess complained to Hadwyn in front of her.

'It's okay, Tess. Look ahead.' The other two leaned to the side so they could see past Hadwyn. In front of them was the largest tree they had ever seen: The Great Oak, with sprawling branches covered with green moss, towered over the woodlands like a massive umbrella.

'Here we wait for something,' Hadwyn announced.

Tess and Jackson were soon asleep, exhausted after a day's trek. Hadwyn sat quietly watching.

14

Bandruí, the Druid

TUESDAY

Darkness had descended and the wee hours of the night were silent, bar the occasional cricket chirping or a distant owl hoot. Gradually, Hadwyn became aware of a green glow becoming stronger around them. He looked around, searching for its source. He peered up into the tree and was taken aback by the vision of a woman sitting quietly, watching him. She wore a long-hooded cape. Her gown was also long and green, but decorated with a pale gold strip of material from top to bottom and a gold braided belt, tied around her waist and trailing down the gown. Long brown hair filtered out from under the hood and cascaded halfway down to her waist. An aura of bright green surrounded her being.

Hadwyn leaned across and shook Jackson and Tess on the legs. 'Hey, wake up, wake up. We have a visitor.'

The other two sat up and looked around. 'Where?' Tess asked.

'Up there,' Hadwyn pointed, looking up, but the visitor had disappeared. A twig snapped as the woman approached them from behind the Great Oak. They all quickly stood, facing her.

'Welcome,' she greeted them, 'have no fear. I am Bandruí, the Woodland Druid. I am here to guide you.'

'A druid?' Tess responded with her hand to her mouth in excitement and wonder. 'A real druid?'

Bandruí approached Tess with both hands reaching out. 'I was expecting Emerald, the young sister druid, but I see you are the same.'

Tess dropped her hand from her mouth and put both hands forward to be held by Bandruí. 'I read about druids and I always wanted be a druid and everyone told me they weren't real,' Tess poured out.

Bandruí looked fondly at the young girl. 'Do you care for your fellow creatures, and the earth that is home to all of us, with all your heart?' Bandruí asked.

'Oh yes, with all my heart,' Tess replied.

'I can vouch for that,' Jackson volunteered.

'I can too,' Hadwyn added.

'Then you are a sister druid,' Bandruí reassured her. Tess's eyes filled with tears of joy. Bandruí turned toward Hadwyn. 'Hadwyn, the lost boy child of Karvaicai village? We all know of you. We have awaited your return. I see you are helping your companions to heal our world. That is good. I must advise you that once the Triado are restored to their rightful place, your debt to us is gone and you are free to return to your people.'

Hadwyn bowed his head and said nothing. Mackenzie felt concerned. Did that mean Hadwyn would not continue on with Jackson and Tess through to the Last Door? Perhaps Hadwyn would be satisfied that his own goals had been achieved and would not want to go further? If Hadwyn refused to go further, could Mackenzie take back control of the character and force him to help Tess and Jackson? He would have to talk with Hadwyn.

'You're not leaving us, are you Hadwyn?' Tess asked anxiously.

'Perhaps, young druid, you must give him time to consider his circumstances,' Bandruí explained. 'He has travelled far for many years to bring about resolution in his home lands. What more can we expect of him? As I have said, once the Triado are released and returned to their rightful place, he is free to go home.'

Now both Tess and Jackson looked worried.

'Let us now converse upon your quest,' Bandruí invited and sat down on the dry leaf-covered ground. The others sat down again, making a small circle under the Great Oak. Buddy stood next to Bandruí, wagging his tail incessantly. Tess listened in absolute awe as Bandruí spoke to them. Every now and then, Tess glanced at Hadwyn but his expression gave nothing away. 'We druids hold ancient knowledge of all things in nature. We are the guardians and teachers. We are all connected in the great web of life. Nature is divine. Trees are sacred to us. They give us the air we breathe and hold wisdom through the ages. I must consider your path for a moment. Please be patient.'

Bandruí arose and stood in front of the Great Oak, leaning in and putting her hands against the trunk. She closed her eyes and began to chant. Several minutes passed. The three travellers looked at each other. Bandruí became silent. 'I will consult the spoons,' she announced, pulling two wooden spoons from within her cape. 'These spoons can provide guidance,' she explained. 'They are carved from a fallen branch of the Great Oak.'

The spoons were placed on the ground. Each spoon had patterns carved in them. One was divided into four quarters, with a small hole drilled into one quarter. Bandruí then produced a small vial containing liquid. She held the spoon with the hole in it above the other spoon and gently allowed a few drops of liquid to drop on to the top spoon. A drop of liquid trickled through the hole on to the spoon below and Bandruí waited. Before their eyes, one quarter section of the lower spoon darkened. 'And so it is,' Bandruí declared. 'There is no other way. You must travel through the swamplands.'

Bandruí stood and asked the group to follow her. They walked downhill behind the Great Oak, pushing thick bushes out of their way. Jackson winced as a branch swung back from Tess in front of him and smacked him in the face.

Eventually, they came to stop at a clearing. In the centre was a beautiful green pond covered in water lilies. Rocks and grassy plants created a picturesque border. Two other druids sat quietly on rocks at the water's edge. 'They are the caretakers,' Bandruí explained. 'This pond is the final holding of the Triado frogs. Here we protect the precious eggs and tadpoles so that the Eye-Pokers cannot destroy them completely.'

'Eye-Pokers? That would be the gigantic dragonflies we were warned about as children?' Hadwyn enquired.

Bandruí nodded. 'Indeed. Once, the Eye-Pokers were small, part of the Triado's food source – but since the Triado spirit was trapped in the amber, they have grown into huge monstrosities. We are unable to control them. They have taken over the swamplands. Their offspring, the larvae underwater, consume all the Triado eggs and tadpoles except for those we save here.'

Tess, ever curious, enquired, 'What happens to the frogs that grow from these tadpoles?'

Bandruí looked fondly towards Tess. 'We take some to other areas in our land where the Eye-Pokers have not yet reached, but many take their chances in the swamplands. We never see them again.'

'Oh no, what can we do?' Tess despaired, shaking her head.

'I will tell you,' a deep voice croaked from the middle of the pond.

'Who was that?' Jackson asked.

'Look closer,' Bandruí encouraged, 'See in the middle of the pond.' They could see what appeared to be a big rock, all green, wet and slimy. The rock moved in several places and eventually they could make out a handful of green frogs perched on top of the rock.

One frog spoke to them again. 'We are the Triado you enquire about. We were born and grew up here in the safety of the druids' care. We are soon to leave this sanctuary and find our way in the Beyond, but before we leave, we will produce eggs to ensure the survival of our species … for now,' he added. 'Our link in the fragile chain of life has been weakened greatly. None of us can exist in isolation. Only together and balanced in the chain of life will we all survive. You have come to free our spirit from the amber. I must tell you what you need to know.' He looked directly at Hadwyn as he spoke.

'I don't think I am going to like the sound of this, given we have no weapons,' Hadwyn mentioned to Bandruí.

'We plan to cause the least harm, Hadwyn,' she advised him. 'All living things in the chain of life must survive. There is no point destroying one creature to save another. We must endeavour to save both. Remember, you do have a druid staff,' she added, looking at Tess.

'I've learnt to make myself invisible, but I'm not sure what other magic it has,' Tess piped up.

'Open all your senses to its wisdom and you will learn. That is what apprentice druids must discover for themselves,' Bandruí replied.

The frog croaked loudly. 'The Triado have a legend. Somewhere in the swamplands, there is a White Amber Burnstone identical to the one which holds our spirit. They are Twin Ambers. You must find the first amber. There is a power of attraction between the Twin Ambers. The first will lead you to the second.'

Another druid approached, holding silvery transparent garments. Bandruí spoke. 'You can wear these coats. They are made of exuviae from many Eye-Pokers. It will confuse them and provide you with camouflage. They are unlikely to attack you if they think you are one of them.'

Hadwyn looked uncomfortable. 'Unlikely?' he repeated.

Bandruí continued, 'Normally they do not hunt at night. However, remember that they are attracted to light, so here is a bag of glow worms. You can use them for distraction if need be.'

Hadwyn looked more uncomfortable. 'If need be?' He really wanted his weapons back.

Bandruí looked at Hadwyn sympathetically. 'Have courage and hope, Hadwyn. You are not alone. You have protectors from the Other World. They will not let you down. It will be daybreak soon. You can get moving then.'

Mackenzie felt a little concerned, given that his friends had been awake since the early hours of the morning. It was going to be a very long day.

In no time, it seemed, they were putting on their exuviae coats and preparing to leave. 'What is this stuff?' Jackson asked.

'It's old skin that the dragonflies shed,' Tess explained to him.

Bandruí smiled. 'It should be safe now in the daylight. You will be travelling south, so you will need to keep the sun to your left in the morning and to your right in the afternoon. I am going to give you this dowsing stick. It has been enchanted to find amber. It will vibrate when it is near.' Bandruí handed Hadwyn a Y-shaped piece of old wood about the size of a walking stick. 'You must be on your way,' she instructed.

Bandruí then walked over to Tess. 'This is for you,' she said, putting a pendant over Tess's surprised head. The pale green crystal, held by a finely braided twine, sat in the middle of Tess's chest. 'This is prasiolite. Keep it near your heart. It will keep your connection to nature strong and help you stay on your spiritual path. When you feel weak or defeated, use this to connect with ancient druid wisdom. Our truth will come to you.' Tess was overwhelmed and could not speak. Bandruí embraced Tess and whispered, 'Take care, little sister.'

Tess didn't think the swamp was a pretty place. The trees were darker and there were no bushes or flowers. There was lots of mud and wide stretches of swamp water that was green and sludgy. 'I don't like this,' Tess grumbled, 'it's so wet.'

Jackson went to his sister's side. 'Get on, I'll piggyback you,' he offered.

'No, let me do it,' Hadwyn suggested, 'I am stronger. I won't get tired as quickly. Besides, you have the dog creature.' Jackson agreed. Tess was hoisted on to Hadwyn's back, much to her relief. 'Keep an eye on the sun, Jackson, and let me know if we are getting off-track,' Hadwyn requested. 'Keep it on our left till midday.'

They traipsed onwards, both with wet muddy legs up to their knees. About two hours had passed when Hadwyn halted in his tracks and held up his hand for Jackson to stop. 'What's that noise? Is it wind?' Jackson asked. They stood still. The sound grew louder.

'No, that is not wind,' Hadwyn warned. 'Tess, get between us. Everyone, keep still.' Tess slipped down off Hadwyn's back, her feet sinking into the mud.

From above, they all heard Mackenzie's voice. 'It's the Eye-Pokers. Just do as Hadwyn says.'

'I'm scared,' Tess confessed.

'It's okay, Tess. I won't let anything happen to you,' Hadwyn assured her. Suddenly, loud whirring and flashes of light shot past them, coming from all directions. 'Keep still,' Hadwyn reiterated. They held their ground, not really knowing what else they could do. For what seemed an endless amount of time, the Eye-Pokers jetted backwards and forwards past them. They could feel the wind created by their wings. Then the whirring slowed and the Eye-Pokers circled them, hundreds of them.

'Oh no! They're hunting us,' Tess cried.

Hadwyn reached into the bag the Spaewife had given them and pulled out a vial. 'Drink this, both of you,' he ordered. 'It will give you courage.'

Tess and Jackson quickly consumed the contents. They felt a rush of warmth through their body. 'Okay, okay, it's working,' said Tess. She was thinking more clearly, and remembered they were safe under the special coats.

At that moment, a particularly large Eye-Poker hovered closer and closer to Hadwyn. 'Keep your hoods over your heads,' he yelled. The Eye-Poker hovered above the group and then lowered itself, coming to rest on Hadwyn's hooded head.

I should be terrified, Tess reflected, *but I'm not. That dragonfly is beautiful.* Another Eye-Poker came in and landed on Jackson's head. They were huge, about the size of a bicycle but light as a feather. 'It's okay,' Tess declared, 'the exuviae capes are working. They think we're one of them.'

'Keep moving, guys,' Mackenzie encouraged. 'You can't afford to stop. You need to get through this swamp before the day is out. I don't want you trapped in this for the night. Just ignore the Eye-Pokers. They're curious but they're not attacking.' The party moved off with one sitting on Hadwyn's head and others continuing to circle them.

About an hour later, Hadwyn felt a vibration in the dowsing stick. At the same time, the Eye-Pokers became agitated. Those that had been perched on their heads flew off and joined the rest of the Eye-Pokers, who had increased their speed of flying in a circle around them. The whirring sound rose to a crescendo. 'We must be close,'

Hadwyn told them, 'they're getting upset. They won't want us to find the amber because they need it. We're threatening their hold on power.' Hadwyn pressed on, following the dowsing stick that vibrated stronger each time he went in the right direction.

'I've lost the sun,' Jackson called out, 'there's too much cloud.'

'Never mind that for now. Let's focus on this first,' Hadwyn answered. The dowsing stick vibrated strongly, shaking in Hadwyn's hands. 'We're getting close,' he reported. 'Wait, I must have gone past it. The vibration is easing off.' Hadwyn turned back around and the vibration increased in intensity again. 'It's right here somewhere.' The Eye-Pokers had moved in very close. The wind they created was almost blowing the companions' hoods off. 'The amber is here somewhere. Feel around with your feet in the mud.'

Unexpectedly, a flash of green emerged at great speed from the murky swamp water and landed on the front of Tess's coat. 'Oh, my goodness, it's a frog,' she called out. It was a Triado. The frog was at least the size of two men's hands together and was gripping onto Tess's coat with its webbed feet. Tess put a protective arm around the frog as Eye-Pokers zoomed past, veering in towards the frog. The frog stared into Tess's eyes, then opened its mouth wide and revealed a white stone sitting on its tongue. 'It's the White Amber Twin,' Tess called out over the deafening noise.

Hadwyn reached over and put his hand out in front of the frog's mouth, who then used its long tongue to deposit the White Amber into Hadwyn's hand.

'They're trying to hurt the frog,' Tess cried out, looking at Hadwyn imploringly. Jackson and Hadwyn both moved in closer to Tess, trying to offer both her and the frog more protection from the Eye-Pokers' desperate attack. The intensity of the attack escalated, getting so loud they couldn't hear each other speak. Tess was becoming hysterical with fear, both arms wrapped around her amphibian friend. 'Help me,' she screamed.

Jackson ripped off his exuviae coat and tried to put it over Tess and the frog. 'It's going to be okay. Here, now you have double protection. I'll look after you,' he yelled near her ear. Hadwyn was on the other side of Tess, swinging his arms at the attackers, trying to scare them off. Jackson did the same, furious that he did not have his swords. Mackenzie called out to Jackson to enact his Skin Shield, but Jackson couldn't hear him. Jackson grew tired and in a split moment, he lost his balance and fell into the muddy water. Hadwyn reached over and pulled him up by the arm. Jackson returned to Tess's side and held onto her.

Mackenzie watched Jackson's protective embrace of his younger sibling and was reminded of when his own father embraced him before he died. Jackson was becoming a really brave and caring guy; someone he was really proud to call a friend. This journey they were on was certainly teaching each of them so much about themselves and each other. Then Mackenzie saw blood oozing down Jackson's back. He'd been hit. He yelled to Hadwyn, 'Jackson is wounded!'

Quickly, Hadwyn sprang into action. 'Have my coat,' Hadwyn yelled to Jackson, ripping his off in a hurry. As Jackson reached over for the coat, the largest of the Eye-Pokers saw a gap in their defence. There was a screeching sound, a flash of silver and blue, and in a microsecond the Triado had been ripped from Tess's grip. Tess let out a scream of despair. Within seconds, the only sound left was Tess's sobbing as Jackson held her quietly. The Eye-Pokers had disappeared, flying off into the darkness of the swamp as soon as they had taken the frog. They didn't seem to realise that the companions had the amber. 'We need to get out of this swamp. They'll be back when they realise they haven't got the amber,' Hadwyn told them.

'What direction do we go in?' Jackson asked. 'It's still cloudy.'

Hadwyn glanced up at the sky. 'Can't be more than midday. Hopefully the clouds will clear soon. We just have to keep moving. We don't want to be dealing with this lot when dark falls. There will probably be more of them and they will be hungry.' Hadwyn looked at the White Amber Twin, wondering how he was going to read the stone for direction. Presumably, the amber's law of attraction would pull it towards its mate – wherever that was.

'Hadwyn, can I tell you something?' Tess asked.

'Of course, Tess, go ahead,' he answered.

'Well, at school, my friends and I looked up the law of attraction and it said that you need to focus on what you desire and then follow where it feels right.'

Jackson looked at his sister with surprise. *That wasn't druidic wisdom,* he thought. That was Tess and her friends exploring romance stuff. He'd overhead them giggling about it at home.

'Well, anything is worth a try. We haven't got anything else.' Hadwyn agreed. He held the amber tight in his hand, put his other hand over his heart and closed his eyes. 'Got it,' he said suddenly, 'Tess, get on my back, keep your hood on. Let's go that way.'

The muscles in Jackson's legs were aching from more than half a day straining through the mud. Hadwyn pressed forward without hesitation. He was focused. Tess was on his back, holding on. The Eye-Pokers could be heard in the distance, slowly getting louder. 'They are searching for us,' he told them. They walked on and on.

'The clouds are getting really dark,' Tess told the others, looking up through the treetops. Then she stopped still. 'Oh no, I think it's a swarm of Eye-Pokers.' The others looked up. The humming grew louder. A big dark circle like a hurricane loomed overhead.

'We need to find cover,' Hadwyn yelled. They searched their surroundings desperately. He saw a bramble thicket. It was thorny but they could probably crawl under it. 'Come on, this way,' he called. They ran over to the thicket and crawled on their bellies under the network of thorny branches. Jackson tried to slide sideways to avoid Buddy getting spiked. In seconds, they were huddled together in a small space, thin spiky branches overhead. They felt safer, but they could see the Eye-Pokers and the Eye-Pokers could see them. Jackson pulled the sling around to his front and patted Buddy reassuringly. And then the Eye-Pokers attacked.

The wind grew stronger and stronger, swirling around them, ripping branch upon branch from the thicket. They were losing their cover and didn't know what to do. Mackenzie feared his friends were about to be killed. 'Just give them the amber,' Mackenzie called to them. 'Throw it out to them!'

Tess was holding her staff at the ready, both hands gripping hard. Surely this couldn't be the end. She saw Hadwyn pull the amber out of his pouch. This couldn't be happening. The last of the branches were swept away. Tess stood up, put her hand up towards Hadwyn and screamed, 'No!'

Hadwyn hesitated. He watched as Tess closed her eyes and raised her staff above her head, gripping tightly as the wind threatened to rip it from her grasp. She yelled, '*Oraibh ort stad. Tá cosc ort. Caithfear an t-ordú nádúrtha a athchóiriú. Téighí abhaile.*' Jackson and Hadwyn watched in amazement as she began to chant a spell over and over. '*Stad mo sheirbhísigh. Stad mo sheirbhísigh. Stad mo sheirbhísigh. Stad mo sheirbhísigh. Stad mo sheirbhísigh.*' The staff glowed bright green in her hands. The chanting continued. Gradually, the wind slowed, the swarm dissipated and the wood became light with sunshine again. Tess collapsed to the ground. The others rushed to her side.

For some time, they were unable to rouse Tess. She lay as though sleeping. 'Get the amber gemstones,' Mackenzie called to them, feeling as shocked as the others. Tess had been magnificent, but had she paid too high a price? Soon, about a dozen amber gems were resting on Tess's body. All they could do was wait. From time to time, Tess stirred, muttering words in a strange language and then settling down again.

It was then that Hadwyn noticed blood on Jackson's trousers. 'Let's have a look at that,' Hadwyn instructed. Jackson pulled up the trouser legs and revealed many leeches attached and blood running down his legs. 'Take your shirt off,' Hadwyn instructed. Jackson was covered in bites on his back and his neck. 'You've had a tough day,' Hadwyn commented.

'I didn't want to complain,' Jackson admitted.

'You should have said something,' Hadwyn reprimanded him. 'It's hard to fight in pain. It makes you weaker.'

Tess's voice interrupted them. 'Well, aren't you in a mess.' She stood up as though nothing had happened to her and rummaged through her pouches. 'I've got just the thing for you. There'll be no more insects feasting off you.' Her hand emerged with a handful of dried leaves. 'It's the bashful plant. I knew it would come in handy.' She crushed the leaves between her hands, added some water from her flask and then started spreading the paste on her brother's exposed areas of skin.

'Whoa … steady on there. Not a bucket of the stuff. It stinks,' Jackson complained. Tess took no notice of his complaints and finished off by putting it on herself as well.

She offered it to Hadwyn, who shook his head and said to Jackson, 'I should have given you this.' He held a vial out. 'This is medicine from Rasa. Please drink it. We can't afford to have anyone sick. Who knows how much further we have to go?'

Jackson drank the liquid. The leeches fell off. The bleeding stopped and the insect bites disappeared. 'I feel so much better,' he announced, hoping his helpers would ease off now. 'I'm ready to keep going.'

Hadwyn and Tess looked at Jackson. He certainly looked much improved. 'Well, if you're certain?' Hadwyn agreed. 'But this time, let me know if there is a problem.'

Tess decided to let her brother know how proud she was of him. 'You really are the bravest, Jackson.'

Jackson chuckled. 'I'm not sure about that. Your performance with the Eye-Pokers was out of this world. I don't know where you pulled that from, but it was incredible. What were you saying to them and what language were you speaking in?'

'I don't really know. Something just took over me. I can't remember everything. I just remember thinking that we were about to die and the stupid Eye-Pokers were going to stop us bringing back the balance of nature. I remember thinking, "Don't they realise the balance has to be restored for all of us to survive?" Then I went blank.'

'Really?' Jackson responded. 'Well, let me tell you what we saw.'

Tess was flabbergasted. 'You know, when you tell me about it, I can remember some of it but it's like a hazy dream.'

'I understand some of that language,' Hadwyn told them. 'In my years of travel, I sometimes heard people speak in that way. For a while, we had a foreign mercenary who had come from across the sea called the land of Eriu.'

'So, what was she yelling at the Eye-Pokers?' Jackson asked.

'I think it was something like ... "I command you to stop. You are forbidden. Go home. The natural order must be restored." The spell was more like ... "Stop my servants",' Hadwyn explained.

'Well Tess, whatever you said and wherever it came from, it worked. You saved us,' Jackson acknowledged. Tess felt very proud.

It was time to move on. The swamplands and Eye-Pokers were behind them, so the companions discarded their exuviae coats. They were in dry woodland again so Buddy was free to run, and was enjoying himself sniffing and weeing on almost every tree he passed. 'I'm getting hungry,' Tess said, looking around hopefully. 'Maybe I can use my pendant to find food?'

'How so?' Jackson asked, equally hungry.

'Bandruí told me that I can use it to connect with ancient druid wisdom. That must include knowledge about food, surely. I'm going to try,' she stated, clasping her pendant and closing her eyes. They waited. 'Mm … maybe I need to work on that,' she concluded.

The group headed off again toward an unknown destination. Not long after, Tess called out, 'Berries, wild berries. We can eat them. I just know it.'

Brother and sister sat down to rest and eat. Hadwyn stood a little way from them. Tess could see him holding the amber twin against his heart. 'He's getting directions,' Tess whispered to Jackson. Hadwyn returned to his companions.

Mackenzie spoke to the group. 'I need to pause the game and have a rest.' He sounded very serious.

'Is anything wrong?' Jackson asked.

'Well, just when you feel like you've been through the worst of it, this game puts up the impossible,' Makenzie replied. Hadwyn had remained quiet but didn't look surprised.

'That doesn't sound good,' Jackson responded, 'dare I ask?'

'Do you want to tell them or shall I, Hadwyn?' Mackenzie ventured.

Hadwyn looked at his companions. 'I have focused as hard as I can. There's no mistake. The Twin White Burnstone is in the knight's castle.'

15

The Amber Room

With the game paused, Mackenzie was able to have another rest. He was losing track of time but he knew he hadn't rested properly since entering the Low Lands. He had asked the group to stay put for a while, in the cover of the trees and undergrowth.

After a short nap, he read up on the Knights of Amber. Their castle wasn't far from where they waited. They were getting very close to securing the third Burnstone. Once that was achieved, they would be past halfway; only two more levels to go. Mackenzie felt a sense of hope. Maybe it was possible to save them after all, but the most pressing task at hand was to talk with Hadwyn.

The game manual had a map of the castle layout. Mackenzie tried to commit it to his memory. He could get Hadwyn to use his Triple Jump to get them over the castle walls, but where was the safest place to enter? He selected the castle. A cryptic clue appeared on the screen. 'An Amber Room found by a hair, the Burnstone travels a crooked stair.' That didn't help but he needed to remember it anyway. He could only hope the Amber Twin would lead them to the exact location of the twin Burnstone. It was time for them to go.

Tess and Jackson were still sitting on the log, oblivious to the amount of time that had passed, as Mackenzie reactivated the game. 'Okay I have a plan,' he told them. 'When it's dark, you're going to jump the castle wall into a servant's area that has a vegetable garden. You can blend in amongst the plants. Hopefully the knights will be eating their evening meal and the servants will be attending them, so there shouldn't be anyone around. If it's clear, I need you to follow Hadwyn quietly through a garden and into a washing room. You can hide in there. Hadwyn, the laundry will be to your left. Head along the edge of the arcade. The pillars may give you cover if the need arises. Once you're in the laundry, you'll be able to focus on the Amber Twin and get a sense of where to go next.'

The group walked south-east through the woodlands. When the castle came into view, they stayed under cover in the thicket of trees and waited for dark to descend. The castle looked impenetrable. Its huge Gothic-like structure had burnt orange turrets atop high towers and high red brick walls. Deep dry moats surrounded the castle, broken only by one heavy wooden bridge that gave passage to the grand archway framing the iron-gated entryway. Guards could be seen standing each side of the gate.

Under the cover of darkness, the group kept silent, sliding down into the dry grass moats and pulling themselves up the other side. The jumps went as planned. Hadwyn got them both over the wall safely. Buddy was quiet in the sling after his long walk. He seemed to sense when to stay quiet now. Mackenzie wondered if even the dog was undergoing changes to help him adapt and survive.

All was quiet. The group moved quickly, locating the laundry but finding the door latched. Hadwyn quickly hoisted the others through the window. They kept very still and waited to hear for any movement in their vicinity. Hadwyn focused on the Amber Twin. He felt a strong sense that they would need to get to the tower in the corner, diagonally opposite where they now were. The castle was roughly square and there was a large stone courtyard in the centre, full of pillars with great wooden beams, covered in hanging vines. Bench seats were situated around the courtyard. A well was positioned in the centre. He needed to avoid open areas and he didn't know where the knights resided overnight. 'Makansee,' Hadwyn spoke quietly, 'I need to get to that tower. Where are the knight's barracks?'

Mackenzie looked again at the castle map. He spoke as quietly as he could to Hadwyn. 'It's quicker through the courtyard. Hopefully there's no one about at this time of night. The barracks are further over to your left. You can't risk going anywhere near there.'

Hadwyn nodded. He beckoned the others to follow. As they crept through the laundry door it creaked, causing them to freeze. After a moment's hesitation, they moved on into an arcade, an undercover walkway with arches that opened onto the courtyard. They made their way between the arches and proceeded slowly across to the far corner. Mackenzie watched their progress as they passed near the armoury and other storage buildings. When they arrived at the bottom of the tower, they could see stairs through an archway, going down. 'Dungeons,' Hadwyn whispered. The Burnstone was close, he could sense it. He beckoned them to come through the door with him.

'Halt!' a voice startled them. 'Who goes there?' someone in the dark demanded to know. The figure moved forward. There were two of them; a man and a woman dressed in servant clothes. 'Guards!' yelled the man, 'Guards!'

Mackenzie was aghast. What had happened? Servants meeting in the dark? Had they come across a romantic tryst? He had not planned for that!

The three companions now sat in a cold stone-walled cell. They had been captured and searched. The Amber Twin had been confiscated. The Burnstones hidden in Tess's hair remained undetected. Mackenzie had no idea what to do next. He tried to reassure his friends that they would find a solution somehow. Tess and Jackson consoled him and told him it wasn't his fault.

The night passed. They could hear prisoners calling out for mercy in other cells. A guard came to their cell and opened the heavy door.

'This way,' he bellowed. They were marched down another dark hallway and herded into another room, where a knight sat behind a table. 'Vagabonds, sir,' the guard spat out. 'Found with this,' the guard informed his superior, plonking the White Amber Twin on the table. The knight picked it up and examined it.

'Worthless imitation, fools,' he announced, 'We have the real thing.' He tossed it onto the floor in the corner of the room. A large wiry hound bent down, sniffed it and walked away. 'Vagabonds, are we? No fixed address? Lock them up again. Maybe the factory for them. Another caravan of workers leaving in two days.'

The day passed into night again. They were tired, damp and cold. They had been fed some type of slush in dirty bowls and thrown lumps of stale bread. Both Tess and Jackson ate, given they had no idea where their next meal would come from. Their bodies rested but they didn't sleep well. It was a long night.

Mackenzie took the opportunity to talk to Hadwyn while his friends slept. 'Hadwyn, we must talk,' he started.

Hadwyn had been expecting the conversation. He had been deep in thought for a few hours about his dilemma. All was going well. Soon they would locate the White Burnstone and he would be free. He had much to consider. His village awaited his return. He wanted to search for his parents. He wanted to join the rebellion to overthrow the cruel control of the knights; that was where he belonged. In his heart he knew that these two from the other world would not survive without him. Should he help them and leave his homeland suffering longer?

'I know what you want to know, Makansee,' Hadwyn responded. 'We both have a choice, as I see it. I could choose to leave. You could choose to try to control me again. Neither of us truly know the outcome of that struggle.'

'What do you choose?' Mackenzie asked with trepidation.

'I will let you know once I have the White Burnstone,' he answered.

WEDNESDAY

Mackenzie knew his friends were in real danger now. He had read everything he possibly could about the game, but there were no answers to these unexpected events.

The companions were relieved to see a glimmer of light coming through the barred window high above their heads, alerting them to the night's end. 'Visitor,' a guard yelled and pushed someone into their cell. She came closer to them and pushed the hood off her head. It was Lorna. Surprised, the group all started talking at once. They were even more surprised to see that she looked heavily with child.

'No time,' Lorna hushed them. 'I have arranged your release.'

'How did you know we were here?' Tess asked.

'Word of mouth is fast around here. My aunt heard in the marketplace that three strangers had been caught at the castle with amber. I knew it had to be you. I went to the Spaewife and she told me what to do, so here I am. Some say The Amber Room is just a legend but the Spaewife is certain it's somewhere in the castle. She said you must go deeper under the castle, so when you leave this room, go right, not left. That will take you to stairs that spiral down. Just keep going and don't come back. If you get caught, you won't get a second chance.' Lorna looked over her shoulder to make sure no one was listening. 'Eadric, there are many who support your return. I have brought your old clothes and your daggers. Quickly, get changed.' With that, Lorna pulled a bundle of clothes wrapped around three daggers from her undergarments.

Lorna and Tess turned their backs while Jackson and Hadwyn got changed, and then they did the same for Tess. Hadwyn rescued the Burnstones from Tess's hair and got them safely back in his pouch.

The group stood silent for a moment. 'And where will you go?' Jackson asked.

Lorna looked down. 'I am leaving for Palanga tomorrow. I am going to become an amber artisan,' she answered.

'But they're prisoners,' Tess reminded her.

'Yes,' Lorna said quietly.

'No,' Jackson argued, 'You can't give up your freedom for us.'

Lorna looked up at Jackson. 'That is my gift to you all. We all have to make sacrifices. Never mind me now. This is far bigger than you or me. There are more important things that must be done and many are depending on you.' She smiled at Jackson. 'Anyway, I can be set free again. All I need is for a free man to offer to marry me. That is the law. Who knows, maybe a Prince will come for me?' Lorna reached under her cape and pulled out an object. 'Keep this to remember me,' she said, putting an amber ring into Jackson's hand.

'Lorna, it was so dangerous to bring amber here,' Jackson protested.

'Not to worry. It is done. The Spaewife told me you would be gone from this land very soon. Now please wear it to remember me,' she implored.

Tess turned to Hadwyn. 'Can I have the last vial, please?' Hadwyn reached into the bag and handed it to Tess. 'Here Lorna, drink this. It will keep your hope alive. Never give up.'

Jackson was staring at Lorna. 'You must go,' she pleaded, 'the guard will return soon.'

Jackson grabbed Lorna's hand. He reached up and stroked her cheek. 'I will never forget you. I think you are the most beautiful person I have ever met.' He had never felt such anguish.

'Go, please, go,' she begged again.

The companions hurried to the spiral stairway and disappeared as quickly as they could. There were at least one hundred steps and it very dark. Hadwyn remembered the glow worms he had been given by Bandruí. *Better late than never*, he thought. They needed light, any light. He scattered them down the stairwell as far as he could throw them. The glow enabled them to move faster and safer.

They came to the bottom of the steps. The underground opened up to a wider passageway with a low ceiling. They continued along, following twists and turns. Jackson stopped. 'There's something wrong with Tess's hair,' he reported. Tess's long hair was standing on end, all of it. Tess walked towards Hadwyn and her hair fell down normal again.

'That was strange,' Hadwyn commented.

'Let me see your hair,' Jackson asked. Tess turned and walked back toward Jackson. As she got closer to him, her hair stood up on end again. 'It must be electricity,' Jackson suggested.

'What is this magic you speak of?' Hadwyn asked.

Mackenzie also wondered what was happening. He thought for a moment. Something about hair? What was it he read? 'An Amber Room found by a hair, the Burnstone travels a crooked stair.' He said it out loud to the companions. 'The Amber Room is near you. Look around for something.'

The three of them searched the floor and the walls. 'Where can it be?' Jackson exclaimed with frustration. 'What's that up there?' he asked, pointing to an iron ring imbedded in the stone ceiling above Tess.

'I don't know, but we are about to find out,' Hadwyn replied. He reached up and pulled, but nothing happened. He twisted it clockwise and anticlockwise and still nothing – and then he pushed it. With a loud scraping sound, part of the wall opened up. They rushed in.

They had found the Amber Room. It was extremely bright. Everything was made of amber. The intricately carved walls and ceiling reflected bright yellows and oranges. 'Don't stop now,' Hadwyn reminded his companions, 'find the Burnstone.'

Tess walked over to the centre of the room, where a short pillar stood. 'I think this is what you're looking for,' she announced. The others rushed over. There it was, displayed carefully in a golden amber bowl. It looked exactly the same as the other Amber Twin. 'Okay,' Hadwyn said, grabbing the White Burnstone and putting it straight into his pouch, 'it's time to leave this land.'

Far off in the Palanga factory, an artisan sat working on a delicate piece of golden amber jewellery. His hands expertly crafted silver metal clasps onto polished gems. He held up the finished pendant and admired the piece. To his horror, the gem began to darken, then turn to a dull grey stone. He let out a gasp. A nearby knight, disturbed by the noise, walked over.

'What is this abomination you have made, fool?' the knight demanded.

'I don't understand sir. A minute ago, it was a beautiful amber gem.'

The knight wasn't listening. He was stunned as he watched all the baskets of amber change into baskets of grey rocks. 'What magic is this?' the knight whispered. Before his eyes, he witnessed the hordes of treasure that their kingdom relied on disappear.

'An Amber Room found by a hair, the Burnstone travels a crooked stair,' Tess repeated Mackenzie's words. 'A crooked stair?' She looked around. 'I think that's a door,' Tess said, pointing to one of the multiple wall panels. 'It looks slightly different to the other panels.' The three of them pushed and pulled hard to get the door open.

'There's no other exit. You can't go back. Keep trying,' Mackenzie encouraged them. The sound of yelling and footsteps reached their ears.

'The guards are coming,' Tess cried out in a panicked voice. Hadwyn put his hand on his sword and stood in front of Tess. There was nowhere to go. The door burst open and two guards ran in.

'Drop your weapons,' they commanded.

'At ease, men,' Jackson ordered in an authoritative voice. The two guards looked at Jackson and each other. 'Do you not recognise me?' he continued, walking towards them. Tess and Hadwyn looked confused. The guards looked confused. 'I am Prince Eadric, son of King Alexander of Juodkrantė. This is my sister, Princess Gabrielle, and this is my bodyguard,' he indicated toward Hadwyn, who didn't flinch. Mackenzie held his breath. He was feeling very helpless. All he could do was watch. There was a moment of silence. Jackson smiled at the men. 'Of course, you could be forgiven for not remembering me. I was a small boy when I was here last. Perhaps I have changed greatly?'

The guards lowered their weapons. Mackenzie watched Jackson's interaction with the guards. Was this Jackson acting or was this the charming Prince taking over?

Tess put her acting skills into practice, walked over to stand beside Jackson and raised her chin elegantly, looking down her nose at the guards.

'Your Highness,' the taller one said, bowing, 'It has been so long. I knew your father before the … before the …'

The other guard finished his colleague's sentence. 'Before the conquest.' He bowed. 'At your service, Your Highness.'

'Yes, thank you. I understand my father's guards were renowned throughout the land. Of the highest calibre.' The two guards straightened up proudly. 'So, things are changing around here, as you can see, but I would like your assistance. Can one of you open this door for me? I don't have time to explain. There is much to be done.'

'Certainly sir,' the tall guard answered, striding over to the door they'd been trying to open. The guard put his hand on the centre of the door and it slowly opened.

'I shall return,' Jackson told the guards, 'keep the faith. I will remember how helpful you have been.' He turned to his companions. 'Let's go.' They went through the door and it closed behind them.

They ran down many passages, all glowing orange. It got darker and darker. Finally, they reached a stairwell. Jackson looked down. 'Crooked stairs,' he exclaimed. He proceeded to navigate his way down steps that veered in different directions every few steps. He was first to arrive at the bottom and face a damp old door. He heaved it open and a small dark room was revealed.

Hadwyn hesitated. This was the moment. What would he do?

Tess was looking up at him expectantly, then a look of fear crossed her face. 'Hadwyn?' she asked in a tiny whisper.

He looked down at the girl. She wouldn't have a hope without protection. His homeland was suffering, but would a few more days really make a difference? Tess reached her hand out towards Hadwyn. He could see her hand shaking. This little maiden had saved his life. He knew what his choice must be. He took her hand and they entered the darkened room. The door slammed shut behind them. They were enveloped in darkness.

Mackenzie took the opportunity to pause the game as soon as they passed through the door leaving the Low Lands. He was so relieved that Hadwyn had chosen to stay with his friends. Now he was starting to feel really fatigued. It had been a stressful few days and nights. He wasn't getting enough sleep. He scribbled on his writing pad; by his calculations, it was eleven nights since his friends went missing. With that thought, he fell into a long sleep.

It was mid-morning on Wednesday. Mrs Jones went into Mackenzie's room. She watched him at sleep for a moment. She picked up a few clothes strewn around on the floor, and dirty plates and cups from near his bean bag. Pieces of paper and empty biscuit packets also littered the floor. She leaned down and retrieved them. Her eye caught note of his writing pad. *That's odd*, she thought. It looked as though he was keeping some type of record. Seeing Jackson and Tess's names at the top of the page caught her eye. She took a closer look.

It seemed he was keeping record of how long the Taylor children had been gone. The heading read 'Jackson & Tess, days in game'. She looked over at Mackenzie again. What was he going through? Was he coping or was he losing touch with reality? How she wished his father was still here to support him though this.

'Good afternoon,' Mrs Jones greeted her son when he finally surfaced from his room. It was past midday now. He had been sleeping for a couple of hours.

'Hey there Mum,' Mackenzie answered, walking over to her and giving her a big hug. His wet hair dripped on her face. He'd managed a quick shower.

'One of the disadvantages of being short,' she laughed.

'Sorry Mum,' Mackenzie reacted, wiping the water off her cheek with his hand.

'Hungry?' she enquired. He was already peering into the fridge.

'Yep, could use something hearty,' he answered. 'What's this?' he asked, pointing to a container.

'Oh, that's a bolognaise I made last night. I'm taking it down to the Taylors' later,' she told him.

'Really? That's nice of you, considering Mrs Taylor is so unfriendly towards you.'

Mrs Jones nodded. 'Well, she doesn't really know me, but now's not the time to be worrying about things like that. She's a mother who's lost her children. That's all I need to know.'

Mackenzie walked over to his mum and gave her another big hug. 'I love you, Mum.'

Mrs Jones knocked on the front door of the Taylors' home. The doorbell appeared to be broken. A minute later, footsteps approached and the door opened. Mrs Taylor looked surprised. 'Hello,' Mrs Jones started, 'I've brought a meal for you and your husband. It can be eaten today or frozen for another day.'

Mrs Taylor hesitated.

'It's just a pasta. And this container has a tossed salad,' Mrs Jones continued. She held the food basket towards Mrs Taylor.

'Look, just bring it in,' Mrs Taylor invited, opening the door and standing back. 'Just in there on the table is fine. Thank you. It really wasn't necessary.' Mrs Jones entered the house and walked toward the kitchen table. Mrs Taylor came into the room behind her. 'Would you like a cup of tea, Mrs Jones?'

'Teri, call me Teri,' Mackenzie's mother encouraged.

'Oh, okay then Teri,' she responded a little uncertainly, 'I'm Margaret. Do you have milk? Sugar? Please take a seat.' Teri placed the basket on the table and sat down.

'I'm sorry, I didn't mean to interrupt your day. I'm sure you don't need any extra visitors at the moment,' Teri said kindly.

'Oh, that's fine,' Margaret answered, 'it's very quiet here with Sam at work and the children ...' She turned toward the stove and began pouring the tea.

Margaret placed two cups and saucers on the table, with a matching pot and a small plate of biscuits. 'I am so sorry, Margaret,' Teri responded.

'No, it's me who must be sorry, Teri. I shouldn't have attacked your boy like I did. I don't know what I was thinking.'

Teri reached across the table and put her hand on Margaret's. 'There's no need to apologise. I can't imagine what you're going through but I'm sure that whatever you've said has come from a place of unimaginable despair.' Margaret's lip trembled. 'Margaret,' Teri continued, 'It was okay to question the messages on Mackenzie's phone. It is strange and I can't explain it – and he can't explain it. All I can tell you, with my hand on my heart, is that Mackenzie had nothing to do with their disappearance. He's devastated too. In fact, he's just stayed in his room since they disappeared. It's been a lot for him to deal with on top of losing his father.'

Margaret looked surprised. 'Your husband died?'

Teri nodded. 'Two years ago. He had cancer. He tried his best to stay with us but it … well, the treatment wasn't successful. Anyway, Mackenzie and I moved to the city so I could get work. Of course, it's expensive to live in this area but that's why I work two jobs. I'm two parents now.'

Margaret poured the tea. 'I see,' she replied quietly.

Meanwhile, Mackenzie was reading the game manual again. The Forest Lands were ahead. They needed to travel through the Terpene Forest, infested with giant centipedes, to find the Green Amber Burnstone that contained the spirit of the Fire Salamanders. A cryptic clue provided a hint to locate the Burnstone: 'First glance unseen, then with amber green, eyes reveal, path be seen.' *Okay*, thought Mackenzie, *I need to remember that.*

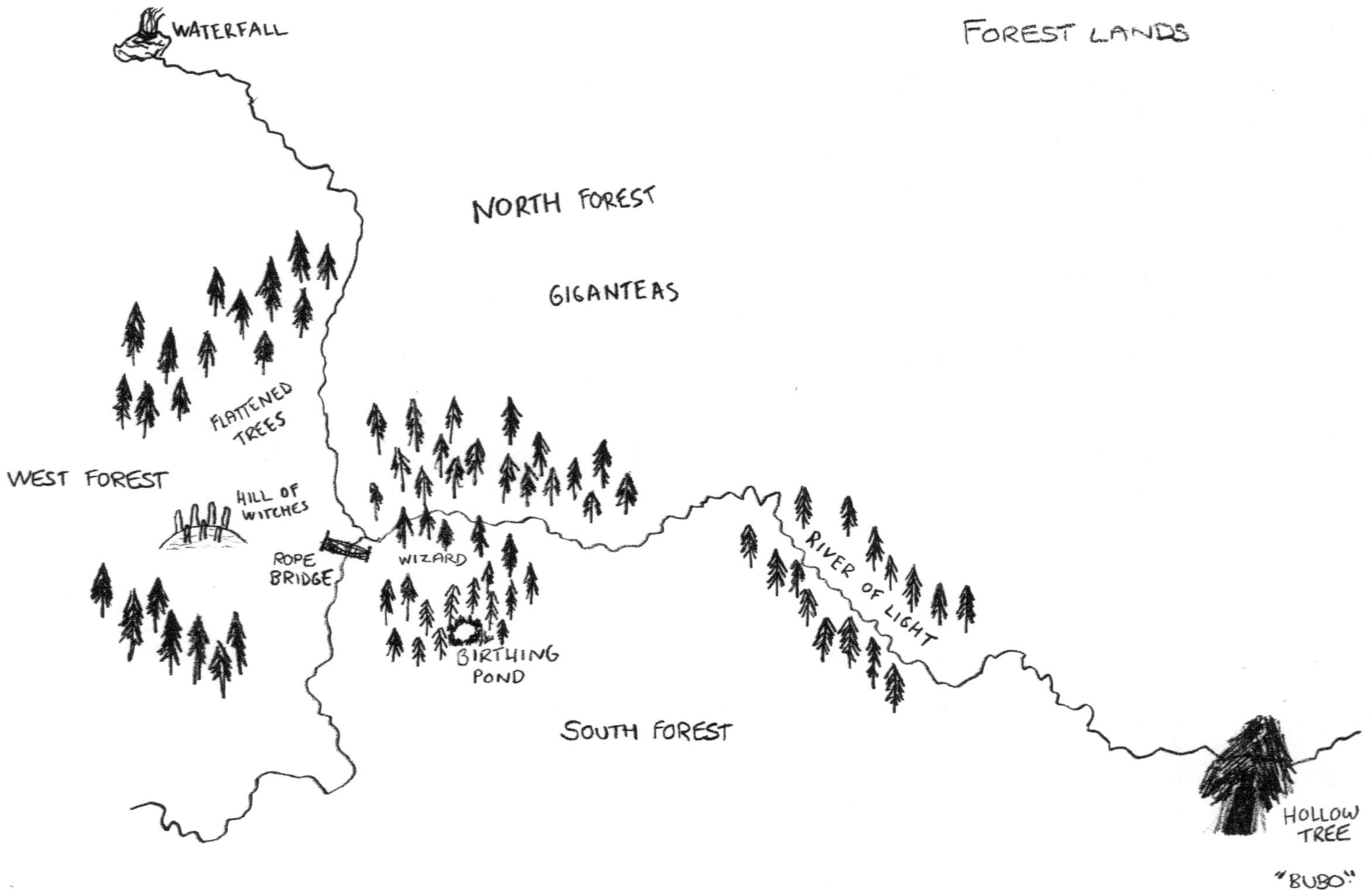

FOREST LANDS
WATERFALL
NORTH FOREST
GIGANTEAS
WEST FOREST
FLATTENED TREES
HILL OF WITCHES
ROPE BRIDGE
WIZARD
BIRTHING POND
SOUTH FOREST
RIVER OF LIGHT
HOLLOW TREE
"BUBO"

FOREST LANDS

16

The Terpene Forest

6 'Where are we?' Tess whispered in the dark.

'I'm not sure, but it's cramped in here,' Jackson replied.

'I can't see,' Tess complained.

'Let's just wait a moment,' Hadwyn suggested, feeling around. 'This wall feels like wood.'

Tess almost jumped on top of Jackson, letting out a squeal. 'What was that?' she asked.

'What?' Jackson exclaimed.

'Something touched me,' Tess cried. A sound like a party horn interrupted their pondering. 'What's that?' Tess squealed again. The noise was then heard by all of them.

'Whatever it is, it's in here with us,' Hadwyn told the others. 'Just keep still and calm, everyone.' Hadwyn reached into a pouch and retrieved a few amber gems, holding them aloft to bring light to their surroundings. It was indeed cramped and the walls were wooden. It appeared they were inside a very large hollow tree. It also appeared that there was a very large owl with them, at least half their size.

'How do you do?' the owl spoke to the astonished group. Tess's eyes were almost open as large as the owl's. 'I am Bubo.'

'Bubo?' Hadwyn responded. They could see that Bubo's feathers were brown and black; his round face had a sharp, black beak and two big reddish eyes peering at them. Bubo had ear tufts protruding from the top of his large, freckled head. His legs were feathered all the way down to his razor sharp, black talons.

'Welcome to our lands,' Bubo answered, bowing his head. 'Time is on the wind, you must leave at once. Traverse the Terpene Forest. Find the ancient River of Light and follow it through the night. You will see a path. Do not cross over into the land north of the river. That land has been taken over by the Giganteas. They have destroyed our way of life in the forest since the Salamander's spirit was trapped in the time of the rising seas.'

Tess put her hand up to ask a question. 'We're not in school, Tess,' Jackson admonished.

'Speak, child,' Bubo responded.

'Thank you, Bubo. May I ask, what is a Gigantea? I've never heard of this before.'

Bubo put his head to one side. 'The Giganteas are what is known as a centipede, but grown all out of proportion. They have become predator to many species – including the Salamanders, which are almost extinct, bar one small group living on the south side of the river. This makes it hazardous for all of us of the forest. Our food chain is altered. The ways of old that ensured our survival have been disrupted. Now I must hasten your departure. Stay with the light of the river. The Giganteas hate light. Keep going until morning. The Fire Salamanders will seek you out. You are expected.' With that, Bubo closed his eyes.

The group emerged from the bottom of the hollow tree into the forest. Moonlight created shadows amongst the pine trees and ferns. Jackson's hand reached up and he felt immense relief as his touch confirmed the presence of a sword hilt. They walked single file along the twisting path for about half an hour. 'There it is,' Hadwyn told them. They looked ahead and saw a river that was lit up from within, like a long winding torch light. 'Okay now, we have a long walk ahead of us. Let's keep quiet. Tess, just tap me on the back if you need me.

Jackson, you come up the rear. Keep your wits about you. We are in unknown territory.'

They trudged on for hours. Hadwyn carried Tess at times and they had a few rest stops for dried meat and water. Buddy walked quietly beside them, secured by a twine lead. As the break of day arrived, the forest came into clearer view. Tall misty pine trees towered over cycads and moss-covered logs. The forest on the north side of the river looked darker and foreboding. The path then veered south-west, away from the river.

'I need another rest,' Tess announced.

'How many rests do you need?' Jackson complained. 'We don't have time for this baby stuff.'

Hadwyn stopped and looked at Jackson, then Tess. 'It's okay. She has shorter legs and she's younger than us. She can't change that.' Hadwyn placated him. 'Take it easy, you're both tired.'

Jackson let out a frustrated sigh. Tess chose a large flat rock to sit on, beside a small pond close to the path. She unloaded her staff, quiver of arrows and bow, and started stretching her tired neck and shoulders. Buddy leaned against her. Tess gave him a chin rub, offered him a few pieces of dried meat and munched on some herself. 'What a beautiful forest,' Tess declared, looking around.

Hadwyn sat down beside Jackson on a log. Mackenzie took the opportunity to touch base with his friends. 'You know, Jackson, you two have been in this game for about nine days now. It's been extremely hard and stressful. You have to expect both of you to be tired and grumpy, but at the end of the day, we're only going to get through this by supporting each other.' Jackson was turning the amber ring around on his finger. 'So how are you feeling about that?' Mackenzie probed.

'About what?' Jackson replied, pulling his hands apart quickly.

'About Lorna?' Mackenzie asked.

'What's there to feel? She's a character in this game. I'm a human. I have to go home. I'll never see her again,' he answered gruffly. Mackenzie realised that it wasn't the right time to talk.

Buddy scampered over to the edge of the pond to lap some water. Tess got up and joined him, ever keen to explore her surroundings. She leaned over to see her reflection in the blackish, brownish water. 'Oh, hello there,' she said as she stepped back.

'Hello to you,' a voice answered.

Hadwyn and Jackson stood up. Buddy was wagging his tail. Two large black and yellow faces with big blinking eyes appeared amongst the palms on the other side of the pond.

Tess was delighted. 'I'm Tess,' she greeted.

The two creatures emerged from the foliage, revealing long lizard-like bodies. They slowly clambered around the pond, coming to a stop close by. 'I am Urodella and this is my wife, Mandra. We belong to the last of the Fire Salamanders left in this land. We are more than hopeful that you will be successful in releasing our spirit from the Burnstone. We cannot survive much longer. There is talk that the Giganteas have been on the move and may be penetrating lands further south.' Urodella shook his head. 'We will be your chaperones for the next part of your journey. My wife is with child and so we are travelling to the birthing pond of our tribe. We must return there every year. After that, we will give you whatever we can to help you on your way.'

The group left the path and followed the Salamanders westerly, walking softly on the forest floor carpeted by pine needles. Liverworts and moss provided patches of greenery on the grey rocks. Colourful fungi clung to trunks and mushrooms gathered at the base of the trees. Tess caught sight of snails and slugs leaving silvery lines behind them. 'Is that a cloud?' she asked, peering up at the mist in the tops of the trees.

'That is terpene mist,' Urodella answered, 'made by these trees. The air in the forest is very good for you to breathe. It is very pure. We call these trees the lungs of our earth.'

Tess looked up again in amazement and took a big breath. 'I didn't know that.'

After several hours of walking, they came across another path, narrower this time with high foliage on each side. 'Our traditional family birthing pond is at the end of this path, well hidden from predators,' Mandra explained. 'We must observe a sacred silence on this path. Many of our dead are buried here. We call it the Path of Sorrow.'

They moved on, resuming single file. Eventually the foliage thinned out and a beautiful, translucent green pond came into sight, surrounded by high rock walls and ferns.

Mandra made her way down into the water and positioned herself with her head above the water. Urodella spoke to the group about their quest to find the green Burnstone. 'From here, travel north until you reach where two rivers meet. The river to your left has a bridge. This you must cross to the West Forest, to avoid the North Forest of the Giganteas. Be wary at the bridge, for there is word of a wizard inhabiting the area. We are uncertain of his intentions.'

Mackenzie pondered the salamander's comment. *I don't remember reading about a wizard,* he thought.

Urodella kept talking, 'When you cross the river, head north. You must keep going to get to the waterfall. That is where the Burnstone is held. It will get very cold, perhaps even snow. Winter approaches.' Mandra had come up out of the water onto the land, and was looking back into the water. 'Excuse me,' Urodella announced, 'I have a job to do.' With that he proceeded to the pool and began swishing his tail backwards and forwards in the water.

Mandra approached the group. 'Our offspring have been born. Urodella must oxygenate the water. That is the father's job.' She smiled. 'So now, you must go. We have a gift for you. Urodella and I have passed on to you our ability to cope with freezing temperatures. This is how we can hibernate in the winter. We hope this will ensure you succeed in your quest.'

Tess looked alarmed. 'But what will happen to you in winter?'

Mandra shrugged. 'We do not know. What we do know is that our young are safe for now. And when you succeed in releasing our spirit, our future will be saved.' Tess yawned. 'Night is falling. You must now wait here till light before travelling,' Mandra advised.

THURSDAY

With an early morning rise and farewells said, the group started on their trek towards the bridge at the joining of the rivers. The land was rising toward the north, so they walked on a slight incline. Sunlight filtered down through the pines. As they gained higher ground, alpine flowers appeared here and there. White and yellow edelweiss and snowbells, mauves and pinks of delphiniums, larkspur and sweet William. Tess enjoyed herself picking flowers – and when they stopped for a rest, she made herself a necklace and bracelet.

'Do you think you could focus on what we're doing?' Jackson asked irritably. 'We should be keeping an eye out for things.' Jackson was feeling on edge. He kept jumping at shadows. Things just didn't feel right. He couldn't wait for this to be over.

Hadwyn walked alongside Tess. 'How are you?' he asked.

'I'm okay,' Tess reassured him, 'he's just grumpy cos he had to leave Lorna. I get it.'

Hadwyn nodded. 'I think you're right.'

Tess lowered her voice to a whisper, 'He's never had a girlfriend. I've never seen him like this. He's always said girls are stupid.'

Hadwyn chuckled. 'Sometimes boys say that because they don't want to say they're scared of girls, or they don't know how to talk to them.'

Tess giggled. 'You're so funny, Hadwyn.'

'What was that? Did you see that?' Jackson called out.

'What is it?' Hadwyn asked.

'I think there's something following me,' Jackson replied.

'Mm, I can't see anything but you go in front for a while and I'll guard the rear,' Hadwyn suggested. After a quick rearrangement, they set off again. A few minutes passed.

'Did you see that?' Jackson called out again, looking very shaken. 'In the bushes up there.' He was pointing to his left.

'What did you see, Jackson?' Tess asked.

'Never mind, I think I know what it was,' Hadwyn stated. 'Just stay calm, Jackson, and look at the path in front of you.' Jackson, who had been peering to the side of the path, turned back around to the front and jumped, startled. Standing in the middle of the path about six metres in front of them, in a long white robe, was the oldest man he had ever seen.

'It's the wizard,' Tess announced.

'Shut up,' Jackson growled.

'Not now, you two,' Hadwyn ordered. He moved to the front of the group and held his hand up in a peaceful gesture.

The old man spoke. 'I am Gwydion, High Wizard of the Trees. I have heard from Bandruí about you.'

Tess's mouth dropped open. 'You know Bandruí?'

'Of course. She is a druid queen. I am a wizard,' he said matter-of-factly, as though it were common knowledge.

'But you live in different lands?' Tess queried.

'Different lands, same world. We are all interconnected,' Gwydion explained. 'Now, you must give me all of the amber gems you carry. Except the Burnstones,' he qualified, nodding towards Hadwyn. Reluctantly, the group emptied the amber gems from their pouches. Jackson felt his amber ring. 'Not that,' Gwydion advised, waving his hand towards Jackson, 'I have no need of your betrothal ring.' Jackson looked at Hadwyn and was about to say something when Hadwyn shook his head silently at him.

The amber gems were placed in a pile at Gwydion's feet. Gwydion gathered handfuls of fallen leaves and covered the gems, and then began to chant a spell and wave his hands around in the air. A moment later, a strong gust of wind sent the leaves swirling, revealing three necklaces of amber beads on red threads. 'Wear these,' Gwydion instructed, 'to repel witches and malicious spirits.'

The companions followed the wizard's instructions and put the beaded necklaces over their heads. 'Witches? Are we going to run into witches?' Tess asked, wide-eyed.

'This is possible,' Gwydion answered. 'It will depend. In the West Forest you will have to walk past the Hill of Witches. They may be there, or not – but they cannot harm you with those necklaces.'

Tess put her hand to her necklace and looked down. 'Well, that's good to hear.'

'Now come,' Gwydion commanded. 'It is time for you to enter the West Forest.'

They followed the wizard for about ten minutes until they arrived at an opening in the trees. There before them was the junction of the two rivers. To their left, a long rope bridge stretched across a wide divide. The rivers were rushing over rocks far below.

'I don't like the look of that,' Tess piped up.

Jackson was busy getting Buddy into his sling. 'Damn you Tess, can you just be quiet and stop whining,' he said, exasperated.

'Get on my back, Tess,' Hadwyn instructed.

Gwydion gave his final guidance. 'Head north, follow the river until you reach the waterfall. It is guarded, so beware.' Then he disappeared.

17

Trapped in Amber

'You go ahead,' Hadwyn suggested to Jackson. With that, Jackson stepped out onto the rope bridge, hanging onto the crisscrossed side ropes. The bridge sagged wherever he placed his feet. Slowly he continued. 'That's it, just take your time,' Hadwyn encouraged.

A sudden flash of black whooshed past Jackson, causing him to lose his grip on one side rope and fall to his knees. He clutched at the ropes. Another swish flashed by, and then another.

'What is it?' Jackson called out, holding one arm over his head, trying to protect himself. Buddy was barking furiously at the darting black shapes.

'It's the witches, Jackson,' Hadwyn called back. 'Don't worry about them. They can't touch you. Just keep your head down, keep your balance and keep going slowly.' Jackson started forward again, his heart beating like a jackhammer. After what seemed like forever, he reached the solid ground on the other side and turned back toward the others. The witches had stopped.

Hadwyn stepped out onto the bridge with Tess hanging on tight. 'Close your eyes, Tess, and don't speak. You might feel some wind but don't worry, I will keep you safe.' As predicted, Hadwyn had not gone far when the witches returned with a vengeance. The bridge swayed dangerously in the strong witch winds. Hadwyn stayed steady until he reached the other side. The wind became still and the witches vanished. 'Vexing creatures,' Hadwyn grumbled.

The river junction separated the North, South and West Forests. Now they were in the West Forest and had turned north to follow the river to the waterfall. As they walked along, they could see the North Forest across the river to their right. It was darker than the West Forest and from time to time, they heard loud cracking and crashing. They guessed it was the Giganteas, but were in no hurry to have that confirmed. They tried to be as quiet as possible.

A short distance from the river, they found a path between the trees, where grass had been flattened recently. 'I wonder what made this path,' Hadwyn pondered, looking around cautiously. He caught sight of a clearing up ahead. 'Maybe you two would like to rest up soon?' he enquired.

'Yes, I would,' Tess replied.

Jackson shook his head at her with irritation. He wanted to keep going. His nerves were frayed. 'It's important to have a rest just before we get killed!' he said sarcastically.

As they approached the clearing, an earthen mound about ten metres high came into view. Atop the mound were what first appeared to be stumps – but as they came closer, they saw that the stumps were three totem poles with carvings of grotesque faces on them. 'I don't like this place,' Tess began.

'Tess, just shut up,' Jackson snapped.

'Hey, hey,' Hadwyn intervened, 'that's no way to speak to a maiden. She doesn't mean to bother you.'

Jackson was shaking his head. His sister's constant chatter was getting to him on top of the uncertainty all around him. He wondered if there would ever be any peace.

Tess was pouting at Jackson when she suddenly screamed and dropped to the ground as a dark shape whooshed over her head.

'Damnation,' said Hadwyn. 'This must be the Hill of Witches. We're in their territory and they're swarming. Come on, let's get out of here. I don't know how long these bewitched pendants will keep us safe.' He pulled Tess to her feet and swung her up onto his back. 'Let's run,' he called to Jackson.

As they ran, the wind of the witches intensified, almost blowing them over. There must have been at least a dozen of them. The travellers ran for about an hour, ducking and weaving their way between trees and jumping logs. Jackson was red-faced and panting heavily.

Hadwyn stopped. They had finally left the witches behind. 'The day is darkening. We need to find somewhere safe for the night,' Hadwyn told the others, looking around. 'Keep your eyes open.' They continued walking slightly uphill. After about another hour, Hadwyn said, 'Look there. We can take refuge under these big logs. It looks like there is a good dry spot under there.'

Through the night, they were disturbed from time to time by loud crashing and cracking. They knew the Giganteas were moving around across the river in the North Forest – but in the night, it sounded much closer. They were relieved when dawn broke and the Giganteas retreated for the day.

FRIDAY

'How are you feeling, Jackson?' Tess asked nicely.

'I'm fine,' he answered gruffly. Actually, he hadn't slept well. He'd been thinking about Lorna and what might have happened to her. He had felt on edge, startled at each strange noise in the night. Quietly, Tess handed him the bag of dried meat and berries and the water flask.

Buddy wagged his tail at her expectantly. 'Don't worry boy, here's a piece for you.' She looked up at Hadwyn, who smiled at her.

Mackenzie stepped in and spoke to them. 'You're doing incredibly well, guys. Can you believe there's only one more level after this?'

'Level?' Hadwyn enquired.

'Land, I meant land. There's only one more land,' Mackenzie corrected. 'This will be another big day ahead,' he announced, 'but hopefully you'll reach the waterfall today. Imagine – maybe you'll be in the High Lands tomorrow. Home is getting closer,' he said encouragingly.

'Mackenzie, how are Mum and Dad? What's happening?' Tess asked.

Mackenzie thought for a moment. He didn't want to tell them their parents were grief-stricken and distraught. Or that the police had scaled down the search – that would take hope from them. 'Well, of course they're upset that you haven't been found yet, but they're working with the police to consider where you might be lost. They haven't given up hope that you'll be home soon.' His friends had enough to worry about. He didn't want them distracted by troubling thoughts of home.

As they continued hiking through the day, they noticed more and more damaged trees. 'Do you think there's been a storm?' Tess asked Hadwyn.

'I'm not sure,' Hadwyn replied, observing the destruction.

'It's like a tornado has ripped a path right through the forest,' Jackson suggested. The broken trees were dripping bright gold and orange resin wherever their branches were injured, trying to heal themselves. The resin glittered in the morning sunlight.

'It' a shame,' Tess determined, 'these poor trees must be hundreds of years old.'

By midday they'd made good ground, despite the trek being uphill. They'd stopped for several rests and to get sticky resin off their boots. The yellowish resin dripped down tree trunks and fell on the ground as the trees responded to their wounds, producing massive amounts. Tess even had it falling in her hair. 'Onward and upward,' Hadwyn encouraged them. Eventually the sun dropped lower to the west, heralding another closing day. 'Keep your eyes open for a camping spot,' Hadwyn reminded them.

'What's that over there?' Tess asked, pointing at what looked like a very large rock amongst the trees up ahead.

'Wait,' Hadwyn ordered, 'that's not a rock.' He motioned to them to crouch down behind some ferns. 'This doesn't look good,' he warned. He put his finger to his lips, ensuring no one spoke. He whispered, 'Sleeping Giganteas.'

They needed to find cover. He looked around and decided to go back down the path. The more distance he could create between them and the Giganteas, the better. Noiselessly, they made their way back for about five minutes when Jackson spotted three huge trunks that had fallen on top of each other, creating a tent-like shelter underneath. He pointed it out to Hadwyn, who nodded. They headed over as quickly as they could, bent down to crawl under a log, and entered the sheltered space. 'What are we going to do?' Jackson questioned.

'I don't know, but for now we stay here,' Hadwyn stated. They sat together apprehensively as night fell.

Soon the crashing and banging started again, this time very close by. Definitely on the same side of the river as themselves. 'I thought they weren't in the West Forest?' Jackson whispered.

'Remember, Urodella warned us that they were on the move. They must have crossed the river,' Hadwyn concluded.

'Great. I guess we're in a world of trouble then?' Jackson pointed out.

Mackenzie needed to step in again. 'Okay team,' he began, 'we need to think this through. You're so close. Let's think about what we can do. You have your weapons back. You have some spells and abilities. We will find a way. Remember, courage and hope. You can do this. Now let's go through this and consider what might be ahead and how we might deal with it.'

'I can tell you a few things about centipedes,' Tess volunteered. 'They can't see very well but they sense vibration through their feet, so if they're coming near you, keep still. And keep away from their fangs or they might inject poison into you.'

Hadwyn glanced at Tess. 'Thank you. Your druid wisdom is of great benefit to our planning.'

Throughout the night, they huddled beneath the logs. The intensity of the noise grew all around them. From time to time, they heard hundreds of footsteps. Peering through the branches of the fallen logs, the moonlight shone on silvery centipede armour and marching legs going past. 'They are hunting,' Hadwyn told them. Buddy growled and shivered with fear. The huge flattened head of a Giganteas came close to their hiding spot. Sharp black mandibles clanged against the wood as a Giganteas tried to reach in to get them. Buddy yelped and shot out the back of the shelter, breaking his twine lead and disappearing into the darkness. 'Buddy!' Tess cried.

'I'll get him,' Jackson insisted, peering out. 'Stay there Tess,' he ordered.

Hadwyn watched Jackson prepare to exit the shelter. 'Don't take any chances out there. If you see anything approaching, get back in here,' Hadwyn instructed. 'I'll keep an eye on this direction,' he added, turning back to the front where the Giganteas continually approached them.

Jackson pulled out a sword and crept out from under the shelter. He thought he could see two bright little eyes under a bush about five metres away. He beckoned Buddy repeatedly, but the terrified little dog would not move. There was nothing for it; Jackson stood up and made ready to run. He didn't realise that Tess was right beside him. Overwhelmed with fear for her beloved dog, she had followed Jackson out immediately. Hadwyn, on guard with his back turned, had not seen her dash out.

Tess's eyes searched their darkened surroundings desperately. She couldn't bear for something to happen to Buddy; she admonished herself for not holding on to him. Out of the corner of her eye, she noticed movement above them. She looked up quickly and to her horror, a colossal bulb of resin oozed rapidly down the great tree towering over them. Tess yelled, 'Look out!' and pushed Jackson so hard he fell to the ground.

In the commotion, Buddy scooted out from under the bush and back to the shelter, cowering next to Hadwyn, who was keeping watch of the Giganteas on the other side. 'Get back in here you two, quickly. The dog is returned,' Hadwyn ordered.

Jackson had been caught off-guard and shocked when Tess pushed him over. 'Damn,' he muttered, trying to get to his feet quickly. He spun around to grab Tess and get her back into safety, uttering a gasp of dismay.

'Tess! Tess! Tess!' Hadwyn heard Jackson crying out despairingly. Hadwyn had fastened Buddy with twine to a branch. He scrambled out the back of the shelter and out into the open, where he could see Jackson leaning over a raised object.

'What's the delay? Quickly, you two need to get back under cover. It's not safe out here …' Hadwyn stopped in his tracks. He could not believe what he was seeing. There in front of him lay Tess, motionless, completely encased in an oval-shaped mass of transparent resin. Tess was enshrined in amber.

18

Battalion of Trees

The sound of splintering branches and falling trees escalated. The Giganteas were returning. 'Drag her in!' Hadwyn yelled. The two boys grabbed the amber casing and pulled as hard as they could. There wasn't much to grip on to. 'I'll push,' Hadwyn called out and hastened to the far side. Within the nick of time, they managed to bring the golden tomb in under the logs with them – just as the Giganteas began congregating around their shelter. The ravenous creatures had sensed movement in their feet and had come snapping their fangs, seeking their prey.

'Fight!' Hadwyn yelled at Jackson, using his sword to chop at the Giganteas feet and antennae encroaching into their shelter. Sobbing, Jackson pulled one of his swords out and swung furiously at the intruding limbs. Ten minutes of intense defending followed. Finally, the Giganteas appeared to give up and move away.

Jackson dropped his sword and turned around. 'Tess,' he cried, throwing himself over the amber casing. 'Why did you do that? She pushed me out of danger. Oh no, Makenzie,' Jackson called, 'She's dead. Is she dead? Tell me she's not dead!' he pleaded, his distraught face turned towards Hadwyn.

Mackenzie had no answer for him. He was distressed himself. There had been nothing he could do to intervene. It happened so suddenly. It wasn't something encountered when reading about the game. Was this the end of everything? He was supposed to protect and save them. He felt helpless and alone, a failure. Mackenzie was completely overwhelmed and at a loss. Defeated, he could not answer his friend.

Then he heard a familiar voice through his headset. 'I am here. Take heart. She is not dead. She is suspended.'

'Dad?' Mackenzie answered, sitting up and looking intently at the screen. He could faintly see both Hadwyn and Jackson under the logs, kneeling down beside the amber tomb. The two of them looked up at the voice overhead.

'Who are you talking to?' Jackson asked with surprise. Mackenzie didn't hear Jackson's words. He was completely focused on the other voice. 'Dad, help me,' he begged.

'Son, listen to me. The girl will be okay but you must do as I say.'

Jackson was devastated. His sister was dead. His best friend wasn't answering him. He could vaguely hear Mackenzie talking to someone but he couldn't hear the other person. The world as he knew it was collapsing around him. He bent his head over Tess's golden tomb and cried, gazing through the amber at Tess's peaceful face.

She looked so young and vulnerable. He felt immense guilt for not protecting her. He had promised to keep her safe. His mind filled with memories of how many times he'd been angry and impatient with her over the past few days. Why had he been so mean to her? Why couldn't he remember she was younger and didn't mean to annoy him? He knew she looked up to him, but he had treated her so badly. She hadn't deserved it and now she was gone. He would never forgive himself.

Mackenzie's father spoke again to Mackenzie. 'The girl is protected by the Salamanders' gift of winter freeze. She is in hibernation. That is what's happening now, but I don't know how long she can stay in this state of suspension. You must get her to the waterfall as quickly as possible. Like all the other creatures trapped in amber, she will be set free when you find the Burnstone of this land.' Mackenzie listened intently.

'I don't know how far we can carry her,' Hadwyn said out loud.

Mackenzie's father continued, 'You must get her to the river. The amber that surrounds her will float, so you can use the water to get her to the waterfall.'

Hadwyn reached over and gently touched Jackson's shoulder. He had heard the words of Mackenzie's father too. 'Hey,' Hadwyn said, moving beside Jackson and putting a comforting arm around his shoulder. 'She's going to be alright.' Jackson looked up at Hadwyn, confused. He had been too overcome by grief to hear what had been said. 'Trust us, Jackson. We know what to do. The wizards have spoken. We know how to save her but we need to get moving.'

A glimmer of hope crossed Jackson's face. 'What can we do? What's going to happen to Tess? How can we help her?' he questioned, looking at Hadwyn for further reassurance.

Hadwyn patiently told Jackson what he had heard from the wizards. He gave Jackson details of the plan at hand. 'It's going to be very dangerous getting to the river,' Hadwyn declared, 'we will have to go from cover to cover. As soon as the Giganteas sense movement, they will come hunting. And once we get to the river, we will have them on both sides. We will have to stick to the middle and hope the river stays wide enough to keep us safe.'

Mackenzie remained quiet, gripped by emotion. He was about to pause the game to gather his senses, but was too afraid of cutting off the treasured communication with his father, so he did nothing.

The boys readied themselves for the arduous task ahead. Jackson secured Buddy in the sling and kept the twine attached between Buddy's collar and his own belt. 'You are not getting away again,' he assured their smallest companion. They dragged nearby fallen branches into their refuge and made a sleigh for the amber tomb.

'This will be easier to drag,' Hadwyn informed Jackson. 'Okay, that's secure,' he said, fastening the last piece of twine, 'one step at a time.'

The boys searched through the moonlight in the direction of the river, looking for a place they could run to and find cover. They waited till there were no sounds of Giganteas close by. When the time was right, they moved out, running and pulling the sleigh together. They travelled short distances at a time, making sure their next destination looked like safe cover. When they reached each spot, they huddled under protective foliage. Repeatedly, the Giganteas came hunting after sensing the vibrations of movement in their legs. Jackson and Hadwyn would wait patiently until it was safe again and move on to the next cover.

'I can hear the river,' Jackson announced after about ten dashes between logs.

Hadwyn peered into the distance. 'There's no cover between here and the river,' he told Jackson with concern, 'we need to run without cover this time. Keep your sword in one hand, okay?'

Jackson nodded. They estimated they needed to cover the distance of about two football fields to reach the river. Could they make it?

The forest was deathly quiet. It was time to make a run for it. Hadwyn and Jackson looked at each other. Hadwyn made a hand sign to go. As quietly as possible, they ventured forth. The sleigh was heavy and scraped along the ground, cracking twigs. They proceeded slowly at first, trying to reduce the vibration in the earth. They were about one third of the way when the sleigh became stuck on something. They pulled harder, trying to dislodge it to no avail. Feeling desperate, Hadwyn looked around. And then they heard the marching footsteps.

Hadwyn yelled at Jackson, 'Get into position!'

'I'll protect her!' Jackson yelled back, now holding both swords at the ready. The two of them positioned themselves back to back, with the sleigh in between them. The Giganteas gathered around them. One came forward; its height was almost to Hadwyn's shoulders. Great black-tipped mandibles opened wide, closing in on them. They fought fiercely against the Giganteas, fending them off with their swords.

Then, a deafening sound descended on the battle. They didn't know what was happening. The Giganteas began to retreat.

Tree branches around them were groaning and straining as they began entwining amongst themselves, until the trees had created a protective enclosure over the top of them. Loud cracking sounds came towards them through the dark as what appeared to be great tree root systems walked like crabs towards their branched enclosure. They then lined up opposite each other creating an archway – a safe pathway towards the river. 'What are they?' Jackson whispered.

A bright light appeared in the centre and as their eyes adjusted, they saw Gwydion standing there. The tree wizard spoke. 'They will not harm you again. They are the Pinaceae Drifters. These sad creatures are the roots of the ancient pines that birthed the amber of our lands. They wander the lands searching for their upper bodies that were destroyed in the time of the rising seas. Do not fear them.' He pointed to his trees and the Pinaceae Drifters archway. 'My battalion is at your service. My part is done. Make haste.'

With the extra light, they could see the sleigh had been jammed against a rotting log. They manoeuvred the sleigh free and headed for the river. To their amazement, the branched archway continued to provide cover all the way along the river for as far as they could see. In no time, the two companions were wading upstream with the amber tomb floating on the sleigh beside them.

The expedition forged ahead. They were wet and Jackson was fatigued, but he was determined to save his sister by reaching the waterfall before her suspension state wore off. The waist-deep water grew colder and colder, but he did not feel the cold. He too was protected by the anti-freeze gift from the Salamanders. Through the night they waded. Each side of the river, the Giganteas could be heard banging against the branches, frustrated that they could not reach their prey. After several hours, they faded away.

SATURDAY

Daylight began to filter through the branches and revealed riverbanks carpeted in snow. The archway came to an end, opening out to a large freshwater pool. On the far side, a waterfall cascaded down a rocky cliff face. 'We made it,' Hadwyn said with great relief. But had they made it in time? 'We have no time to lose,' Hadwyn told

Jackson. 'You stay here with Tess and I will go for the Burnstone.' He swam across the pool and disappeared behind the waterfall. He pulled himself up onto a ledge of slippery black rocks – in front of him were many steps carved into the rock, leading back into the cave. He pressed on.

After he had climbed at least one hundred steps, he came to a landing. The rock walls were bathed in orange light. Against the back wall, a great stalagmite rose from the floor like a grand golden cathedral. Nestled in a crevice near the top, a glow of green revealed the Burnstone.

Hadwyn made a move toward the stalagmite when two red antennae appeared from behind the structure. Hadwyn pulled his sword out and prepared for battle. A great Giganteas lurched forward and he struck its head repeatedly and furiously. It did not seem to have any effect on the beast.

Hadwyn stepped back and tripped, falling backwards on to the floor. The Giganteas, sensing a quick meal, lurched in his direction again and then was abruptly stopped in its tracks by an unknown force. The Giganteas appeared to be battling something invisible. Hadwyn was bewildered.

Mackenzie knew in that moment, his father was still helping. Somehow, he was stopping the Giganteas from further attack. 'Get the Burnstone and get out of there,' he instructed Hadwyn confidently. Hadwyn paused for a moment. 'Now, Hadwyn!' Mackenzie's voice urged again.

Hadwyn gathered his wits, pulled himself up, raced past the Giganteas, scrambled up the stalagmite and seized the Burnstone.

Back in the pool, Jackson witnessed the amber tomb, still holding Tess entrapped, begin to dissolve in the water. As it disappeared, he reached down and hung on to Tess's body to stop her sinking further into the water. Then she began to cough and splutter. Jackson supported her as she tried to stand up. 'Where are we? Where's Buddy? Why are we in water?' she asked, looking very confused.

For once, Jackson was greatly relieved to hear her questions. 'It's a long story, Tess,' Jackson told her. 'Come here,' he beckoned and grabbed her in a big hug. 'I am so glad to see you.'

Tess smiled widely. 'I don't know what's going on,' she said, 'but I like it.'

Hadwyn appeared through the waterfall and swam towards them. 'I'm glad to see you.' He smiled at Tess. 'Let's get out of this water.' They waded over to the water's edge and stood on the snow-covered ground.

'What's that in your hand?' Tess asked. Hadwyn held up the green Burnstone. It was the most beautiful thing she had ever seen. Deep within the amber was a miniature world of tiny plant life, frozen in time. 'I don't see any Salamanders in there,' she queried.

'That's because like you, they have been set free,' Hadwyn told her.

Mackenzie called to the companions. 'Well done, everyone. There's just one more task here in the Forest Lands. Look around you. There must be a door somewhere.'

The group searched their environment to no avail. 'Maybe it's under the water?' Jackson suggested.

'First glance unseen, then with amber green, eyes reveal, path be seen,' Tess reminded the companions.

'That makes no sense,' Jackson quipped.

Mackenzie tried to help. 'There's something you can see now that you have the green Burnstone.' They continued searching high and low, under rocks, along the rock walls. 'It has to be here,' Mackenzie told them. 'You're at the edge of the map.'

Tess was too tired after her ordeal to search any longer and sat on a flat rock near the water's edge. She noticed a few tiny fish swimming by – then, slowly, the water became as still as glass. The surroundings were mirrored beautifully in the water.

'There it is,' Tess exclaimed excitedly. They looked where she was pointing at the mirrored surface of the water and saw a reflection of a door in the rock face beside the waterfall. When they looked up at the actual rock face, there was no door to be seen.

'It's over there,' Hadwyn calculated. 'We will have to swim over and climb to it.'

Several minutes later, the water-drenched companions were feeling the rock wall for the invisible door. Tess almost fell and grabbed onto a shrub. The plant came away from the wall in her hands. Jackson reached out and steadied Tess. 'Well, that was a fortunate stumble,' Jackson told the others. 'Look what we have here.' A rusted door handle had been jutting out of the rock behind the plant. Jackson pulled, but it wouldn't budge. Hadwyn made his way over and pulled as hard as he could. A part of the rock wall began to move. Jackson wedged his dagger in a crack that appeared and then Hadwyn was able to get into a better position. He pulled again and this time the heavy door scraped open. All they could see was a white mist.

'I can't see anything,' Tess queried.

'Never mind,' Mackenzie reassured them all. 'It's time. You're so close to home. Remember, Tess: courage and hope.' One by one, they jumped into the cloud.

HIGH LANDS
NORTHERN LIGHTS
CRAG OF DREAD
HIGH TATRA
FINAL BATTLE
PASS
IRMINSUL
MOTHER STONE
BEEHIVE HUTS
CAVE

HIGH LANDS

19

Austeja, the Bee Goddess

Finally, they had made it to the last level of the game, the High Lands. Hadwyn sat on the dirt floor, leaning against the rock wall, peering out to a great mountain range. They weren't in a deep cave, more of a den.

Jackson, Tess and Buddy lay on the ground fast asleep. Hadwyn waited patiently. He pondered this journey he had been on, the friends he had made and the approaching goodbye. 'Makansee?' he said quietly.

Mackenzie was reading the game manual. He was very hopeful now. They had made it through four levels. Surely, they would make it through the last level. He was reading about the Golden Burnstone.

'Makansee?' Hadwyn said again.

Mackenzie looked up. He closed the game manual so he could see the screen. Hadwyn was still sitting in the cave while the others slept. 'Yes Hadwyn, I'm here,' Mackenzie answered, adjusting his headset so he could hear better.

Hadwyn nodded and began to speak. 'Makansee, I wanted to say thank you for trusting me with your friends' safety. I don't know what you look like. I don't know what your world looks like. But I have learnt that you are a good man and I have become very attached to your friends. I want you to know that I will do everything in my power to get them back to you.'

'Thank you, Hadwyn. I know you will. I know that you could be back at your village, helping your people and searching for your family. We are indebted to you.'

'You too, Makansee? You have family here that you must miss? I hear your father speak. He is a wizard, yes?'

Mackenzie could not explain to Hadwyn how his father was communicating with him, that he had in fact died. He couldn't explain it to himself. He just knew it was happening. Part of Mackenzie didn't want the game to end, but he knew he had no choice. 'Yes Hadwyn, my father is like a wizard. He speaks to me from another world.' If only they could be together in the same world again, Mackenzie wished.

Tess and Jackson slowly began to stir. They sat up, squinting and adjusting to their new surroundings. 'Well, we made it. Look out there,' Hadwyn told them, waving his hand towards the opening. 'The High Lands,' he announced, 'and somewhere out there is the Last Door you speak of.' The three of them stood and walked to the front of the cave, looking out over the High Tatra. They had a vast view of the alpine forest and meadow leading up to the towering, rocky mountain range with snow-covered peaks.

Mackenzie spoke. 'Well, that was really heavy going yesterday and last night, and you haven't really had much sleep. I vote you stay here and rest. I'm going to pause the game and have a rest too, and get all the information I can. We're so close to getting you home … we need to get this right. I suggest you empty all the amber from your pouches and make a barrier across the front of the cave; that will not only keep you warm, it will keep unwelcome visitors away.' And with that, Mackenzie paused the game.

Mackenzie re-assessed everyone's spells and strengths. Both Hadwyn and Jackson still had Furious Strike with their swords. Hadwyn had the Statue and Triple Jump spells. Jackson had Fireball and Skin Shield. Tess had Invisibility, Charm Stare and Replenish Quiver. On top of that, they were all immune to cold thanks to the Salamanders' gift. He would have to talk to Tess and Jackson about how and when to put their weapons and abilities to good use.

Then he read up on the enemy. They would be coming up against a formidable foe: the Great Ambush Bugs. He looked at the picture in the manual. Ugly green and black creatures, with a large upper and smaller lower body separated by a tiny waist. They had big knife-like pincers, long black antennae and bulging yellow eyes. Apparently, once they had their victims in their pincers, they could inject a poison into their prey, causing paralysis. After that, they would suck the insides out of the body. *Well*, Mackenzie thought, *I hope there aren't too many of them.*

Mackenzie kept reading. In the High Lands, the Ambush Bug has taken over the land. The spirit of the bee has been trapped in a Golden Burnstone. The bees have been weakened, no longer able to out-fly their predators. The Ambush Bugs have taken advantage of the bees' weakened state and almost destroyed the whole population. The flowering plants have withered as the pollinators died. The landscape was being changed irreversibly to a time over 130 million years ago, when no flowering plants existed. Mackenzie kept reading. 'Your task in the High Lands is to take on the characteristics of the sacred bees, known since ancient times as bringers of order – hardworking, cooperative and ensuring the welfare of all.'

Mackenzie considered this situation. He was uncertain of how much this game world was blending with the real world, but at school he had learnt that without bees, humans would lose one third of their food supplies. Pretty disastrous, really. If this game world was interconnected with his own world, as he increasingly feared, then this level may be the most crucial of them all. He was feeling a lot of pressure now. He needed to save Tess and Jackson's lives, but maybe he was also saving the connection between humans and bees.

He was getting so tired. It was now two weeks since they had gone missing. He had been playing this game for so many days and nights that it was all starting to blur in his mind. He had to sleep.

Mackenzie tossed and turned through the night. The responsibility ahead weighed heavily on him. He dreamed of battles and giant creatures, of Tess and Jackson being lost, of him not being able to return to the game – and of his father's voice. He awoke in a sweat.

He opened the in-game manual again and re-read it, trying to commit the information to memory. The house was empty, so he assumed his mum had gone out somewhere. He decided to go for a walk to clear his head. On the way out, he grabbed a drink from the fridge; as he walked past the table, he saw a note balanced up against the flower vase. 'Dear Mackenzie, I am at the Taylors'. Help yourself to the sandwiches made up in the fridge. Love always, Mum.' *Interesting*, he thought to himself. He had never thought his mum would be visiting there. Still, he knew his mum. She was very caring. Maybe she had worked her charm on them?

An hour or so later, Mackenzie had returned home and was sitting at the kitchen table, eating his sandwiches and guzzling an enormous glass of chocolate milk. It was 11 am on the wall clock. The back door opened and Mrs Jones came in with her basket full of apples and lemons. It was good to see her. Mrs Jones observed the demolished sandwiches with a look of satisfaction. 'Finally, he emerges from the deep dark cave,' she commented good-humouredly, looking intently at his expression. 'How are things?'

Mackenzie smiled at her poorly disguised investigation into his health. He put his head to one side and gave her a reassuring smile. 'I've just been for a walk in the sun and filled the belly.'

She sat down opposite him at the table. 'That's good, sweetheart. I've been worrying about you. You've been in that room for many days now, you know?'

Mackenzie nodded. 'I know.' He thought for a moment. 'I know it's not ideal but you know, Mum, in the big scheme of things, it's really nothing and it won't be forever. Just for a while, you know. It's a hard time at the moment,' he explained.

'It's okay,' Mrs Jones responded, reaching over and holding his hand.

Back in his room, with a big breath, Mackenzie sat in his bean bag. His bedroom door was closed. A water bottle with some fruit and biscuits sat by his side. He had no idea how long this might take. 'Let's do this,' he said to himself. He grabbed the controller and became alarmed when it would not respond. After some pushing of buttons and turning the TV on and off, he worked out the batteries were possibly flat, so he jumped up and went to his bedside drawer, retrieving two new batteries. 'Thank goodness,' he muttered to himself as he started the game again.

Hadwyn sat waiting for several hours while Jackson and Tess slept. Buddy sniffed around occasionally and spent the rest of his time sitting next to Hadwyn, who unfastened the tie on his pouch and pulled out the four Burnstones. He laid them on the ground in front of him. Red, blue, white and green gems.

It seemed like a lifetime ago when they had met Bemmung, Grand Ruler of the Leliyn Lizards in the Desert Lands. Bemmung had told Hadwyn that he had a strong and courageous heart within him – all he needed to succeed.

Hadwyn then reached over and picked up the Red Burnstone. He thought of Bunyip and the gift of water in a drought-ravaged land. He looked at the Blue Burnstone and remembered Kulibari, Queen of the Leatherback Turtles, who had sacrificed her life so that they could survive underwater. The Green Burnstone had been recovered successfully because the Salamanders had gifted their ability to survive freezing temperatures. The White Burnstone reminded him of the solders responding to whom they thought was Prince Eadric, and showing support for the overthrow of the Amber Knights. He wondered how Lorna was coping, giving up freedom for them and working in the amber factory. Maybe he could return to his homeland and bring about her release.

So many were dependent on the success of this mission. So many were involved and fighting together. They had come so far, been through so much. They were now on the precipice of victory or disaster.

Tess and Jackson had adjusted their clothes, checked their weapons and repacked their amber gems into their pouches. The three of them then sat and considered their final journey in their quest to deliver the five Burnstones to the Last Door. Mackenzie filled them in on his understanding of the Ambush Bugs and how the adventurers might engage with them if a battle ensued. He reminded them of their weapons, skills and spells. 'Keep Buddy in the sling at all times unless we know it's safe,' Mackenzie instructed Jackson. 'Now, firstly you're going to walk down there, through that grassy valley,' he said, 'and later you'll begin climbing into the mountains.' The companions looked at the mountain range. There was much ground to be covered.

The companions set off, finding their way between grey rocks and alpine flowers. Buddy was very much enjoying a scamper alongside the group. They climbed higher and higher as the day wore on. Up ahead, they could see craggy mountaintops covered in snow. 'I wonder if the Last Door is up there somewhere?' Tess queried.

'Well one thing we can be sure of,' Jackson replied, 'is that it won't be a walk in the park.'

Hadwyn spoke. 'Somewhere we will meet a guide, who will let us know where to go.'

'Did you say it was the bees in trouble in the High Lands?' Tess asked for clarification. 'Because there are lots of bees buzzing around these flowers here.'

Mackenzie answered, 'Yes, it's definitely the bees. I guess we'll just have to wait and see how things unfold.'

The valley narrowed. Their path travelled along one side of the valley, following a rocky wall. As they came around a bend, they caught sight of several odd-shaped structures built up against the rock wall. Hadwyn paused in front of the others. Jackson grabbed Buddy and secured him on a twine lead. The structures were made of rock and mud, shaped like domes with small front entranceways. Hadwyn walked forward slowly, looking for signs of activity. There appeared to be none.

Finally, he reached the doorway and peered in. It seemed to be empty. Cautiously, he stepped inside. The other two followed. 'Um, these walls look like honeycomb,' Tess volunteered. The inside of the hut was completely circular. Small openings served as windows or air vents. At the rear of the hut was another small doorway, leading into a small dark tunnel. 'I can smell honey,' Tess said, venturing into the tunnel.

'Who goes there?' a voice spoke.

Jackson reached in and grabbed Tess's cape, pulling her back towards him. 'I'm not losing you again,' he insisted.

The voice spoke again. 'Is that the wayfarers?' Hadwyn stepped forward and bent down to enter the tunnel. He made his way along the dark tunnel, which was about two metres long, and then came to the opening to another circular room. The others followed. He straightened himself up and looked around. To his left sat a beautiful woman dressed completely in gold: a shining gown, sparkling necklaces and bracelets, jewels in her golden hair piled high up on her head. The golden attire complemented her flawless bronze skin. Her lips shone gold and her eyes were brown. She sat upon a golden throne in front of a honeycomb wall. 'I see you have arrived,' she announced.

The other two had bustled in behind Hadwyn and now stood each side of him, speechless. The golden lady stood up. 'I am Austeja, the Bee Goddess. Your arrival has been anticipated. Please sit down,' she invited, indicating towards stone benches that circled the room. Once they were seated, she returned to her throne and sat down. 'You are here to save us. Our land is in peril. We depend on nectar and pollen to survive. Flowering plants need us to survive. The humans are dependent on the foods of these plants. You must understand that we are all connected in a sacred system. We are all in this together. And remember,' she added in an ominous tone, 'this is not a game. This is life and death.'

'Yes Goddess,' Hadwyn responded, 'we are definitely aware that this is no longer a game. We await your guidance.'

Austeja continued, 'In the past, we could fly faster than these Ambush Bugs. Now they are overgrown, hunting all insect life with voracious appetites. They have destroyed our hives, so now we build these places, hiding where they cannot enter. Our population is shrinking. The flowers are neglected and dying. You must find the Golden Amber Burnstone and release our spirit,' she said in a commanding voice.

At that moment, a swarm of bees came hurtling through the entrance tunnel and flew straight over to form several hundred lines in front of Austeja. Their buzzing was very loud. She appeared to listen for a time then raised her hand. The buzzing stopped. Austeja then moved her hands in some type of sign language. As fast as they had appeared, the swarm flew through to a deeper tunnel and out of sight. 'You have a question, child?' she asked, looking straight at Tess.

Startled, Tess blurted out, 'Yes, I was wondering how come there are flowers and bees out there?'

Austeja looked very serious. 'The Ambush Bugs are yet to cross the Great Gap. Beyond the Gap, they have destroyed almost all the insects, bees and flowering plants. We seldom venture there except for patrolling and monitoring their movements. For now, this side of the Great Gap is safe. We have built our shelters here and we nurture our eggs and infant bees. We have also been developing our drones into larger soldier bees by raising them on the precious royal jelly. This is our attempt to adjust, to find a way to defeat these monsters, just in case you never came. But now, we can depend on your intervention to put things right.'

'What's the Great Gap?' Jackson asked.

'The Great Gap is a deep ravine that breaks the path to the high mountains. There is a great fallen tree which you can use to cross. Make use of the Sticky Sap from the milkweed flower that I will give you. Apply it to your hands and feet to help your grip and don't cross in the wind.' Austeja rose and walked over to a cavity in the wall that held wax candles and bowls. 'I must consider the divination of the beeswax,' she announced. Austeja brought a few items to a stone in the centre of the hut. She held wax in her hand that warmed and melted, dripping into the bowl of cold water below. Then she watched as the wax formed into particular shapes as it solidified in the cold water.

She stood for a long time, looking into the bowl. Eventually she turned to the companions. 'You must await the appearance of the Bee Hive Cluster, a constellation of stars that will inform you when good weather is ahead so that you may travel east. The Golden Burnstone is imprisoned in the great Irminsul, the Mother Stone of our land. The Ambush Bugs guard the Irminsul. You must try to harness the gift of the bee spirit to maintain focus and perseverance on this dangerous quest.'

Jackson asked, 'Please, Goddess. Can you tell us more about Irminsul?'

Austeja continued. 'The Irminsul is a sacred rock structure in the mountains. When our land was in harmony and balance, this was a meeting place for all the creatures in our lands to meet at the beginning of our Tatra season. This is when the high Tatra is painted blue by the sky and all creatures come together as one. This has been a safe place where predators and prey could meet without fear, to explore factors impacting on our shared survival. We would meet for three moons. This way, we all worked together and maintained the ancient knowledge of balance, life and death. We called the Irminsul our Mother Stone, a place of safety and nurturance.'

'It sounds like a beautiful place,' Tess responded earnestly. 'I hope we can rescue the bee spirit and return things to the right way.' A buzzing sound preceded several small swarms of bees re-entering the chamber from within the hive system, with each swarm carrying various items to the Bee Goddess. They carefully lowered the items onto the stone table like a hovering helicopter, then departed.

Austeja spoke again. 'Supplies for your venture. For each of you, a vial of honey to sustain your energy, the Sticky Sap to help climb, and beeswax twine – also for climbing.' The three travellers moved forward and took the gifts, finding space in their pouches and attaching the twine to their belts. 'Now you must await the appearance of the stars. On your travels, take heed of caves that have empty carcasses around their entrance. These are the remains of the Ambush Bugs' meals after they have sucked the insides out of the poor creatures. Remember that they are superior hunters. They can alter their colour to camouflage themselves in their surroundings and lie in wait, ready to ambush their prey – and now, you are that prey.'

The travellers were made to feel at home as they awaited the sign to commence their journey. They were well fed with honey and flower petals, and shown where fresh berries grew close by. Austeja took them deeper into the hive to see the egg chambers and precious larvae readying for the birth of baby bees. Finally, they were taken to a special chamber where the male drones were being fed and bathed in royal jelly by the worker bees. The drones had developed to the size of a small horse. They were hoping that soon, the drones might match the Ambush Bugs in battle.

The only area that was forbidden was the Queen Bee's chamber. They were told that her work producing eggs was imperative for their survival, so she could not be disturbed. Austeja also explained that normally, new queens would be born and fly off to make new hives – but because of the Ambush Bugs, this was no longer possible. This was their last queen.

The travellers had learnt a great deal and rested well. Finally, after waiting through Saturday and Sunday night, a surveillance bee came on Monday evening with news of the Bee Hive Cluster stars becoming visible in the eastern sky. It was time to leave.

20

Assassins of the High Tatra

TUESDAY morning

They waited for first light to make their departure. The uphill climb continued towards the east as the morning sun rose higher. Clear skies prevailed, just as predicated by the stars. Buddy had scampered alongside them for a couple of hours when Tess noticed a change in their surroundings. The flowers were gone; just grey rock and grass beneath their feet.

After stopping for a rest, they marched on, finally turning north through a narrow pass into a higher valley that ran alongside high rocky cliffs. After they had ventured along for a while, Hadwyn turned to the others and suggested they get their weapons at the ready, as he had spotted a mound of insect, reptile and bird carcasses ahead. 'Remember, Tess: if you get into trouble, activate your Invisibility spell. Jackson, I suggest we burn them with your Fireballs and freeze them with my Statue spell before trying to battle these beasts.'

They managed to get past the carcasses without trouble but were on high alert, as they knew now that they were in Ambush Bug territory.

The wind picked up, whipping their capes against their legs. They pulled their hoods down over their heads. Although they had the gift of withstanding freezing temperatures from the Salamanders, they still felt the cold. Buddy was tucked into the sling once again, worn out. As the day progressed and their slow climb continued, the wind howled around them. 'So much for good weather,' Jackson commented.

'I think this is good weather for the High Tatra,' Hadwyn suggested, 'no rain, no snow, no blizzard.'

'Really?' Jackson answered, 'perhaps you spoke too soon.' They all looked up and saw snowflakes beginning to float down.

'Well, no blizzard,' Hadwyn corrected.

They pressed on for another hour or two, their legs working harder as they trudged along the ground that was becoming carpeted in a fine coating of snow. The howling wind made it hard to hear each other. Up ahead, Hadwyn noticed a stand of pine trees and he could just make out a fallen tree with what looked like a dry space underneath. 'Let's take shelter in there for a while,' he yelled. They turned into the wind and made for the shelter.

Huddled together under the tree, they reflected on what might lie ahead. 'Do you think we're going to make it home, Hadwyn?' Tess asked, stating what was on all their minds. 'I mean, even if we get to the Last Door, what's on the other side? It could be another level, another world.'

Hadwyn looked down for a moment. 'Well, I can't promise to know what is behind that door, but I can promise you I will get you to the door and we will face whatever happens together.'

Jackson tried to lighten the mood. 'Well, imagine Mum and Dad's faces when they see us.'

Tess smiled, nodding. 'And we get to see Mackenzie again,' she remembered happily. She put her head to one side and looked at Hadwyn. 'But wait. What will happen to you, Hadwyn?'

Jackson and Hadwyn were silent until Hadwyn answered. 'We will face whatever happens together.' Tess was very confused.

Over the howling wind, the three of them heard another howl, but high-pitched. Buddy's ears pricked up and he let out a whine. 'It's a puppy,' Tess told the others, 'I can hear a puppy out there in the cold.'

Jackson looked doubtful. 'Why would a puppy be up here?'

Tess looked distressed. 'I don't know, but we need to help it,' she declared.

'Now wait a minute,' Hadwyn interjected, 'it could be dangerous out there. You mind Buddy, and Jackson and I will go and look around.' The two boys headed out into the wind and snow, which was reducing their visibility to about ten metres now.

'It's coming from over there.' Jackson pointed with his sword. They turned in the directions of the cliffs and tramped on. The sound became much louder; before long, they spotted the pup alone in the snow, howling.

The pup was quite large, bigger than a normal dog, but its young age was given away by the soulful cry. Just as they were about to approach the terrified creature, something much bigger appeared through the swirling snow. It was an Ambush Bug and it was ready to devour the pup.

'Here we go,' Hadwyn yelled. 'But we're too close to the pup to use our spells,' he warned.

The boys ran at the Ambush Bug together, ready to strike and defend themselves against attack. Their swords clanged against the pincers of the Ambush Bug. The wind howled around them. Out of the corner of his eye, Hadwyn saw the pup being pulled toward the shelter. Tess had heard the commotion, tied Buddy up in the shelter and raced out to help, using her Invisibility spell to avoid being attacked by the Ambush Bugs.

The boys continued holding the Ambush Bug back when another appeared at its side. With the pup now out of danger, Hadwyn employed his Statue spell, causing one Ambush Bug to freeze. A third Ambush Bug appeared through the mist. 'Fireballs, Jackson. Now!' he yelled, swinging his huge sword back and forth towards the two Ambush Bugs.

Jackson fumbled with cold hands in his pouch, but soon was casting Fireball and flinging the glowing flames in the direction of their attackers. The two Ambush Bugs exploded into hissing flames.

'Let's get out of here,' Hadwyn called to Jackson. They turned in the direction of the shelter, ready to run when, to their horror, another two Ambush Bugs blocked their way. The Ambush Bugs came at them – huge green monstrosities with black lumpy backs and bulging red eyes. The boys made ready their defensive postures when abruptly the Ambush Bugs became distracted, writhing and squirming around. Something was attacking them from another direction. Hadwyn thought he saw huge dogs but didn't want to waste time investigating, instead taking the opportunity to escape. He grabbed Jackson and pulled him from the fray.

Back under cover, they could hear the sound of the fight continuing for another ten minutes or so. Finally, it came to an end. Tess was cuddling the pup and giving it comfort after its terrifying ordeal. Buddy was wagging his tail and trying to make friends with it. Then they heard a long wolf howl.

'Uh, oh,' Hadwyn commented, looking at the pup, 'that's not a dog, it's a wolf cub … and I think that's its mother howling.' They saw dark shapes moving about in the falling snow. The shapes came closer and closer – and seemed to be circling them. 'Keep your swords ready,' Hadwyn whispered to Jackson.

Out of nowhere, a great snarling wolf appeared in front of them, teeth bared in a deep growl. Just as quickly, another wolf pounced on the first and they fought ferociously. They were huge, at least as tall as horses. The other wolves continued circling. The snarling wolf let out a yelp and ran off cowering, while the wolf that attacked it now turned and walked slowly over towards the group. To their surprise, the wolf spoke. 'You have my child.'

Hadwyn reached for the pup and placed it on the ground toward the front of the shelter. The pup scampered over to its mother.

'I am Conwennam, mother of Felan,' The mother wolf bent down and licked the pup's head. 'I am in your debt. You saved Felan's life. I apologise for Gunnolf's aggressive behaviour. He has just come from battle and acted in haste. We mean you no harm.' A larger wolf came up beside Conwennam. 'And this is our leader, Bodolf,' she introduced.

'We have smelt you on the wind,' Bodolf told them. 'Would you be the travellers of the prophecy?'

Hadwyn came out from the shelter and stood in front of Bodolf. 'Yes sir, I believe so. I can only hope that our quest succeeds, but we still have much to get through.'

Bodolf gave a long slow nod and looked at Conwennam. 'We are at your service. Our children are not safe and these abominable creatures are destroying our land. We will escort you to the Mother Stone.'

With great relief, the companions were soon hanging on to the wolves' manes as they galloped across the land at great speed. Conwennam had taken her son back to the lair. Bodolf and two of his fastest and bravest wolves, Ulmar and Kader, carried the travellers on their backs with great ease. They leapt across ravines and bolted up slopes heavy with snow. Nothing stopped them. They kept running and leaping until the sun had disappeared and the moon was rising.

They came to a stop on the edge of a frozen lake. 'The Irminsul,' Bodolf announced. They looked across the lake and caught sight of the massive stone structure, the Mother Stone. In the moonlight it looked magnificent and ancient. Glowing lights escaped from crevices in the rocks, lighting up its unique shape and sacredness. The Golden Amber Burnstone was somewhere within. There were also about six giant Ambush Bugs perched at different locations on the rock, standing guard.

'Our Mother Stone must be restored,' Bodolf declared. 'She is our symbol of hope and wisdom. She holds the memories and wisdom of our ancestors – of the balance that we must not lose. We will get you safely behind the Mother Stone and then we will distract the Ambush Bugs. You must find the stairs hidden near the bottom. Climb as far as you can. You will find a holding place carved out in the rocks, and within this a shallow well. In this, you will find the Burnstone.'

'I can go,' Tess suggested. 'I can be invisible.' The boys looked at each other. Bodolf waited.

'Very well,' Hadwyn agreed. 'Jackson and I can wait at the bottom of the stairs and defend any attack.'

Bodolf nodded. The three great grey wolves crept stealthily around to the rear of the structure, under the cover of trees. 'Wait till you hear them – then you will know we have their attention,' Bodolf instructed. The companions slipped down to the soft snow and the wolves ran off.

There were loud rasping sounds, like sandpaper on wood. It was the Ambush Bugs reacting to intruders out front; they were responding by rubbing two parts of their body together.

The companions at the rear of the structure quickly located the stairs. Tess nodded silently to them, commanded her Invisibility spell and was gone from sight. The boys waited, on edge, hearing the sound of disruption from the front and hoping Tess would not take too long.

Tess raced up the stairs and, to her dismay, discovered an Ambush Bug in the room. The Golden Burnstone lay immersed in sacred water, in a bowl-shaped indentation on the floor. After pausing a moment, she remembered she was invisible – so she went forward, grabbed the Burnstone and fled back down the stairs.

The startled Ambush Bug, aroused, pursuing the floating Burnstone. Tess jumped the last few steps to the ground and warned the boys she was being chased. Hadwyn quickly raised his arm and waited for the Ambush Bug to appear before he threw his Statue spell, freezing it in its tracks. They quickly fled back to the tree line and waited.

The wolves reappeared and the travellers were instructed to climb aboard. With angry Ambush Bugs in pursuit of the wolves, they bounded away from danger.

Once a good distance from the Irminsul, the wolves stopped. Back on firm ground, Tess handed the Golden Burnstone to Hadwyn for safekeeping. They had done it. They had all five Burnstones.

'This is where we part,' Bodolf informed them.

'I am uncertain of the location of the Last Door,' Hadwyn confessed.

'I understand,' the great wolf answered. 'I will summon the northern lights.' With that, Bodolf began a long howl, his neck extended towards the night sky. Slowly, the sky became illuminated by swirling blue and purple lights. Bodolf turned back to the travellers. His eyes were vibrant blue and purple, matching the northern lights. 'Now watch where the lights reveal.' The dancing lights swirled around, eventually gathering over one particular high mountain peak on a distant mountain range. 'There is your door. The door where everything ends,' Bodolf announced. 'Follow the light.'

They parted company and the companions set off toward the mountain. Their way was lit by moonlight and the bright glow of the northern lights reflecting on the snow.

Back in his well-worn bean bag, Mackenzie became alarmed when the TV and game console suddenly stopped working. 'What could possibly have happened?' he asked himself worriedly. He jumped up and raced out to locate his mother. She was in the kitchen, lighting a candle. 'What's going on, Mum?' he demanded in a stressed voice.

Mrs Jones looked a little sheepish. 'I'm sorry Mackenzie, I forgot to pay the electric bill. With everything that happened, it just got lost under other papers and I forgot. Never mind now, I can ring them tomorrow and maybe get it back on tomorrow or the next day.'

Mackenzie was beyond comprehending this. It was more than two weeks since Jackson and Tess had gone missing and they had spent about fifteen nights in the game. Now they were so close to the end. It was really starting to take a toll on his nerves. 'I can't wait that long, Mum. I need it back on now,' he demanded.

Mrs Jones looked at Mackenzie. It wasn't like him to speak this way. 'Now listen, I realise this has been a terrible time but you still need to be understanding and respectful. You're not the only one struggling.'

Mackenzie shook his head. 'No, Mum. You don't understand – I need power. I'm in the middle of something extremely important.'

He was indeed acting very strangely. Was it stress? She was uncertain how to deal with this. 'Mackenzie, you have to be realistic,' she started.

'You just don't understand. You'd never understand,' he yelled.

Taken back by his anger, Mrs Jones paused. Her son was deeply disturbed by whatever was going on for him, so she decided to take a chance. 'Just try me. Maybe I will understand.'

Mackenzie didn't know what to do. He sat on the couch next to his mother and swore her to secrecy. She sat, patiently wondering what could possibly be so distressing. Mackenzie told his mother everything that had happened. She sat quietly, trying to listen respectfully and not make light of what he was telling her, no matter how far-fetched it sounded. She watched him cry when he spoke of communicating with his father. She listened to the fanciful stories of battling monsters and saving his friends. What was she do with him?

'You don't believe me, do you?' Mackenzie demanded.

Mrs Jones had a helpless look on her face. 'I can't believe it.'

'When have I ever lied to you?' he challenged.

'Mackenzie, you are asking me to believe that two humans are inside an electronic game,' she said.

'You can't prove I'm wrong,' he contested.

'No, that's right,' she agreed.

'But I can prove I'm right. Please help me, Mum.'

Mrs Jones was at her wit's end by now and willing to do just about anything. 'What do you need me to do?' she asked.

'Take me to the Taylors,' said Mackenzie. 'They have a console and it's about time they know what's going on with their kids anyway.'

'Mackenzie, I don't think we should be upsetting them any more than they already are,' Mrs Jones replied.

'I should never have told you,' Mackenzie shouted and stormed off to his room.

Desperate, Mrs Jones rang the Taylors and spoke to Margaret. They had become quite close and mutually supportive over the past week. 'Look, I'm terribly sorry to bother you but I have a problem on my hands,' she began. 'I'm not sure that Mackenzie isn't having some type of breakdown. He's imagining that Jackson and Tess are in his game and he wants to show us all. Our power is off and he's insisting I bring him to your place.'

Margaret asked for a moment to speak with her husband Sam and soon came back to the phone. 'Teri, bring him down. If there's anything we can do to help, so be it. Maybe he needs to see for himself that it's just his imagination. I guess we all respond differently to loss.'

In less than an hour, Mackenzie was setting up the game in the Taylors' house. Margaret, Sam and Teri sat quietly on the couch, watching as requested, occasionally looking at one another. The game began, and the screen lit up to a mountain scene. Three game characters appeared to be walking along a mountain path. Mackenzie used his controller to make Hadwyn tap Jackson on the shoulder.

'Hey, you two,' Mackenzie spoke, 'turn around and look up at the sky.' The two characters turned and as they looked up, their faces became clearly visible to the three adults sitting on the couch. It was Jackson and Tess.

Margaret screamed. Sam rushed to the TV and looked closer at his children, calling out to them. Teri looked at the TV and then her son. Her eyes filled with tears. She now realised what he had been going through, what he had been carrying alone, and she remembered him telling her of his communication with his father. 'Oh Simon,' she said under her breath.

Mackenzie paused the game again to allow them to calm down. They were all in shock. There was no way he could concentrate on the final quest with all this going on around him. With the game paused, all they could see was a still shot.

'I am so sorry, Mackenzie,' said Teri.

'It's okay, Mum. I get how hard it was for you,' Mackenzie reassured her.

Margaret was asking multiple questions and crying. 'Margaret, I think Mackenzie should tell you both what he has shared with me,' said Teri. 'He really needs to try to help them come back to you, but he won't be able to do that until we let him do what's needed without interruption.'

Mackenzie proceeded to repeat the story to the Taylors, from the very beginning. 'Why didn't you tell us before?' Margaret asked.

'Would you have believed me?' Mackenzie put to her.

21

The Last Door

It took Mackenzie at least an hour to relay his story to the Taylors and answer all their questions. Eventually, they grasped the reality and the gravity of the situation. 'Do what you need to do, son,' Sam told Mackenzie. 'Just tell us if there's anything we can do to help.'

Mackenzie nodded. 'Thanks, Mr Taylor, but all I really need is that no one interrupts. I can't afford to be distracted. It's extremely dangerous.'

Mr Taylor looked over at his wife. 'Did you hear that, Margaret? If it gets too hard to watch, you'll need to leave the room.' Margaret nodded anxiously.

Teri grabbed her hand in a comforting gesture. 'He's got them this far, Margaret – he'll get them home,' she said reassuringly.

The sound of howling wind could be heard as Mackenzie resumed the game. Buddy had been packed in the sling with amber gems and his head covered to keep him warm. The companions continued to tramp through the snow, leaning into the wind as the night wore on. The path became rockier and nearly all signs of vegetation had disappeared. Brown and grey rocky areas were interrupted by increasingly larger patches of snow. Jackson kept close behind Tess, reaching out and steadying her each time she stumbled. The path was becoming more and more precarious on the steep climb. They slowed down to carefully negotiate safe footing. From time to time, when their view opened up, Hadwyn looked up to locate the northern lights and keep them on track.

WEDNESDAY

Finally, a hint of morning light appeared through the snowy mist. They could see better where to put their feet, but visibility ahead was limited to about five metres. Hadwyn had been carrying Tess on his back for a few hours and her sleeping head bumped against his shoulder blade with each step. Snowflakes had accumulated on top of her hood. Oblivious to her surroundings, Tess did not see the steep ravine they had travelled through, with slippery rocks and treacherous ledges. When she did begin to wake up, they had started climbing a very steep slope with knee-deep snow. It was slow progress. She looked up and saw high mountain peaks all around them. She knew that somewhere above her, they would find the Last Door.

Hadwyn had used the beeswax twine to attach Jackson to himself for safety. Jackson was struggling the most, with no one to carry him and having to use human legs, unlike Hadwyn. The climb was exhausting him. Every so often, Hadwyn turned around to check on Jackson and could see his red cheeks and panting breath steaming from his mouth. They stopped every ten minutes or so, allowing Jackson to recover his breath.

Back in the Taylors' house, Margaret clutched her husband's hand for support. She held her breath. Her heart felt as though it had stopped beating.

At one point the travellers came across a gap in the rocks, a crevice that they could climb into to take cover from the wind for a while. The sun was higher now and they had more light, glaringly so where it reflected off the snow. Jackson sat against a rock wall, eyes closed, recovering. Tess was by his side, offering water and food while patting Buddy reassuringly. Hadwyn was walking around to different vantage points, investigating the climb ahead. When he looked back at the path they had traversed this morning, he could see they had climbed above the clouds.

Mackenzie spoke to Hadwyn, providing information from the maps he could read. 'You're going through a valley of rocks. Up ahead you'll eventually come to a wide-open area of snow slopes surrounded by the highest peaks. We have to get up those slopes and locate the beginning of the climb to the Crag of Dread.'

'I don't like the sound of that,' Hadwyn replied. 'I have heard of this place where others have climbed and never returned.'

After a good hour's rest, Hadwyn encouraged the others onward. 'While we have light, we must press on. I don't fancy climbing cliffs in the night,' he explained. Hadwyn continued carrying Tess. Jackson had Buddy safely tucked away.

A couple of hours passed. They took rest breaks, especially for Jackson. They were so grateful for the everlasting water from Bunyip and the anti-freezing ability from the Salamanders. The Bee Goddess's honey gave them much-needed energy to continue on the long, arduous trek.

Finally, they came to a gap between high rocks and as they stepped through, before their eyes and stretching all the way to the base of the distant mountains ahead, they saw the great white slopes. 'The Crag of Dread is up there,' Hadwyn told them, pointing to a row of sharp mountain peaks. 'Let's get you home,' he said, stepping down on to the snowy slope.

Soon, the three of them looked like tiny ants making their way up the great white slopes. The day was getting on. Midday came and went. Lengthening shadows crept across the vast expanse of snow as the sun slowly disappeared behind the great mountain range. They chatted amongst themselves, reflecting on the journey they had shared and the approaching goodbye. 'I don't know if we will ever see you again, Hadwyn,' Tess began, 'I wish you could come with us.'

Hadwyn looked fondly at his young friend. 'I too will struggle with this farewell … but my people, my family need me just as yours need you. We have all grown close and parting is difficult, but I am very glad that I had the chance to meet you. It is hardest to say goodbye to those we care about the most,' he added, glancing over at Jackson, who was looking down at his hand and feeling his amber ring. 'You saved my life, Tess. You and Jackson have helped me restore my reputation with the druids and I am now free to help my people. I will be forever grateful and I will never forget you.'

Tess ran over to Hadwyn's side and hugged him. Hadwyn hugged his young friend back as his eyes took in the almost vertical cliff ahead. *Courage and hope*, he thought, *a lot of hope*.

At the pace they were walking, Hadwyn and Mackenzie had estimated they would be at the base of the cliff in about thirty minutes. Mackenzie was on high alert. His friends were out in the open. The snow was starting to fall again and the wind was picking up. He just hoped all the battles were behind them. Sitting beside him, transfixed, his mother and Mr and Mrs Taylor barely breathed.

Off to the left on the map, Mackenzie noticed something moving towards them. To his horror, it looked like an army. 'Hadwyn, look to your left. We have trouble.'

The group turned and looked with dismay. There were at least one hundred horsemen coming through between two mountains. They made no noise in the snow. Hadwyn could see the unmistakable black crosses on the tunics. 'Amber Knights … and we have nowhere to hide,' Hadwyn stated. 'Just leave this to me,' he advised the others. 'If we get separated, try to get to those boulders at the base of the mountain. You might get cover in there. If I don't return, start climbing.'

Both Tess and Jackson looked alarmed. Mackenzie sat still, full of apprehension. His mind was racing. How did the Amber Knights turn up in this level? If they had broken through the game barriers, what else had broken through? Surely, they weren't going to be captured, not now, not so close to home?

Within minutes the knights were upon the group. 'Name!' the leader demanded.

'Darius,' he answered, remembering one of the names of his mercenary band.

'And where are you from?'

'I know not my origin. I have been with the mercenaries since boyhood,' Hadwyn replied.

'A mercenary?' the leader repeated. 'We are in need of more men,' he said, laughing with his men. 'And who are your companions?'

'Children,' Hadwyn responded, 'I found them lost.'

'We are in need of more workers at Palanga,' the leader spoke menacingly.

'I am taking them over the mountains in search of their family, sir,' said Hadwyn.

'Perhaps you will all kindly empty your pouches and pockets.' The leader smiled. 'We must always check that we do not have amber thieves on our hands.'

Hadwyn's heart sank. Mackenzie felt sick. They were so close to the climb, to the Last Door – now this.

The sound of a battle horn pierced the wind. Hadwyn looked behind the knights and saw another, equally big group of horsemen charging towards them. 'Formation!' the leader of the knights yelled. The Amber Knights rapidly swung their horses around, preparing for the onslaught coming from behind them.

In the confusion and disruption, Hadwyn motioned to Jackson and Tess to follow him. They ran from the scene toward the cliffs. As he looked over his shoulder, Hadwyn saw that the other horsemen were villagers. They were rising up. The two groups were in earnest battle. The knights had not noticed the companions' escape.

Several moments later, Hadwyn stopped. He could not believe what he could see. Mackenzie too, sat helplessly, feeling absolute dread. Amassed across the slopes ahead, in between the companions and the cliff they needed to climb, were throngs of enemies facing them. There before them in great numbers were all the creatures from previous battles, joined as one: the Whistling Spiders, Trap-Jaw Ants, Spider Crabs, Giganteas and Ambush Bugs. Somehow, they had broken through from their own lands, through to the final level of the game – and they had no intention of letting the companions achieve their final goals. They were going to fight to the death before giving up their power. 'What the hell?' Jackson yelled.

'We're going to die,' Tess cried. Behind them, they could hear the battle between the horsemen. The three companions stood frozen to the spot. They didn't stand a chance.

The massed army moved towards them. The ground shook. Tess, who was on Hadwyn's back, buried her face in Hadwyn's cape, feeling absolute terror.

'Something's happening,' Jackson called out. They looked up at the sky behind them and saw the northern lights approaching from behind them. Soon the whole sky was vivid blue, green and purple. Through the mist, hundreds of wolves sped towards the companions. They recognised Bodolf, Ulmar and Kader.

'Climb on,' Bodolf instructed as Ulmar and Kader waited with him. The rest of the pack continued towards the enemy army. 'You have more defenders,' he told them, pointing to hundreds of giant Frilled-Neck Lizards led by Mungo Man, riding Bemmung towards the battle from their right. 'And there.' He indicated up towards the crest of a smaller mountain on their right. They could see Gwydion, the High Wizard, standing atop the mountain with his staff pointed towards the battle, as hundreds of Fire Salamanders raced down the slopes towards battle. The Salamanders glowed red with flames all over their bodies. 'We must make haste,' Bodolf called out. The three great wolves ran towards the cliff with the companions safely on their backs.

'I can't bear it,' Mrs Taylor called out. Mr Taylor held his wife closer to him.

'Don't watch, Margaret,' he told her. Mackenzie's mum was now sitting right beside her son, leaning up against his bean bag. Mackenzie stared intently at the screen. 'Can't you do something?' Mr Taylor called out in anguish to Mackenzie.

'I can't. I've just got to trust Hadwyn,' he informed them. 'He hasn't let us down yet.'

As the three wolves sped across the great snow slopes towards the cliff, the companions could see the defenders and enemies clashing to their left. Hundreds of creatures battled on the slopes. The gathering of the Burnstones in each level had freed the spirits of those who had been trapped for centuries, and now they sought recovery of the balance. They now matched their enemies' size and each side fought for supremacy.

Blood-curdling screams and shrieks reached their ears. Blood spread across the battlefield. Dead creatures and severed limbs littered the slopes. The battle continued to rage.

As the wolves made ground leaping though the snow, about five Giganteas came rapidly from the battleground, launching an attack on the wolves. Bodolf commanded the travellers to climb off their backs and get behind them. The companions quickly dismounted. At least five Giganteas were swinging their sharp pincers at the wolves. Ulmar let out a high-pitched yelp as pincers closed in around his body, piercing his lungs and squeezing the life out of his body. Within seconds, his bloodied carcass lay dead in the snow.

Kader and Bodolf continued to fight the Giganteas, but were struggling to hold them back. Behind the Giganteas, Trap-Jaw Ants and Whistling Spiders were approaching. Flame-covered Salamanders were leaping onto their backs and trying to destroy them in flames, many erupting into fire. It looked very bad. Hadwyn decided they should make a run for it. There was about sixty metres between them and the bottom of the cliff. He motioned to Tess to get on his back and beckoned Jackson to follow.

They started running but to their dismay, the remainder of the giant creatures on the battlefield turned and moved rapidly in their direction. Jackson tripped and fell into the snow. Hadwyn stopped and turned around. The enemies were almost upon them. Hadwyn yanked Jackson upright and looked at the approaching hoards. They weren't going to make it.

Hadwyn's head bent down and he closed his eyes in a moment of defeat. He was a skilled mercenary, but this was not a battle that could be won. He felt an overwhelming sense of failure.

'Hadwyn, look,' Tess called, tapping him on his shoulder.

Looking out towards the enemy. Hadwyn now saw what looked like long branches emerging out of the snow, like large wooden hands with long fingers walking across the ground. 'The Pinaceae Drifters,' he almost whispered.

The group looked on in amazement as the Pinaceae Drifters fully emerged from the earth and snow, walking like giant wooden hands, joining together to make a great wooden fence that prevented the enemy from coming further. From high above, standing together on top of the smaller mountain, Gwydion, the High Wizard of the Trees and Bandruí, the Woodland Druid watched their handiwork. Gwydion had his wand pointed towards the Pinaceae Drifters and Bandruí held her druid staff high above her head with both hands as it glowed with power. Hadwyn caught sight of them. 'They are protecting us. Run, Jackson!' he yelled.

Within minutes, they had reached the bottom of the Crag of Dread. They looked up at the almost vertical cliff face that rose up about as high as a twenty-five-storey building. Mackenzie called out to them, instructing Hadwyn to tether the others to him with the beeswax twine. Hadwyn would be leading the way. He attached a shorter length of twine to Tess so that she was close behind him, and Jackson was behind her. Mackenzie hoped Hadwyn would be able to hold them if either or both fell. He reminded them to apply the Sticky Sap, given to them by the Bee Goddess, to their hands and feet to help with their grip on the rocks. He instructed Jackson to enact his Skin Shield spell. This was the final climb.

It was slow going as Hadwyn looked for footholds in the rock wall. Tess couldn't always reach them with her shorter legs, so he would turn and hoist her up behind him. The snowstorm was worsening again. The wind whistled past their ears and snow splattered on their faces. Onward they progressed, step by step.

Hadwyn heard Jackson's yell over the top of the wind. He turned and saw Jackson swinging his sword against at least five Eye-Pokers flying nearby, trying to attack him. Their huge bodies were being tossed around by the high winds, impeding their ability to get at him.

Back in the Taylors' house, Margaret rushed from the room. She couldn't bear watching anymore, and she didn't want to break Mackenzie's concentration and put her children at further risk. Mr Taylor sat beside Mackenzie, tense and deadly quiet.

Hadwyn climbed back down to Jackson's side and tried to keep Tess behind him. They were about halfway up the cliff face. They both hung on to a rock with one hand and swung their swords at the beasts with the other hand. Jackson let out a yell as one of the Eye-Pokers got hold of his arm. He lost his footing and his swords fell away below. The Skin Shield spell was protecting Jackson's arm from injury, but he couldn't break free. Hadwyn grabbed Jackson by his other arm and pulled him closer, but to no avail; the Eye-Poker was too strong and ripped Jackson from Hadwyn's grasp. The twine between Hadwyn and Jackson pulled violently as Jackson fell, swinging in the air in the grip of the Eye-Poker. They were all going to be pulled off the rock.

Then the Eye-Poker released Jackson, who fell hard back against the rock, hanging precariously by the twine attached to Hadwyn and Tess. The jolt strained the twine connecting them all. Tess and Hadwyn grabbed at the rocky crevices to prevent themselves from being pulled off the rocks and falling.

'Dad! Dad! Are you there? Please help us. Please, if you can,' Mackenzie called out in anguish. Teri's eyes filled with tears. She felt so helpless. This was a nightmare.

Hadwyn used all his strength to slowly winch Jackson up to them. Just as Jackson found safe footing, Hadwyn was struck by an arrow, piercing him through his shoulder. Blood spurted from the wound. He put his hand up to try to stem the bleeding. Mackenzie quickly checked Hadwyn's health. Alarmingly it was down to twenty per cent. Would he make it to the top?

More arrows hit the rocks beside them. They looked down and saw Amber Knights gathered below, taking aim. They needed to climb higher, out of the arrows' range. They heard the battle horn again and saw the villagers' rebel army coming in for a second attack. It looked as though they had lost half of their men.

The hooded leader of the rebel army galloped his horse to the bottom of the cliff and dismounted, leaving his army to continue the fight. He made his way to the cliff and began to climb; he looked strong and sure-footed. Soon he was beside the companions. He pulled Jackson up to safety effortlessly. As he turned toward them, they saw, beneath the hood, a man who was partly transparent. 'Who are you?' Hadwyn asked with some trepidation. He wondered if he was seeing a ghost.

'Simon,' he replied.

'Mackenzie's father?' Jackson gasped.

Teri and Mackenzie were crying. 'Simon!' Teri called out.

'I am with you always,' he whispered, looking up towards the skies. 'Now keep going,' he instructed the companions. 'I must return to the fight. We will hold them at bay. Don't give up.' And then he disappeared back down the rocky cliff face, as mist obscured any trace of him.

Teri Jones had both hands clasped tightly against her chest. Tears poured from her motionless face.

The Eye-Pokers had now turned away and were battling an army of giant bee drones. Hadwyn remembered what the Bee Goddess had told him; the spirit of the bee sacrifices itself to achieve a common goal. The bees had come to their rescue too. The scene below was a bloodied, screaming battlefield. Tess cried out as she saw many Frilled-Neck Lizards and Fire Salamanders dying. 'Hadwyn,' she called, 'can't we help them?'

Hadwyn shook his head. 'Tess, they are dying for all of us. We must keep going and restore their worlds or they are dying for nothing.'

Tess was distraught. Hadwyn tied her to his back and continued to climb as she sobbed. Jackson followed, still attached to Hadwyn by the twine. The snowstorm swirled around them, eventually hiding the tragedy below. The crevice in the cliff was now in view. The Last Door was in that crevice.

The final part of the climb was the most dangerous. The last ten metres or so was straight up with no footholds. Hadwyn didn't know how to get his friends up this part. He didn't want to jump with one and leave the other.

Within seconds, a large bee came right up to them, hovering next to the cliff. It was the Queen. 'I am here to take you to your destination. Please climb on my back.' She managed to hover at a lower level than them so that they could jump on to her back.

'We are going to have to do this together,' Hadwyn yelled over the howling wind to his companions. 'It's the only way.' There was no way he was going to untie them. There was quite a gap between

The Queen and the rocks they clung to, and she was battling to keep in one spot against the wind. With Tess on his back he yelled to Jackson, 'Okay, on the count of three,' and they jumped.

Landing on the Queen, they grabbed hold of her furry back. The whirring of her wings increased as she made her way upwards. Through the pelting snow, they watched the grey rock whizz past them, travelling higher and higher. The Queen slowed her pace and hovered next to a narrow ledge. At the back of the ledge, they finally saw it. The Last Door. It was identical to the front door of the Taylors' home.

'What's happening?' Mrs Taylor cried out as their home began to shake like an earthquake. Outside, lightning and thunder had risen from nowhere and became deafening. Teri was holding her breath and had one hand gripping her son's arm.

'They're almost here,' Mackenzie yelled, glancing at the front door and then back at the television screen repeatedly. 'Oh, please make it,' he pleaded inwardly. He checked Hadwyn's health. His heart sank. It read three per cent. Hadwyn was about to die.

The Queen swayed as close as she could without banging into the cliff. Hadwyn readied the group again. The High Lands was erupting with thunder and lightning. The blizzard was intensifying. The earth and mountains shook violently. This time he had to untie them. The ledge wasn't big enough for all of them to jump at once. 'I'll go first and then you jump to me,' he yelled. Within seconds, Hadwyn was on the narrow icy ledge. It was dangerously slippery. He beckoned to Tess.

'Courage and hope,' she said to herself and leapt towards him.

Hadwyn grabbed Tess and pulled her in behind him. He nodded to Jackson, who stood up and leapt to the ledge, slipping on the ice and skidding into the side wall. The Queen Bee disappeared into the storm.

Battling the extreme winds that were threatening to unbalance them, they huddled close to the Last Door. Hadwyn, with a firm grip on Tess, reached for his pouch containing the Burnstones and handed it to Jackson.

With the wind ripping at his clothes, and his body swaying in the gale force winds, Jackson reached into the pouch and, one by one, pulled out the Burnstones. Facing the door, he saw the familiar wrought ironwork tree covering the full length of the door, with its five circular indents at the branches' ends. Carefully, and hanging on to the doorknob for support, Jackson wedged each Burnstone into a hole. As each one found its home, the Burnstones began to glow – first red, then blue, white, green and gold. Finally, the door brightened, glowing with a golden light. The time had arrived. The power of the Burnstones was culminating as the five lands returned to balance and the Last Door prepared to open.

In the Taylors' home, Mackenzie was more focused than he had ever been in his life. The front door of the Taylors' home was rattling and glowing. The crucial moment had arrived … Mackenzie dropped the controller and raced to the front door. Teri and the Taylors stood desperately behind him. The door was wrenched open from the other side. Wind and snow swirled through the door. Immediately, Mackenzie saw Jackson.

Mackenzie lurched forward and pulled Jackson and Buddy through the door, pushing him towards the waiting arms of his parents. Mackenzie then reached for Tess, who was hanging on to Hadwyn. Hadwyn pushed Tess through the door towards Mackenzie. Tess stumbled in and fell to the floor. Her parents were at her side in seconds.

Mackenzie stood up straight and looked at Hadwyn. Hadwyn looked at Mackenzie. Hadwyn put his hand up toward Mackenzie. His hand was fading from sight. Wordlessly, Makenzie lifted his hand and placed it against Hadwyn's hand. Tess looked up and cried out 'Hadwyn!'

In that moment Hadwyn slowly fell back, fading from sight as he disappeared downward into the blizzard. The Last Door slammed shut.

Acknowledgements

I would also like to acknowledge my great appreciation for the efforts and support from the alpha readers.

<table>
<tr><td>

Young Alpha Readers
(aged 9–16)

Claudia Miller
Anna Green
Callum McKeown
Grace McKeown
Anna McDonald
Isaiah Bassett
Jared Glover
Jess Taylor
Shreya Kapitan
Jack Canty

</td><td>

Adult Alpha Readers

Jade Rhianna Grey
Joshua Palmer
Elle Señalista
Merrin Taylor
Kate Fitzsimons
Bronwyn Lee

</td></tr>
</table>

About the Author

T. D. DELANEY (Tricia Dawn) has dreamt of being an author since she was nine years old. She still remembers a pivotal moment as she sat in the classroom daydreaming, looking out the window at the sun dancing on the shrubbery and wishing she could write a book that made people kinder. Growing up in the small country town of Barmah on the Mighty Murray River, which borders Victoria and New South Wales in Australia, she had already come to understand that unkindness caused great sadness.

Home was an old weatherboard homestead with great verandahs all around. Much of her childhood was spent outdoors – climbing trees, yabbying in local channels, building cubbies from branches, fishing, swimming in the river, and walking to school along the Murray. Unlike the town, this home had no electricity. As the sun went down each evening, Tricia took great wonder and delight in reading by candlelight. It was in those books that she travelled far and wide in magical wonder. Just holding a book brought a sense of excitement and friendship.

Just over the river was Cummeragunja Mission, an Australian Aboriginal reserve established in 1881. It wouldn't be until attending high school in a nearby town that Tricia would learn that ignorance and prejudice permeated society, leading to much social injustice. She learnt that her Indigenous school friends were treated differently. These early experiences cemented a passion for writing, for the preservation of the environment, and for advocating for those who are marginalised in society.

Years later as a parent, she continued to immerse herself in nature with her children at every opportunity, even climbing trees with them. As a working single parent, time was scarce and it was hard to know what one could do to help the environment and her children's future. And so, the dream of writing an adventure book for young people, that highlighted the need to protect the balance of nature and honour Indigenous wisdom, was born.

The urgency to complete the book became stronger in 2010, when her daughter landed the role of a Joey Ambassador for Australia Zoo Wildlife Warriors. Tricia delved into environmental issues to support her daughter, undertaking community education and fundraising. As a parent, the urgency to protect the environment became ever stronger. It has taken thirteen years to complete. She hopes that the book will excite, inform and inspire young people.

Tricia has worked for many years as a community-based palliative care social worker. Tricia is proud to be an activist for Indigenous rights and environmental sustainability.

www.ingramcontent.com/pod-product-compliance
Lightning Source LLC
Chambersburg PA
CBHW060930190726
48286CB00002B/706